The Columbian

Molina knew that the powerful drug lords loved the game and were known to bet heavily whenever there was a soccer match. When a block of owner's investment became available in the club Atletico Nacional de Medellin, he decided to buy it and become a major shareholder. This elevated his status amongst the Cartel and gave him access to the soccer players as well.

The Colombians had great aspirations of taking the World Cup soccer games, which were to be played in 1994 in the United States. Their desire to become world champions rested with their national hero and goalie: Pibe Valderrama.

All of Colombia knew that not only was the good name of Colombia at stake in the World Cup soccer games, but certain governmental officials had high hopes of eradicating the country's image as the world's largest cocaine theme park. Rene Higuita had even been quoted, saying that "The Colombia National Soccer team will be on a dual mission: to win the World Cup and to eradicate the country's image."

The Columbian

by

Howard A. Losness

𝔠ommonwealth
𝔓ublications

A Commonwealth Publications Paperback
THE COLUMBIAN

This edition published 1997
by Commonwealth Publications
9764 - 45th Avenue,
Edmonton, AB, CANADA T6E 5C5
All rights reserved
Copyright © 1995 by Howard A. Losness

ISBN: 1-55197-234-4

Designed by: Patrick Earl

Printed in Canada

This book is dedicated to my parents, Hans and Lillian Losness, who have encouraged and supported me throughout my life. Without their guidance, love and understanding I would not be the individual I am today.

Special appreciation goes to my wife and best friend, Myrna. It was with her support and understanding that I was able to write The Columbian.

Thanks to Guillermo for his encouragement and technical assistance in this manuscript.

Chapter One

On the day of his birth, June 30, 1961, Molina Cesar Marquez named his first son Juan Molina Marquez. They were a poor family, living in the section known by the inhabitants of Medellin, Colombia, as Comuna Nororiental—shanty town, the most undesirable section of that mountain city.

Molina Cesar Marquez, although he was poor, was a proud man. He knew that in the caste system of Colombia, given his lack of formal education and the fact that he possessed no occupational skills, he would never in this life rise above the station he occupied.

In addition to those who worked hard to maintain their families in this shanty town, there were those who resorted to drugs, crime and, of course, prostitution. The "homes" in Molina's area consisted of makeshift, unhealthy structures haphazardly constructed on land confiscated by the poor of Medellin so long ago that no one remembers when it wasn't known as Comuna Nororiental.

As a young man, when he came of age and had decided to strike out on his own, Molina Cesar Marquez located a vacant site and constructed his house. It was made of cardboard boxes framed onto discarded pieces of lumber taken from construction sites. The sparse furnishings were simple, consisting mostly of wooden boxes and a discarded cushion here and there. His bed was a pile of straw laid upon cardboard which had been placed over the dirt floor to help ward off the chill from the ground.

When, at the age of 20, he took a wife, Juanita, it was with the heartbreaking understanding that he had little more than love and devotion to offer his bride. At that time, she was only 17, the oldest of seven children. She, too, had come from the same poor environment as Molina, and knew that the time had come for her to move out, relieving her parents of the responsibility of caring for her. Given their mutual background, she expected no more from their relationship than Molina's love, and asked for no more than his devotion to her and the family.

When they first met, Molina had been immediately taken in by her quiet personality and was challenged by her quick wit. She was frail, yet seemed to possess a strong constitution, born, no doubt, from the responsibility of being the eldest of seven children. They fell in love and, six months later, were wed.

They lived in Molina's modest abode until Juanita became pregnant with their first child. By this time, Molina had acquired a broken couch here and a discarded chair there, all of which he had repaired to the best of his ability. Although he wanted more for his family, he never apologized for his station in life. He just accepted it as God's will and lived the role that that life had dealt him.

Juanita loved her husband and never allowed him to see the tears she often shed when they lacked for proper clothing or enough food to put on the table for their children. Molina was not so easily deceived, however, and never let on that he, too, suffered with heavy heart, wanting more for his family, yet knowing that he could not provide for them as he desired.

Although they were poor, Molina Cesar Marquez never let his two sons Julio and Juan think for a moment that they would ever be anything less than successful Colombian citizens. The key to their future, he would constantly preach, was hard work, drive and, most of all, education. He felt that if his children had a formal education they would one day be able to pull themselves out of their station of having to toil in the coca or marijuana fields and make something of their lives instead of working for la compania, "the company", otherwise known as the Cartel.

The owner of the fields was Pablo Pizano. He was ranked as one of the most powerful and wealthy men in Medellin, and a member and leader of the Cartel—he was also one of the most ruthless. His power reached deep into the police and political arenas, including judges and magistrates. No one doubted nor dared challenge his authority. Those few fools who were brave or stupid enough to speak out against the powerful drug king usually ended up either dead or with body parts missing. Some of the decedents were severely punished by having family members killed in order to keep them in line. Killing a child of the family or a family member was his way of putting one on notice that one had made the mistake of crossing the most powerful man in Medellin.

Whenever a member of a wealthy or well-to-do family was murdered by a member of the Cartel, it was common practice to kill all of the male members of that family, regardless of their age. The rationale was not to leave any male member of the family alive who could and would grow up to avenge his father's death. Even a male child as young as two years of age whose father had been murdered was trained from that day forward that his utmost role in life was to avenge his father's death. It made no difference if the murderer was a member of la compania or not. That was the Colombian way of life.

Molina Cesar Marquez worked hard for his meager daily ration of pesos in the marijuana and coca fields of the drug king, Pablo Pizano, as did most of the poorer men of Medellin, earning barely enough money to feed his family. It was a rare occasion when there were funds left over for treats. Somehow, he was able to save a few pesos for special occasions, such as Christmas and birthdays, but most of the gifts were hand-carved toys or jewelry crafted from stones and metals found discarded or lost by someone in the city.

On those days when the fields didn't require Molina Marquez's attention, he would take his two sons to the main boulevard of El Poblado, where the exclusive restaurants, bars, boutiques, stores and art galleries were located. There, the elite of Medellin spent their time and money. Molina and his sons would look into the store windows, barely daring to even think that they could one day own such possessions as silk shirts or real leather shoes. He would then take them to see the spectacular mansions and white stucco villas of Las Diagonales and Las Lomas, pointing out villas where the "patrones" lived. Almost every house was surrounded by wrought iron fences or stone walls. It was not uncommon to see guards armed with automatic weapons patrolling the grounds with guard dogs. The largest and most grandiose villa was that of Pablo Pizano.

"You, too, will someday have a casa like this," Molina would whisper to his boys. He knelt with his arms around their shoulders as they looked upon the magnificent structures. His eyes would dance with excitement as he spoke with conviction. "You need only remain in school and study hard. Education is the universal ticket for success. Without it, you have no chance to elevate yourself from this way of life. Set a goal for yourself and never lose sight of it. You must rise above the level in which you now find yourself," he would say with firmness. "This way of life is only temporary. God will show you the path, but it will be up to you to achieve wealth and happiness. You can be great—only if you believe!" He would then look at them admiringly and ruffle their coarse hair which had been carefully combed by their mother. His voice carried the message of conviction. He knew he had opened the door of the future and lit the fire of desire in their souls. It only needed the fuel of education and his constant nurturing to make them succeed.

The boys were young, but they never forgot the magnificent villas of the patrones, with their high fences, manicured rose gardens, the tall trees and their park-like settings with lawns that seemed to go on forever. Juan could but attempt to visualize how one must live within those walls. *One day I will live in such a place,* he thought to himself as he looked over his shoulder one last time as his father led them home.

At times he had difficulty maintaining this dream, especially during those times when his father took him to the boulevard of El Pablado. He could not shake from his mind the look of disgust that they received from the rich people. This disgusting pauper dared venture within their midst with his two ragged, ruffian, shoeless waifs who obviously came from Comuna Nororiental. "Vamosnos" they would snarl, hoping to send the three of them scurrying back to their dirt floor shack.

Once in a great while a compassionate woman would hand them a peso accompanied with a weak smile, taking care to drop it into their hands so as not to touch them. Their father was always quick to make them return the money. "We do not beg," he would tell them with a quiet but stern voice. He condescendingly smiled to the lady as the boys grudgingly returned the money. For this embarrassment, Juan vowed, they would one day pay.

One day after school, Juan had returned home early with a note from his teacher stating that he had been suspended from school for a week for fighting. He had been constantly taunted by the boys in his sixth grade class who had proper clothing and wore shoes. Juan had neither. With his father's instruction, he had learned to ward off their barbs and mask his anger by remaining alone and ignoring them.

On this particular day, however, they had crossed the line by hurling insults regarding his father...a topic of insult that no self-respecting Colombian would tolerate—poor or not.

In the ensuing battle, Juan had broken the nose of one of the boys and had badly beaten the other two before the fight had been broken up by Manuel Degasa, the principal. The three 12-year-old boys had been sent to the infirmary for repairs while Juan had been given a severe tongue-lashing and expelled from school for a week.

That night, when his father returned home from the fields, he carried under his arm a pair of walking shoes that he had purchased for Juan in town. When he read the note from school, he became intensely angry. Setting the shoes aside, he brought out a small switch which he used exclusively for disciplining the children.

It wasn't that Molina was so angry that Juan had beaten the three boys. As a matter of fact, he was secretly proud of his son for standing up for his principles. It was the fact that Juan had been expelled from school, an act in itself not severe enough to endanger his educational future, but an event that he wanted to be sure was never repeated. He needed to be sure that Juan understood the severity of the repercussions of fighting that had resulted in his being expelled.

Molina switched Juan so severely that the stick finally broke. To drive the point home, Juan was given three more hits with his father's hand on his bare bottom. By this time, Juan's skin was so numb from the punishment that his feelings were more hurt than his bottom by the blows he had received.

His younger brother, Julio, and his sister, Teresa, had been forced to witness the punishment. Their father wanted to set a clear example of what would happen to them should they encounter such difficulty in school themselves. There was to be no margin of misunderstanding on how strongly he felt about their education.

Once the punishment had been administered, Juan was banished from the house for the rest of the day without dinner. The shoes that his father had purchased for him sat on the table like an unpresented trophy waiting for the victor.

Juan sat atop a large rock overlooking the shanty camp and was nursing his feelings when several men drove up in an open jeep brandishing automatic weapons. The vehicle skidded to a halt on the loose gravel and slid into one of the wooden shacks, knocking it down.

A man within the shack, not knowing who had knocked down his house, ran out, cursing the driver. One of the young men in the jeep responded by hitting him on the side of the face with the butt of his gun. It knocked him to the ground, bloodying his face.

Although their village was heavily populated with children—as birth control was all but non-existent in this basically Catholic village—the area was amazingly quiet. From time to time some of the rich and pugnacious youths, drunk and bored with their lot, would vent their boredom by going on a vicious rampage, terrorizing the poor people of Comuna Nororiental by knocking down and setting fire to portions of their village. The people were too scared to protect themselves or attempt to thwart the youths for fear of retaliation by their parents, so they usually retreated to safety, waiting for the attackers to tire of their malicious game.

For the most part, the law ignored such outbursts, rationalizing that it would be best for the city to rid itself of the plagued little village anyway. Besides, most of the youths came from well-to-do, influential families. The families of the wealthy and powerful young men were aware of the control they had over the officials of Medellin, knowing the desire of the officials to remain in office of the community.

This time Juan watched, much to his horror, as the men from the jeep marched unerringly towards his house. While two of the men kicked down the walls of his home, the other two stood in front, firing their automatic weapons into the house, filling it with bullets.

Screams could be heard throughout the camp

as people from every corner of Comuna Nororiental
vacated their homes, running for cover. The shooting lasted less than a minute, but it seemed an
eternity as Juan watched, frozen with terror. Although logic told him that no one could have survived such a barrage of bullets, he refused to believe the worst, hoping that it was only a prank by
the rich kids to scare his family—for what reason
he could not fathom.

Once the shooting was over and his house had
been leveled the four men made a hasty retreat
back to the jeep, shouting and laughing as they
jabbed their guns into the air, discharging the remaining bullets. The tires of the jeep spat gravel
over the village as they sped down the road in their
hasty departure.

The whine of the jeep's engine faded into the
distance. The long silence that followed was soon
filled with the murmurs of the villagers as they
cautiously returned from behind rocks and trees.
This had not been the first incident where the drug
lord's men had raided their village and killed people, and they knew it would not be the last. It was
just a fact of life that must be endured, they rationalized. Those still alive were just grateful that,
this time, they had not been the target of the senseless brutality.

Juan was the first person to reach his house.
Onlookers stood in a semi-circle gaping at the damage, holding their hands over their eyes or mouths,
fearful of looking under the bullet-riddled debris.
Slowly at first, then rapidly, Juan flung aside the
sheets of cardboard that had once been the walls
of his home.

He saw his father first, his body riddled with
bullets. A look of fear was imprinted on his face,
his eyes showing the horror he must have felt when

he realized what was happening. At his father's side lay the blood-splattered shoes that he had purchased for Juan.

Slowly Juan searched for his mother, his brother and sister. All were dead. Each had been shot several times. As the villagers cautiously approached him, many sobbing and murmuring to each other, Juan grabbed the blood-spattered shoes and ran past the people, through the village and into the woods. Tears of sorrow and fear ran down his face. He had seen the massacre, but couldn't bring himself to accept the fact that his entire family had just been murdered before his very eyes.

He would later learn that the previous day his father had apparently stolen a small marijuana plant from the fields where he worked, which belonged to the drug king, Pablo Pizano. He had been successful in smuggling it past the constant, watchful eye of the armed guards.

In town, he had used the small plant to barter, trading it for a pair of shoes for his son. That theft had cost him and his family their lives. As Juan slowly wiped the blood from the shoes, tears of anger spilled onto his cheeks. He made a silent vow to his father that one day he would avenge his family.

As he slipped on the shoes, he made a sacred promise that his father's name would not be forgotten. "From this day forward," he said aloud, raising his arms to the sky with clenched fists, "I will be known not as Juan Molina Marquez, but as Molina J. Marquez!"

Chapter Two

Molina never returned to his home after that fateful day, nor did he return to the schooling that his father had felt was so germane to his future. Instead, he fell in with a gang of small-time hoods known as Los Hombres. They lived in an abandoned warehouse in the industrial district and specialized in breaking into the homes of the middle class, robbing them while they were at work, then selling the stolen goods to second-hand dealers, pawnbrokers or tourists. The pay was not great and he knew would never become rich, but, more important, at the age of 12, Molina had become his own man. He vowed that he would never be laughed at again or be told how scruffy he looked by sympathetic onlookers who grudgingly handed him a peso.

By the time he was 17, he had accumulated his own gang—a group of young men numbering seven who were not unlike himself, homeless and without any positive direction. The modus operandi remained the same: rob from the middle class and tourists, and sell to merchants or the other tourists that visited the city. As boss of his little gang, he was able to participate in a greater percentage of the profits. With the money he made, he eventually purchased tailor-made silk shirts, wore imported alligator shoes, and owned a white cotton suit with a Panama hat. He always carried a small Beretta in a shoulder holster when he wore the suit; otherwise, it was carried in a small concealed belt holster.

Years passed and he lived in a modestly-furnished studio apartment where, for the most part, he cooked his own meals in order to conserve money. Benefiting from the lessons of frugality taught by his father, he eventually saved enough to purchase a used Mercedes.

Each day he awoke with the name of Pablo Pizano on his lips, swearing on his father's grave that one day he would avenge his death. Not a week went by when he didn't drive by the Pizano estate. Gaining access to the estate was all but impossible, as the villa was set on the northwestern hillside high above the town, nestled in the shade of the jagged, bluish mountains. The road to the villa was paved and unobstructed by trees or bushes. A twelve-foot-high rock fence surrounded the 28-acre villa. The grounds were constantly patrolled by armed guards with trained Doberman pinschers. The electronic gate was manned by armed guards 24 hours a day. To even approach the gate without specific, sanctioned business with Pablo Pizano could result in death. His soldiers had been instructed to shoot first and ask questions later.

Like the other major drug lords of the city, Pablo Pizano had the mayor and police officials in his hip pocket. The amount of money he spent on under-the-table monthly tariffs was astronomical, but it bought him security and peace of mind. The police had been instructed to keep a watchful eye on the villa and to regularly patrol the road leading up to the gates.

The bribes afforded an additional luxury: freedom from prying questions relative to periodic reports of missing field workers. It was a policy to summarily execute a worker from time to time, just for exercise or as an example to others of what would happen should anyone get out of line or attempt to steal a coca leaf or marijuana plant for themselves.

Any official, police or judicial, had been whipped into shape over the years by the Cartel's dominance over the city. Anyone opposing their power was first intimidated by telephone or had unpleasant personal visits by the Cartel's thugs, or they were subject to beatings. If the unfortunate party continued their opposition, the Cartel simply had them executed. They regarded no one to be beyond their reach. It had been reported that over the years the Cartel had executed in excess of 200 Colombian governmental officials, policemen, judges and journalists in Medellin.

As a young man, unattached and ambitious, Pablo Pizano had managed to work his way into the confidence of Gabriel De Angelino, the most powerful drug czar in Colombia. It wasn't long before Pablo was courting his eldest daughter, Estrella De Angelino. She was somewhat less than a raving beauty and had no other suitors, a fact that her mother attributed to her father's position in the Cartel rather than her lack of wit, charm and good looks.

Little did they know that Pablo Pizano had greater goals than love and affection in mind when he courted her. Through careful planning and deception, they were married a year later.

Gabriel's wife Lupita De Angelino had borne Gabriel three daughters, but no sons. As tradition dictated, the eldest daughter, Estrella, was to be the first to marry. For this reason, the mother and Estrella's sisters breathed a sigh of relief when Pablo Pizano asked for her hand.

Having no wealth nor a suitable home for his bride, through the insistence of Lupita De Angelino, Pablo and his wife were invited to live in the spacious villa. A short time after the newlyweds occupied part of the house, Gabriel De Angelino was overcome with a sudden, unexplained illness, rendering him incapable of running the family business. Through the persuasion of his wife and daughter, and against his better judgment, Gabriel De Angelino, from his sickbed, appointed his new son-in-law, Pablo, to take charge of the business. Shortly thereafter, the old man mysteriously died, leaving his distraught wife to care for her two remaining daughters. As head of the family and the only male, Pablo Pizano had succeeded in taking over the most powerful drug trade in Colombia.

Because the marriage to Estrella was one of convenience, and to gain the position of power he had so carefully planned to enjoy, he was careful to tender lavish attention on his wife the first few years of their marriage. He knew the importance of securing himself in the social and business community. In time, Estrella would come to learn that there was little love lost between them, and would discover that there were numerous mistresses who shared the bed of Pablo Pizano.

By now, Pizano was so firmly entrenched in Gabriel De Angelino's business that in reality, De Angelino's business had become Pizano's. In his rise to power, Estrella had lost all leverage over her unloving husband. Only during important social events, when he felt that a show of family unity was necessary, did he give her the social due she deserved.

With a significant amount of cash and the promise of lucrative employment within his organization, Pablo Pizano managed to entice a few eligible gentlemen to court and eventually marry the remaining daughters, leaving only himself, his wife and Lupita De Angelino to occupy the villa. A short time after the last daughter was married and out of the villa, Lupita De Angelino was overcome with a sudden illness that took her life.

After her mother's death, a period of soul searching took place, during which time Estrella came to realize that not only had she lost her parents, but now she had all but lost control over her father's financial holdings. She came to the decision that the time had come to begin putting her shattered life back together.

Estrella found solace in women's social gatherings and her one vice—shopping for clothes. It was the latter that gave Molina J. Marquez the opening he had long been seeking into the life and surroundings of drug czar Pablo Pizano.

On this particular day, Estrella Pizano had been shopping in La Madam's Boutique on El Pablado. Her arms were full of packages, and she was fumbling to get the car keys from her purse while balancing her load. She had located them and was trying to unlock the door of her Bentley when suddenly three youths accosted her. One grabbed the packages and started down the alley while the another snatched her purse.

"Stop! Help! PLO..." she began, but the third youth hurried to hold his hand over her mouth, allowing his accomplices to escape without alarming passersby or the storekeeper. The third thief's job was to disable the helpless woman and make off with her automobile, an item worth several thousand dollars, even on the black market.

Molina happened to be driving by the boutique at the moment the assault was taking place. Immediately recognizing the Pizano's red Bentley and seeing the elderly woman in trouble, he swerved his Mercedes in front of the fleeing youth who was carrying the packages. Molina stepped out of the car and took aim at the man with his Beretta.

Seeing Molina, the youth dropped the packages and ran down the alley, yelling, "Don't shoot! Please don't! I'm sorry!" he screamed, as he ran with his hands above his head.

Molina then ran to the man holding Estrella Pizano, hitting him solidly on the base of his head with the Beretta. "Take that, hombre! Maybe next time you will pick on someone more your size."

The man dropped to the ground like a sack of potatoes, hitting the pavement with a sickening thud. The blow had severed his spine, killing him instantly.

Seeing his companion lying still on the cobblestone road while the other member of his gang disappeared around the corner at the end of the block, the third youth realized that he had no chance against Molina. He released the purse and escaped down the street, screaming for mercy as he ran. "Sorry! It was a mistake in identification! Don't shoot! Sorry!"

"Oh!" was all Estrella Pizano could say as her knees started to buckle under the strain. She was dressed in a simple black dress that buttoned high on the neck. She wore a large cabochon ruby tightly bound around her slender throat by a double strand of pearls. A small gold watch was strapped around her thin wrist with a gold band. She wore no other rings, save a gold band around her left-hand ring finger.

Upon examining her closely, Molina could see that her face was heavily covered with make-up. Dark mascara hung from her eyelashes, and the deep, red lipstick she wore had been painted far above the upper lip line. Heavy powder had been applied to her face in an attempt to cover the age lines.

At first Molina was repelled by the thought of touching the wife of the man who had killed his family, but seeing her in a stage of helplessness, he realized that she could have had no part in her husband's brutal acts.

"I've got you, Señora," he said softly, supporting her by holding onto her arm. "It's all right. They're gone. You're safe now."

Helping her to the seat of her Bentley, he asked, "Are you all right?"

She gasped for air, her face ashen. She held onto Molina's shoulder for support as she looked up into his eyes. "Oh, thank you. I don't know what would have happened to me if you hadn't saved me from those dreadful men." In that brief moment, Molina could see the unhappiness that time had etched on her face. He thought of his mother and how she had always looked more than her age.

"Are you hurt? Are you all right?" he continued to inquire, gently holding onto her elbow to sustain her balance.

"I...I think I'm all right. Thank you, young man," she said, studying his face for the first time. He was a handsome young man with his black hair combed back, parted just off-center. The small, manicured mustache made him look like a movie star in one of her novellas. She managed a weak smile. "You saved my life." She looked at the youth lying at her feet. "Is he dead?"

"I should hope so, for his sake." He smiled for the first time.

She didn't seem surprised nor shocked by his answer, as if she had been familiar with death's hand. "How can I repay you?" she asked, automatically reaching into her purse to find money to reward the brave young man.

"No. No money," he said, holding up his hand in protest. "It is not necessary. I'm just happy that I was in the vicinity and was able to be of some help. I'm grateful that you were not harmed. You're obviously a woman of refined stature. You should not be out alone on the streets like this," he said, looking around for effect. "Have you no one to watch over you?" His words were well chosen, and his concerned mannerism was played perfectly.

"I—I like to shop alone. My husband, you see, well, he…"

"He should not let a fine lady such as yourself go out alone," he said, with a furrowed brow. "The streets of Medellin are not safe, even in this part of town, as you yourself can testify. Many men would kill for a gem such as that," he said, eyeing the ruby around her neck. "It would bring more than most see in a lifetime. Allow me to accompany you home." He delved into her eyes with a look of trust and concern. "You never know when those thugs might return."

"I could not impose," she weakly protested, although it was obvious that she would be most grateful for the security of his company. "It would not be…"

Molina cut her off, "Nonsense. Please, allow me to drive you. I would never forgive myself if anything were to happen to you," he said, continuing to look around for effect. "I feel responsible. Do you live nearby?" he asked, knowing full well the way to her villa.

"On the other side of town, just up the hill," she nodded. "But...your car?" she inquired, looking towards Molina's Mercedes.

"It will be all right. I'll phone a friend to pick it up. Come now. You're looking faint. Can I get you some water?" His manner was impeccably attentive.

Estrella Pizano immediately felt at ease in the presence of this strong, capable young man who had suddenly come to be her savior. She felt comfortable and protected.

"You're looking a bit peaked," he added as she allowed him to lightly press the back of his hand to her forehead.

Molina's suggestion that she was looking pale reinforced the feeling that she was indeed feeling faint. She smiled weakly as she closed her eyes and laid her head back on the headrest. Molina gently closed the door and walked around to the driver's side.

He eased the Bentley out onto the street, towards the Pizano villa. He stole a look at himself in the rear-view mirror. A slight smile of self-satisfaction crept at the corners of his lips.

* * * *

As he approached the gates of the villa, his pulse quickened. He braced himself for what he knew could become an ugly situation. He glanced at his passenger as he slid his Beretta out of its holster and concealed it under his left leg. The guards immediately recognized the Bentley, but were surprised at Molina being at the wheel. One of the men stood in front of the car with his automatic weapon pointed at Molina while the other approached the passenger side.

"Señora Pizano? Is everything all right?" He studied Estrella Pizano's face and then that of Molina. "Who is this?" he demanded to know, pointing his weapon at Molina.

Molina's fingers tightened around the Beretta as he slipped it from under his leg.

"This is..." *My goodness, I didn't even ask his name,* she thought as she looked into Molina's eyes. "This is my new bodyguard," she said, with a smile and a slight nod towards Molina, as if asking him if this was all right with him.

Molina smiled back and said to the guard, "Marquez. Molina J. Marquez. I'm bringing the Señora back from a shopping trip in town."

Having said that, he rolled up the window and put the Bentley in gear. The guard standing in front of the car barely had time to get out of the way as Molina drove past him, giving him a quick smile. As he looked in the rear-view mirror he could see the guard talking on the portable phone. He knew who would be waiting for him at the house. He slid the Beretta back into his shoulder holster.

* * * *

Pablo Pizano was shorter and fatter than Molina had expected. His hair was greased back and he wore a bolero-type white shirt that seemed to be a size too large. His hair and shaggy mustache were gray. He had bags under his eyes, as if he had been on a binge the previous night. He appeared to be in his early '60s, Molina thought as he pulled in front of the villa. A large man stood beside Pablo at the foot of the verandah, wielding an automatic weapon. *A bodyguard*, Molina thought. Pablo had an angry look on his face as he opened the passenger door for his wife. "Where have you been and who is this?" he demanded, pointing to Molina.

Molina decided it best to remain in the Bentley. *The Señora will explain,* he thought. He would wait. He slid his hand under his coat. If he needed his weapon, he would be ready. He figured he could drop the guard before he had time to become alerted to the fact that Molina was armed. Pizano would get the next bullet, of that he was certain. After that, it didn't matter.

Estrella relayed the events of her shopping trip, dramatizing it with wild arm gestures, stretching the truth for sympathy. The results were desirable. Pablo Pizano helped his wife up the stairs of the villa and ordered the bodyguard to fetch the packages.

Molina waited in the car until Pizano returned. Pizano informed him that his wife had requested that he be hired as her personal chauffeur and bodyguard, pending ongoing approval, of course. There was no inquiry as to his availability.

Molina could tell that Pizano was suspicious of the sudden events that had brought this young man to his sanctuary. He could but guess what was going through the mind of his new patron as he studied his aging, stoic face. Pizano could be thinking that, perhaps, Molina had staged the whole affair to gain entry to the grounds. Maybe he was an assassin hired to kill him. Then again, maybe everything was as it appeared. Molina would have to prove himself. That much he knew.

He was ushered by the bodyguard to a small cottage behind the main residence, where he was given a room with a bed and a dresser. Once he had settled in, he strolled over to the bunkhouse, where the gardeners were housed. He introduced himself as the Señora's chauffeur. As expected, they were common, simple, uneducated men. He was given no more respect from them than any of the other hired help.

Molina returned to his quarters, satisfied with his position. He had finally gained access to the one man he had vowed to exterminate. Time was on his side. Now he had but to wait and carefully study his adversary.

The game of revenge that he had planned all these years was now afoot.

Chapter Three

Six weeks after Molina had been hired as a chauf-feur-bodyguard for Estrella Pizano, he walked into the gardeners' bunkhouse. It was a Friday evening after dinner. He had a bottle of anisette in one hand and a bottle of rum tucked under his arm. "Today is my birthday," he announced to the six men lying on their bunks. "I have purchased Colombia's finest to celebrate," he said, holding the bottle in the air. "Muchachos! Let's party!'

The men were only too willing to share Molina's bottle, not caring whether or not it was his birth-day. Molina had thoughtfully supplied heavy glass tumblers, and he poured each man a portion of anisette.

They raised their glasses to Molina, their new best friend, said "Salude", and downed the con-tents. It wasn't long before he had them arm-in-arm, singing robust songs of women, and consum-ing the rest of the rum straight from the bottle. Molina was careful to keep his glass full, but did not drink its contents as he toasted each round, feigning drinking with the men.

Around midnight, the gardeners were so drunk they couldn't stand on their own two feet. Happy and inebriated, they collapsed onto their bunks and instantly fell into a deep slumber.

Molina carefully shook each man to be sure that they had passed out. When he was satisfied that they were beyond this world, he stepped outside the door, where he had previously stored five gallons of gasoline in a glass container.

Setting the bottled gasoline on the gas stove, he turned the burner on low. Before departing, he took one last look around to see if he had misplaced any personal item which could link him to the catastrophe that was about to occur. Satisfied that there was none, he turned out the light, locked the door behind him and returned to his quarters behind the main house.

Molina had no sooner laid his head on his pillow when the sound of the explosion brought a smile to his face. "I guess the patron will be in need of a crew of new gardeners," he said quietly to himself as he heard startled voices from the main house.

* * * *

The bunkhouse had burned to the ground by the time the fire could be put out. Molina stood near Pablo Pizano, who was dressed in a long, flowing nightshirt, and said, "Poor bastards. If I told them once, I told them a dozen times not to drink that cheap tequila. Look at the mess they have caused you, Patrone," he said, looking at Pizano.

"Stupid bastards," was all he said.

"Excuse me for being so bold at a time like this, Patrone, but I know of some very knowledge-able and capable gardeners that you can depend on. And they will work cheap, too."

"Eh? What do you mean?"

"I think I could get these gardeners to work

just for room and board, and they would be willing to rebuild your gardener's cottage in their spare time." Molina knew Pizano's weakness for getting cheap labor, even if he was one of the wealthiest men in Colombia.

"Are they any good? I don't want another bunch of drunken bums up here," he snarled. "I've already had that."

"Oh, no. They are very experienced. They have worked for the very best families. It's just that things are slow right now, and I think I can get them for peanuts. Beside that, they owe me a favor," he said with a wink.

"Very well. Have them report to me tomorrow at noon. I will interview them. They had better be as you say." Pizano looked hard at Molina, as if threatening him. His bodyguard eyed Molina as well. He had always distrusted Molina, yet, because he had been hired by Pizano to be the wife's chauffeur, he held his tongue.

"I guarantee satisfaction," Molina said, bowing in retreat. "You will not be disappointed. Tomorrow at noon."

* * * *

Molina left the villa before the sun was up. He knew if his men had partied the night before they would be sleeping late. Now that he was not there to run herd on them, they tended to be lax and to drink far into the night. Although he had spoken to them many times about his plan, no one was certain when and if it would be implemented. Once he had been hired, he had told them to be ready, as the time for revenge was imminent.

There was much to be done before they would be ready for presentation to Pizano at the Villa at noon. He spent the morning checking on the grooming of each man, taking care that each was wearing clean clothing, that their hair was cut and combed properly and they were clean-shaven. Above all, he made sure that they were sober. He went over the game plan again, for the nth time, assuring himself that each man knew his role, what to say and what his job entailed. If they were not hired, Molina's plan had no chance of succeeding.

* * * *

At twelve sharp Molina had the men stand at attention in a line in front of the lawn, awaiting Pablo Pizano's inspection. When Pizano arrived, an hour late, he stood in front of the men, along with his bodyguard. He examined the group for a moment, then simply said, "We have a lot of grounds here. I expect perfection. I have no time for questions, and above all, I tolerate no indiscretions. One slip-up, and you're gone." He emphasized the words with a quick motion of his forefinger across his throat. "You will confine yourselves to the grounds and concentrate on your work. You are not to speak to any of the family nor to the guards. You will be directly responsible to Molina, here, and I will look directly to him for satisfaction," he said, looking at Molina critically.

Molina returned the look with a nod and slight bow, then said sharply, "All right, muchachos! To the toolshed. There's much work to be done!" With that, he led them directly to the toolshed at the back of the house before Pizano could say any more.

"So that is the great Don Pizano," Mario said with a sneer once they had entered the confines of the toolshed. "He's an old man. He doesn't look so tough."

"Don't make the mistake of thinking you're dealing with just any old man," Molina said sharply. "Did you happen to notice the bodyguard with the automatic? He's ruthless. He goes everywhere Pizano does. He shoots first and doesn't ask questions."

"Does he even wipe the Patrone's ass?" one of the men asked, hitting another on the shoulder, laughing.

Molina held up his hand to quiet their laughter. "The man you just met is the most powerful man in la compania. He orders the executions of more judges, policemen and bugs like us than you can shake a stick at."

"Bugs like us! What makes him so special?" he shot back.

"Power, compadre. Power and money. He has both, and it's my intention to relieve him of that burden." He smiled. "In the meantime, we mow lawns, trim hedges and wait for a window of opportunity. Soon this will be all mine," he said, "and you men will be patrones," he laughed. "No more sleeping in sleazy hotels and bagging street putas. You will have real wealth, power and fancy women," he said, slamming his fist into the air with a large grin.

"Hey, man. I can hardly wait. I'm tired of hustling TVs and camcorders and stealing women's purses. This is the big time!"

"You have no idea," Molina said. "No idea at all."

* * * *

The next two months sailed by without incident. Molina's gardeners stayed discreetly in the background, trimming bushes and cutting lawns.

As time passed, Pizano and his bodyguard became more relaxed with the presence of Molina and his gardeners.

Molina's window of opportunity came on New Year's Eve, when Pizano and his wife were invited to the annual party in Bogota given by the Cartel to celebrate their continued good fortune.

It was the holidays and Pizano gave the majority of his bodyguards the week off, as he planned on staying in Bogota.

There were no crops to harvest, and the country as a whole was caught up in the Christmas celebration. The only staff left on the grounds were a few men left to guard the gate and the grounds. A skeleton housekeeping staff remained, as did Molina and his grounds crew.

No sooner had the Bentley departed through the gate with Pizano, his wife and their bodyguard, than Molina gathered his men in the toolshed. "Our time has come, muchachos. Today we take the first step in becoming landowners and kings of the Pizano empire. Today we begin to take our place in destiny as members of the elite Colombian Cartel. Only no one knows it yet." He laughed.

Molina unlocked the door in back of the toolshed, where the power tools were kept under lock and key. Over the past six weeks, he had smuggled his own personal arsenal into the shed and had purchased additional automatic weapons, handguns and ammunition.

"Wow! Would you look at that!" Mario said, taking one of the Israeli automatic weapons with a silencer attached. "This is where the fun begins. You have enough firepower here to take over Medellin," he joked.

"That's exactly what we're going to do," Molina said with a serious look. "We start by taking control of the villa and grounds. But first, let me caution you, we're dealing with expert military men here. Don't make the mistake of being careless or cocky. From this moment forward, each move we make is to be carefully calculated, with exact precision. A mistake can not only blow the plan, but cost you your life. Now, here's what we do first..."

* * * *

Pizano had left only two men to roam the grounds and two more to guard the gate. Because of the similarity in their ages, the relationship between Molina and the guards was anything but cordial. They resented the way he had wormed his way into the organization, the cushy job and fine clothes. Motoring the lady of the house around in the Bentley just added insult to injury. It was with this alienation in mind that Molina approached the two guards cautiously. They were standing under one of the large oak trees smoking when Molina walked up. They stopped talking the moment he arrived.

"I know it's hot out here, and I thought you guys might appreciate a beer," he offered, handing each a container. "With the boss away, I had the kitchen make you each a sandwich, too. Thought you might like a bite to eat."

Without waiting for a response of gratification he knew probably wasn't forthcoming, he left them holding the bags and turned to return to the house. The men, not ones to look a gift horse in the mouth, sat under a tree and consumed the beer and sandwiches. Five minutes later, they lay dead from the colorless, tasteless drug Molina had laced in their sandwiches. It had been purchased from one of his pharmaceutical friends, at a handsome fee, of course.

Molina's men quickly stashed the bodies in the gardening shed before anyone in the house took notice of their absence. Two of Molina's men replaced them, roaming the grounds far enough from the front gate and the house so they wouldn't be recognized. Aside from the gate guards, the remaining staff consisted of the cook—an elderly woman who had been with the family since before Pizano took over—for whom there was no love lost, and the housekeeper, an attractive young girl of 22 who Pizano had rescued from the coca fields. She was young and beautiful, with a vivacious body. Pizano had plans for this young miss...plans that included making her his personal in-house bed-servant.

Molina and Mario drove his Mercedes to the gate and waited for the guards to open it. They were the youngest of the six that rotated guard duty. Because they were the youngest they were also cocky and the least experienced. They had been chosen to work while the rest of the army enjoyed the day off. This was one of the few times that Molina had been without Señora Pizano, so the young guards decided to take advantage of the moment and make sport of him.

"Hey, pretty boy. You and your green-thumbed friend gonna go in town and try to get lucky?"

"Yeah, with another guy," the other guard laughed, slapping his buddy on the back.

"How did you guys guess?" Molina said good-naturedly. "Look what I'm bringing for bait," he said, motioning the man to look at his lap.

When the two stuck their heads into Molina's car window, they were shot between the eyes with the Israeli automatic with the silencer attached. A few moments later, the guards were laying in the Mercedes' trunk.

Molina dialed a number on his cellular phone.

"Get Montilla and Alverez down to the guard house. They're on duty," he said with a light voice and a smile of satisfaction. Everything was going as planned.

When he returned to the garden house, the men had already dug a deep grave with the back hoe and had put the guards' bodies in the hole. Moments later, the gatekeepers were added to the collection.

"Shall I cover them up?" one of the men asked Molina, throwing a shovel full of dirt down on their faces.

"No, not yet. We'll have a few more to add to the pile before we're finished. Just cover the hole with a tarp for the time being. Let's adjourn to the house and prepare for the next stage."

* * * *

Stage two began with the changing of the guard, when the second shift came to relieve the gatekeepers. Molina's men were in the gate house with their backs to the road when the guards walked up to relieve them. Moments later, these guards, too, lay in the trunk of their car, each with a single hole in his surprised face.

All was quiet until the day after New Year's Day, when Pablo Pizano and his wife returned. As expected, they were chauffeured by Pizano's body-guard. Alverez and Montilla stayed in the shadows of the guard house, opening the electronic gate and waving them on as they approached. It was late at night and Pizano, his wife and the body-guard were obviously exhausted from too much wine and food and the long trip home. No one spoke to the guards nor noticed anything amiss as they passed through the gate.

The bodyguard let Pablo Pizano and Estrella off at the porte cochre at the entrance of the villa before driving the Bentley around into the garage. As he exited the auto he was met by Mario, who took great pleasure in greeting him by first shooting him in the kneecap, then in the stomach. The bodyguard lay on the floor, writhing in pain.

Mario was enjoying the slow death of the villainous man so much that he neglected to observe that, in the process of squirming around on the floor, the driver had slipped his weapon from his shoulder holster. He succeeded in getting off a shot at Mario before passing out.

The bullet passed through Mario's chin and exited through the top of his head, killing him instantly.

Inside the villa, Pablo Pizano stopped short of the stairs as he heard the shot. "Did you hear that?" he asked Estrella, who was already on the landing. "Sounded like a gunshot!"

He ran for the door, where he was met by Molina Juan Marquez. Pizano glanced at Molina, wondering why he was in the house, but temporarily dismissed it as he angrily brushed him aside and opened the door.

"Pizano!" Molina shouted with a tone of authority to the aging man.

Pablo Pizano stopped short. No one ever spoke to him in that tone of voice, let alone used his last name. He spun around to face Molina, who was holding his Israeli automatic weapon with the silencer.

"Marquez! What in the name of God is this all about? Drop that weapon this instant," he demanded, "or I'll have you shot!"

"Sorry, Pizano. I'm giving the orders now," he said softly, with confidence. "I don't quite know how to break this to you, but your killing days are over."

Molina's face took on a somber appearance. He walked close to Pizano, his eyes searching the tired face. "You probably don't remember my father, but years ago he used to work for you. He worked long and hard each day in the coca fields for a few measly pesos to buy food for his family.

"He lived in Comuna Nororiental, a place I doubt you have ever seen, let alone visited. One day, he stole a marijuana plant to buy his son a pair of shoes.

"That son was none other than me, Pizano. And for that minor infraction, the act of taking a simple plant," his face was stoic, with piercing eyes now, "you ordered the death of my father, my mother, my brother and sister. I happened to witness that execution, Pizano. That day, after I found their bullet-riddled bodies, I vowed to exterminate you, patrone." He spat the word at him. "And today is that day."

"Why, you little tramp!" Pablo Pizano screamed as he lunged at Molina. "I'll..."

Molina calmly stepped aside, letting the man fall clumsily to the floor. As he looked up, Molina slowly and deliberately pumped 10 bullets into the heart of Pablo Pizano. As the man lay at his feet, blood pooling on the white oriental wool carpet, Estrella Pizano entered the room. She screamed when she saw her husband lying dead on the floor. The look of horror was soon replaced with hatred as she looked at Molina.

"I am sorry to have to do this, Señora Pizano," he said, with a look of regret. "I appreciate everything that you have done to facilitate my goal. Without your assistance I could never have fulfilled my promise to exterminate the man who killed my family. This day, the Pizano dynasty has come to an end."

Molina Cesar Marquez leveled the automatic weapon at her heart and fired a burst of shells. "I'm sorry that you have had the unfortunate luck of being a Pizano," he said softly, as she fell to the floor without uttering a sound. She had always known that one day she would die a violent death—she just didn't know when or by whom.

"Juan! Check on Mario in the garage. See what that firing was about," Molina ordered. "Mario was using a silencer on his weapon, so something has gone wrong. Be careful!"

* * * *

The remaining men who worked for Pablo Pizano were executed, one by one, as they returned to the villa. Soon all had been accounted for and eliminated. Molina Marquez had succeeded in accounting for and executing all of the army attached to Pizano's home base. The next task would be to take possession of his coca and marijuana fields, which were hidden high in hills of Colombia.

The following day, Molina and his henchmen drove into the lush hills and visited Pizano's fields one by one, announcing to the field hands that he had taken over the Pizano empire. Having announced that fact, much to the delight of the workers, he then summarily executed Pizano's field patrones in full view of the workers as they whistled and threw their hats into the air. This display of brute force was Molina's way of demonstrating to the laborers that there was no doubt who was now in charge. To the workers, it simply meant someone else would be paying their pesos. It was of no importance to them who that person was.

Their plight was the same. They only hoped the new patrone would be more lenient than the last.

Seeing the field workers and recognizing the look of defeat etched on their faces, Pablo vividly recalled the time when his father occupied that station in life. He had spent and lost his life working in the coca and marijuana fields. Molina vowed to himself that he would not be an uncaring taskmaster.

The first task he undertook was to take one of the poorer-producing fields, the one closest to their village, and disc the crop into the soil. He then ordered the construction of multiple housing units with playgrounds and a day-care center. He was taking the first step in fulfilling his promise to help and aid the disadvantaged workers who toiled in his fields.

* * * *

The fall of Pablo Pizano and rise of Molina Marquez was met with mixed reviews in the world of Colombia's Cartel. Those who knew and hated Pablo Pizano could not have cared less about his recent demise or those who took his place. Others, like Hugo Garcia, the second-strongest member of the Cartel, who also lived in Medellin, viewed Pizano's death as an opportunity to expand his own holdings. The bloody territorial battle took place at Pizano's prime coca field.

Garcia's men were waiting at the crack of dawn to ambush Molina's new field foremen. Unbeknownst to Garcia, however, Molina had foreseen the possibility of a violent takeover by Garcia, and had previously planted one of his men in Garcia's army. He was thus forewarned of the impending attack.

The field workers arrived to work on schedule that morning and, finding no patron, began their daily work. It was not all that unusual to have the gunmen periodically arrive late after a night on the town, drinking and whoring with putahs in the cantinas.

By 10 a.m., the guards still hadn't arrived. Hugo Garcia laughed as he stationed four of his best men at the field. He had gained possession of Pizano's prized coca fields without firing a shot.

"Molina Marquez had apparently gotten the word that I was taking over his newly acquired territory, and doesn't have the huevos to show up and fight for what should have been his," he boasted. "Your monthly income just increased, Muchachos!" he laughed, shooting his silver Beretta pistol into the air.

"Vamasnos," he said, jumping into his jeep. "Let's tour our next acquisition."

As the jeep rounded the turn at the top of the hill, Garcia was hit by a barrage of bullets from both sides of the road. The jeep spun to the side of the road and the driver slumped over the wheel, dead. Hugo Garcia sat in the back of the jeep. A startled look fixed on his face as blood seeped from the small bullet hole that had pierced the middle of his forehead.

"Let this be a lesson to all who make a move on Molina Marquez, self-proclaimed king of the Cartel!" Molina laughed, jabbing his automatic weapon into the air, discharging the balance of his bullets. "Muchachos! Finish the job," he said, nodding towards the field where Garcia's four men had been stationed. One of the four men had been Molina's plant, and, upon hearing the gunfire, the other three made a swift departure into the hills through the fields. Molina let them escape to tell the rest of Medellin that he was now the king of cocaine. From that day on, the name of Molina Juan Marquez demanded respect.

* * * *

At first, Molina Marquez was somewhat cautious about appearing in public, uncertain of his position in the community. It was not unusual for those in the drug business to be assassinated as they drove down the street, sat in a restaurant sipping wine, or while they were bagging someone's woman in one of the local hotels.

When he did venture outside the villa, it was always under a heavily armed guard. He decided that his first social-business visit would be to police headquarters, where he would buy local protection. He met with the chief of police, one Joseph Diaz. Chief Diaz was a man of small stature, impeccably dressed in a sharply creased, fresh-pressed jacket and pants with highly polished, knee-high black boots. He spoke with a clear, high-pitched, articulate voice. Small of stature, he pranced around his office like a bantam rooster, his black swagger-stick jammed under his arm when he wasn't waving it about for effect.

When Molina departed his office an hour later, he left a small eelskin briefcase full of unmarked bills on Chief Diaz's desk. Along with the money came a clear understanding that in the event any of his men were ever picked up for violations of any kind, they would be released on their own recognizance and the charges shuffled to the bottom of the ever-growing pile of papers on his desk, eventually to be lost forever.

Additionally, and most importantly, the information highway that inevitably flowed through the

Medellin police squad, 90 percent of whom were on someone's payroll other than the police community—usually members of the Cartel—was to be made available to him at all times. Molina made it clear that if any word was spoken or heard relative to a movement against Molina Marquez, the chief and/or his staff was to notify him immediately.

Molina made it abundantly clear that any violation of this agreement would result in severe reprisals. To back up his claim, Molina left two photos for the chief to retain in his possession. One was a photo of his children at play while they were at school. Two unidentified men stood beside the children, their hands inside their jackets exposing the handles of their weapons. The other photo was of Hugo Diaz sitting in his jeep with the bullet hole in his forehead, blood trickling down his forehead. Hugo Diaz and his henchmen had not been seen since that fatal day on Molina's ranch.

The message was clear. Molina had just taken the second step in establishing himself as a force to be reckoned with.

Chapter Four

"Chris, what time are your folks coming over again? I want to be sure to leave enough time to visit with them before the ham is done and we have dinner. I don't want them to feel like we're giving them the bum's rush." Jana Murray had been up since 6:15, setting the table, putting last-minute touches on the fruit salad, hitting her favorite porcelain sculpture pieces with a dust cloth for the third time, while periodically checking her hair in the hall mirror to be sure that each well-coifed, blonde strand was in place.

"They said that they'd meet us at church and follow us home after Easter services. That way they'll have lots of time to visit with the kids," Christian replied as he briskly rubbed his hair with a towel. It was still thick and dark, thanks to his Colombian heritage.

"That's what I mean. I want them to be able to relax and enjoy themselves and have time to visit with the family before dinner."

"You know as soon as we've eaten Larz will be at our door to pick up Kara. Then they'll be out of here like a duck on the first day of huntin' season." He was always the practical one, not easily flustered by his parents' visit, Easter or no. He really appreciated all the time and effort that Jana put into family gatherings, but social appearances just weren't his thing. Eat dinner, have a cup of coffee, then put on the Bull's basketball game was his idea of a family gathering. He might even have a beer and a bag of potato chips at half time, just to fill in the empty spaces. After the game, maybe he would retire to the backyard and throw a few horseshoes, or just sit on the patio and enjoy another beer while he watched the hummingbirds sip nectar from the liquid feeder and listened to the mourning dove's haunting coo.

"Not before she helps me with the dishes," Jana said, adjusting the distance between the forks and spoons for the third time. "No 16-year-old of mine is going to leave me with all that mess."

"Mom can help. I just don't want any family arguments, especially today," he said as he entered the family room trying to adjust his tie. Christian Murray had access to all the tension he wanted at work, and then some. In his home, he demanded peace and tranquillity. Family arguments, especially when his parents were around, were met with stern opposition. Jana knew this, but she was a strong-minded Irish-Catholic who stood her ground. When her feathers were ruffled, she didn't hesitate to give you a piece of her mind, whether you wanted it or not. That was one of the reasons Christian had fallen in love with her. He hated those wet wash rag, Mary-milk-toast-type, what-ever-you-say personalities.

"Chris, get serious. Your mom is 85. She deserves to be served and to spend her time enjoying her grandchildren, not cleaning up or washing dishes. Kara and Kal will just have to do kitchen duty, like it or not."

"Aw, Mom. I'll get dishpan hands," Kalvan complained, dropping over the arm of the couch and sliding onto the seat with all the grace of a newborn calf. "What will the guys on the team think when I show up for basketball practice with soft, dishpan-white hands?" he asked with a scowl, holding out his young, unblemished hands as if presenting an incontrovertible argument. He had obviously inherited his mother's flair for logic.

"They'll think that your mom made you do the dishes, that's what they'll think," she said, giving him a sly but firm look.

"You're a senior now, a leader among your peers. You're not to supposed to care what everyone thinks," their father replied, matter-of-factly.

"Aw, Dad," Kalvan said, furrowing his brow, appealing to a higher authority.

"Your father used to not only help prepare dinner, but he dried the dishes when we were first married," his mother argued, nodding towards his father, who was still struggling with his tie, looking frustrated. She was interrupted by the soft chime of the telephone.

"Get the phone, will you, Kal?" she said, twisting the plates a fraction. "My hands are full at the moment. And if it's Larz, you can invite him over for dinner if you like..." She added quietly to herself, "then maybe you'll hang around for a while."

Christian had given up trying to tie a Windsor knot in the new Bill Blass tie that Jana had bought for him just for Easter, and had switched to an easier forehand knot as he looked into the hall mirror, frowning. "Can you give me a hand here, Jana? These new wide-body ties just aren't meant for guys with four thumbs." He scowled, dropping his hands to his sides in resignation.

"It's for you, Dad," Kalvan said, handing his father the portable phone. "Business," he added, with a knowing look towards his mother.

"The office?" he asked, furrowing his brow. He was chief of Drug Enforcement Administration, otherwise known as the DEA. The main office was located in Washington, DC, and it was not unusual for him to receive calls from his subordinates at all times of the day and night. "I told them not to call me at home," he said apologetically to his wife, who shot him a sharp glance. "Especially today," he emphasized with a stern look at the phone, as if it were responsible. He shook his head in mock disgust as he took the receiver from his son. "Looking pretty spiffy," he said with a wink. "Got a date after dinner?"

"Nah. Me and the guys are going to shoot a little pool, that's all."

"On Easter Sunday?"

"Why not? Nothing else to do. The malls are all closed, so we can't go girl watching."

Christian watched as his son grabbed the Sunday comics and fell back onto the couch with the grace of a sack of potatoes. *All boy, that one*, he thought as he studied his son's rugged, handsome face. He was the school's quarterback, point guard in basketball, and first baseman and alternate pitcher in the spring sport. Girls threw themselves at his feet, but at this age his only interest was sports and his buddies. *Oh, to be that age again*, Christian thought to himself as he looked at Kal admiringly.

He put the phone to his ear. "Murray!" he said sharply with a voice of authority.

He listened intently as his look changed from one of irritation to intense concentration. His eyes darted around the wall, as if he viewed a hologram of the conversation.

Finally, he took a deep breath and quietly said,

"Be there in 20. Round up the rest of the team."

His wife put down the cake she had been frosting and shot him an angry glance. "Not on Easter Sunday, Christian Murray!"

He looked at his wife apologetically. "This is a big one," he said, removing his tie. His eyes darted around the room, not wanting to lock on his wife's eyes. "We've been working on this bust for over a year now. The mob's bringing in a shipment that's so large it could reduce the national debt by a ton. And it's going down today." He emphasized by pointing to the floor with his index finger.

"What are we supposed to do?" she said, throwing her hands in the air. "Sit on our hands, waiting for you to bring in the bad guys? What about dinner? Church? Your folks? I'm not your entertainment committee, you know!" She angrily tore off her apron and threw it on the floor, but stood her ground, glaring at him.

He could see that she was fighting back tears of anger and frustration. He felt a temporary pang of guilt, which quickly disappeared as his mind started to focus on the gravity of the job that lay ahead.

They had been married for 18 years now, and 14 of those years had been spent with busted vacations, lonesome nights and cold dinners. He had missed Kara's lead in the play *Oklahoma*, been absent at countless of Kal's games, and had missed anniversaries and birthdays, but the most unforgettable, unforgivable sin was when he had missed Kara's birth. It had been a premature birth, and Kara had to be put into an incubator, diagnosed with hyaline-membrane disease, a serious lung deficiency. For a while there, the doctors thought that the baby might die, but Kara's will was strong and she had pulled through. Jana never forgave him for not being there when they had needed him most, nor did she let him forget it.

"I'll take the Bronco and catch up with you guys at the church," he said, trying to muster a cheerful voice. "You guys can have the Mercedes. Be sure and save me a seat," he said with a wink, trying to defuse the situation with a note of frivolity as he turned to leave the room.

Both he and Jana knew that he would be lucky to make dessert, let alone church.

"Jeez, Chris! Why on Easter?" She stamped her foot. It was a rhetorical question to which she already knew the answer—the same answer she had received for 14 years.

"It's what I do, Jana," he repeated for what seemed like the millionth time. "We want to build a world safe for our children and their children, don't we?" It was another repetitive rhetorical question, but a safe response.

The situation was obviously out of her hands. She had learned years ago that inquiring into or challenging the nature of his business was futile. At first it had been exciting to be married to a government agent who went out into the cold night to fight the bad guys, but over the years the excitement had deteriorated to a mundane pain in the neck. Oh, sure, she was the envy of the ladies at the tennis club and her weekly bridge group, who were always eager for any tidbit they could take home for gossip or to flaunt at their husbands, who had boring jobs such as building houses, driving trucks, being lawyers or selling.

He leaned over to kiss his wife, but she merely turned her cheek, demonstrating her displeasure. Fifteen minutes later, Christian Murray drove down the driveway, waving at Kara and Kal as they stood in the doorway watching the black Bronco disappear down the street. This had become a familiar scene, as common as Beaver and Wally watching their father go to work in *Leave It To Beaver*.

His children were aware that the work he did was dangerous, and, although their father never spoke to them about his job, they inferred from periodic hushed conversations between their parents that several of his associates had been killed over the years in the line of duty. They had once even seen their father on national television, walking next to the President of the United States during a funeral. In one unforgettable instance, several men of his own team had been killed. The Mob, it was later learned, had a mole in the administration, and had set a trap for the agents in a sting operation of their own.

They didn't consciously think about the danger he might be in, but, in the depths of their minds, they always feared the day when there might be a call telling their mother that their father wasn't coming home that night—or ever again.

"Come on, kids. It's time to get going," she said, looking at her watch. "We're meeting your grandparents at the church," she said, surveying the pre-set dining room table one last time. Although it had been a lot of work, she loved to entertain, to show off her fine china and decorate the house. She was an excellent cook, and the family always looked forward to her Sunday dinners. It was the one day when they would all sit in the formal dining room, where she would set the table with her fine china, crystal glasses and cloth napkins. She would usually prepare a roast, bake homemade biscuits and have mashed potatoes and gravy. Those were special times.

Kara was dressed in a new pink dress, bought especially for Easter. She wore a small hat, a custom that Jana's family had engaged in so long ago that it had become a family tradition. Kal wore his blue blazer with brass buttons, a blue striped tie, and gray pants. He had put a little mousse on his crew cut, so it glistened in the sunlight. Jana wore a dark blue knit suit that accentuated her size nine, five-foot-seven frame. A string of freshwater pearls hung loosely around her neck.

The Murray family looked like the typical American family on its way to Easter services... sans Father, of course.

The Mercedes was parked in front of the house, on the circular driveway near the front door.

"Can I drive, Mom?" Kal asked, his eyes dancing. "I washed the car yesterday, especially for Easter. Looks great, doesn't it?" He loved the heavy road feel of the 450 SEL. It was a gun-metal gray, government issue for the select few, of which Christian Murray was one.

"I guess you deserve it. But no driving fast," she warned, tossing him the keys with 'that look' in her eyes. "Seat belts, everyone," she said as she closed the passenger door.

Kal buckled his seat belt and gave his sister a knowing look through the rear-view mirror as she buckled up in the back seat. He smiled at his mom as he inserted the key into the ignition. He pushed the second button on the radio, which had been pre-set to his favorite rock station, and turned the key. At that moment, there was an ear-splitting explosion that blew the hood off the car and shattered the windows of both the car and the front of the house. A burst of deep red flame mixed with black smoke filled the air, simultaneously incinerating everything within.

Christian Murray's family had just been executed.

Chapter Five

Christian parked his Bronco behind the large, vacant steel building in the older section of Washington, DC's, industrial district. It had an old, deteriorated For Lease sign hanging on it. The building had been purchased by the Drug Enforcement Administration three years ago, when Director Christian Murray had formed his special, secret, elite group of eleven men, known as The Team. The faded telephone number on the sign rang through to a federal answering service which bore the name of Investments Limited. In the event anyone ever called for information regarding the dilapidated building, their name and phone number was taken, and they were told that a sale of the property was pending. They were told an agent would contact them in the event the sale fell through.

From all outward appearances the building was vacant, with numerous broken windows. The gate was half hanging on its hinges, and the grounds were littered with empty 50-gallon barrels, stacked wooden pallets and broken, rusty, run-down machinery. It was too scary for anyone to venture into at night, and too ugly and dangerous looking to explore during the day.

Access to the interior portion of the building was through a locked rusty steel door which had a camouflaged electronic eye positioned over the entrance, which looked much like an old, broken EXIT sign. Christian put his hand around the cold steel handle and punched in a code on the numbered face-plate that had been installed under the rusty hinged mailbox lid. There was a pause, then the steel door silently swung open.

Inside the large tin shed a windowless structure had been built within the building. The room was lit with a strong pure white incandescent light, powered by a silent generator in a small room of its own which was encased within a four-inch sound proof styrofoam structure. In the middle of the 20x40-foot conference room was a 12-foot plank table with a dozen black tufted leather chairs surrounding it. The walls were bare sheet rock with soundproofing on the outside. Television monitors lined one wall, displaying the entrance as well as the entire perimeter of the building. Christian faced nine men as he entered the room, surveying each man quickly with piercing, expert eyes.

"Where's the Safety?"

"Chet's got the flu," one of the men replied.

Murray shot him a sharp look. He had instructed the men countless times against using names, even within the confines of the building. This was a very elite team, known to only Robert Macaffe, the US Attorney General, and a select few members of the DEA. No one outside of the administration, not even the President of the United States, knew about it. For that reason he had assigned each man a position on the team in place of a name...a position on a football team. He was the quarterback, and was to be referred to as such at all times during an operation, although many simply called him "Coach".

"Sorry," the man said. "It won't happen again."

"I know you men think that using your real name in the confines of this building is acceptable, but if you don't get used to protocol here, when you get out in the field, during the heat of battle, you'll slip. As sure as the day is long, you'll call one another by your real names."

They had heard the speech a hundred times if they had heard it once.

He looked sternly at his team. Christian Murray was a firm taskmaster. He had seen enough combat—both militarily and in civilian life—to know that a man's discipline could make the difference between survival and death.

He had joined the marines right out of high school, just in time to be sent to Vietnam. Through a combination of bravery, dumb luck and self-preservation, he quickly rose through the ranks. By the end of his first tour he had been awarded the rank of staff sergeant.

He had decided to re-enlist when, the day before signing papers, his outpost had been hit by incoming VC shells. All but two of the men had been killed in the attack: Sergeant Murray and Lance Corporal Koslowski. They had been on guard duty on the outer perimeter when the camp was hit.

Murray took this as a sign that the war in Vietnam was just a land mine away from impending doom, and shipped out when his tour of duty was completed a week later. The war had instilled in him a fascination with anything to do with law enforcement and correctional work. After a few weeks of R&R, he applied for and was accepted by the University of Virginia, where he majored in criminology. Four years later, he graduated with honors and entered the master's program.

One day he walked into the gymnasium when they were having "Career Day" and spoke to agents representing the FBI, DEA and the Secret Service. Robert Macaffe, the man in charge of the Drug Enforcement Administration, was so impressed with Murray, his war record and academic credentials that he offered him a job on the spot.

Murray spent the next 18 months at the DEA training facilities in Virginia. His skills and ambition soon elevated him to a leadership position in the organization.

"Protective identity is mandatory in this line of work. If you have any doubts about that, recall the feeling you had when we fished Jim Laferty's body from the sewage treatment pond last year," Murray said with a firm voice and an intense look. "The mere slip of his name heard by the wrong people cost him his life!"

The man studied his feet, not wanting to look at Murray or his colleagues, whom he knew were looking at him.

"All right. Having said that, let us concentrate on the task at hand. Center! Brief the team."

A husky, powerfully built man with a military-type haircut unraveled a street map and laid it on the table. He wore a tight-fitting khaki T-shirt. His muscles rippled with each movement of his arm. "The targeted shipment is believed to be pure Colombian coke. Our source indicate that the Colombians have carried the cocaine from the interior jungle of Colombia down to small boats. The shipment was then transported along the San Juan River until they reached the Pacific Coast. Their destination was Japan. Once it reached Japan, the coke was packed into the those metal cases that house computers, except the components will be missing and bags of coke have been inserted in their place.

"The shipment departed Japan three weeks ago and arrived off our shore last week. Yesterday it was off-loaded onto a river boat which traveled up the Chesapeake Bay, where they diverted the craft up the Rappahannock River, docking at Tappanhonnock last night."

"Crafty buggers," one of the men said.

"Careful and watchful," Murray said. "They know if they go up a smaller tributary than the Chesapeake it'll be easy to spot anyone following, in which case they'll simply abort the mission and return to the mother ship."

"After coming halfway across the world?"

"Better to abort than die or go to jail," Murray said.

The man nodded as he cocked his head and shrugged his shoulders, as if to say, "I guess you're right".

"Once there, they unloaded their cargo and placed it in an unmarked 16-wheeler..."

"If it's unmarked, how will we know which truck it is?" one of the men asked.

"Our source reports that the truck is painted black and the trailer is silver. We also have the license number."

"Yeah! Raider's colors," one of the men quipped with a smile, raising his fist into the air.

Murray shot him a quick glance.

The man diverted his eyes and looked at the map again.

"Do we have a chopper tailing them?" another asked.

"Too risky. They might spot it, and then all our work would have been for naught."

The man nodded.

"Right," Murray said. "On with it." He nodded toward the map again.

"The truck is expected to drive to Arlington, Virginia, where we believe a meeting has been set up with their buyer here in the States..."

"Mafia," Murray added.

"But Arlington is next door to the Capital. Isn't that a bit gutsy?" one of the men asked.

"These are gutsy times. Remember, these men are pros. They know it's Easter, and who's going to expect drugs to be delivered on the President's front lawn on Easter Sunday? Remember Pearl Harbor? The Japs knew everyone would be lounging around with no one minding the store before they even decided to hit Pearl. Same scenario." Murray nodded towards Center, indicating for him to continue.

"Right. And that's where we'll intercept them. We'll bag the Colombians and the Mafia, and get the drugs and the money," he said, drawing a circle around the city of Arlington, hitting it with his pointer for effect.

"Quite a catch," one of the men said.

"We've been tracking this particular supplier since before the shipment left Colombia," Murray said. "Bagging these scumbags will send a loud and clear message, not only to the Mob, but to the Colombians as well, that we mean business. We've got their number now," he said with pride.

"How did we find out about this deal?" one of the men asked curiously.

"Let us just say that I've cultivated an inside source. Close to the game, so to speak." He smiled to himself.

"In the Mob?" the man asked in awe. "I thought that was near impossible."

"It probably is. My contact is in the thick of

the jungles of Colombia, where the coca fields are located." He looked at his men with an apologetic look. "Now, I know this is Easter, and I'm sorry to have to drag you men away like this, but if this is the day they plan on us having our guard down, they're mistaken."

He looked over the group of young faces, all serious, eager to serve. None of the men were married nor had family obligations. Murray had purposely hand-picked each man, not only for their military skills. Being unattached was mandatory. Most had no family at all. He wanted no outside influences clouding their judgment. Most of the men had been trained by the military with special units, such as seals, marines or rangers. They all had intensive jungle survival training and all had their paratrooper wings. When they had been discharged from the service, normal civilian life had just become too mundane for them. If they hadn't been working for Murray, they, in all probability, would have been social misfits.

"Well, they'll have another think comin' when the see the end of my piece," one of the men said, smiling, holding up his forefinger as if it were a gun.

"I assume that there will be no locals to assist?"

"You mean interfere," Murray was quick to add.

The man smiled.

"You assume correctly," Murray said. "I don't want any amateurs mucking up this job."

The men nodded, each with a self-satisfying, smug smile. The group prided themselves on self-sufficiency and independence. Asking for outside assistance would be an insult to their abilities, and would jeopardize their identities as well.

"All right, Center, proceed," Murray said, nodding to the large man leaning over his map with a pointer.

"The truck is expected to arrive at Arlington in about two hours. The two Ends will pick up the truck here," he said, pointing to an intersection on the map. Then the Backs will take over," looking at the two men who nodded. "You will follow for four blocks, then turn right, go down two blocks and pick up here again." He indicated with his pointer. "The Guards will pick up where the Backs left off, picking up their trail. The Tackles will proceed parallel, one block off route, in the event either the Guards or Backs are spotted. The balance of the team will follow in the assault trucks a block behind, waiting for instructions from Quarterback." He nodded towards Murray.

"We expect the meeting to be on open ground, where it will be difficult to surprise the offense," Murray said. "So, when the blitz signal is given, it's imperative that you attack as quickly and as effectively as possible. The Ends and Guards will hit their right flank. Halfbacks around to their rear. The Tackles will strike their left flank, while the rest of the team blitzes up the middle, hitting them with everything you've got."

"And if there's gunfire?" the Safety asked—a rhetorical question, but he wanted to be clear on his actions. He was the one member of the team who required a clear, precise picture of his duty.

"Take no prisoners." It was standard orders to shoot to kill, not to just wound with the intent of interrogating the prisoner later. "This is a major drug bust between the Colombians and the Mob. With a payload of this magnitude, it's expected that there will be significant resistance. The element of surprise will be our only advantage. Once they're aware of our presence, there will be a moment of confusion, as the Mob will temporarily think the Colombians are after the money, and the Colombians will think the Mob is after the drugs. That moment of confusion will be our only ace in the hole. Any questions?"

He looked at his men, pausing momentarily to study each face before moving on. Having satisfied himself that there were no questions, he nodded. "We'll use radio frequency 6.1 on band 'B'. No one is to use the air unless it is absolutely necessary. It's highly unlikely that they'll pick us up, but they could have a roving band monitor and accidentally pick up a transmission, so, as I said, silence is imperative." He paused for a moment to study the men once more. "If there are no questions, mount up."

They filed into the equipment room, where each man drew an automatic assault weapon with a silencer and an automatic handgun, also equipped with a silencer. As they exited the room, the Center passed out ammunition belts with clips for each weapon. Murray handed each man a dark gray combat helmet equipped with a built-in, highly sophisticated headset that was to be worn during the operation. Each headset had been previously tuned to 6.1 and contained a small battery pack. Each individual could now easily hear and speak without breaking stride. The table near the door contained a bulletproof flack jacket for each man with his position-name imprinted across the back.

Outside the metal building, they paired off to their vehicles: black and gray windowless vans equipped with sophisticated electronic equipment, including a two-way radio. Murray drove his black Bronco.

"Check time," Murray said into the mike attached to his headset.

"Roger, Tackle."

"Roger, Ends."

"Roger, Backs."

"Roger, Guards."

"Roger, Safety and Center."

"Quarterback, clear and out."

They drove in silence from Washington, DC, to Arlington, keeping approximately 100 feet between each vehicle so as to not draw attention to themselves.

Chapter Six

When Christian didn't show for Easter services, it was no great surprise to his parents. Over the years they had become accustomed to their son's unpredictable schedule. They could be having breakfast at Denny's or having dinner at the Red Lyon hotel or enjoying a movie, and Murray's beeper would invariably go off. They would look at one another, full well knowing that their evening was about to be disjointed—and it usually was. For that reason, they made it a rule to take two cars, just in case Christian had to leave and they had to take Jana and the kids home.

When Jana and the children didn't show up for church, especially for Easter services, that was another matter. Jana was not only fanatical about going to church—she was a devout Catholic, firm in her faith and stoic about instilling that faith in her children. She was also fanatical about punctuality.

Christian's parents kept checking their watches and looking back to see if maybe they had arrived late and had decided to sit in one of the back pews so they wouldn't interrupt Father Mather's sermon. As a rule, if Jana said she would be at a given place at a given time, she was not only punctual, but could usually be counted on to be early.

So, when the service was over, after shaking Father Mather's hand and offering a lame excuse for Christian's and Jana's absence, Ted and Alice Murray rushed over to their son's house. As they turned onto the street that led into their neighborhood, traffic was at a standstill. They could see fire engines and black smoke rising ahead. It seemed to be coming from the general vicinity of their son's house!

Unable to move their car, they abandoned the vehicle and walked up the street, where they encountered a crowd of people. Shock registered on their faces as they made their way through the crowd and found that the area in front of their son's house had been cordoned off with yellow police tape.

Fire trucks, police, ambulances and a tearful crowd of neighbors were huddling together, talking in hushed voices.

Officer Lawrence, a friend of the families, spotted the elder Murrays as they stood frozen in unmasked, silent hysteria. "A terrible thing has happened," he said as he rushed to take them aside. "It would be best if you don't go near the house."

They could see the broken windows on the front of the house. The Mercedes was black from smoke and was unrecognizable, but Ted Murray knew it was his son's automobile. Alice Murray snapped out of the trance she had fallen into and immediately went into hysterics, fearing the worst.

"What happened? Where's Christian? Where are Alice and the kids?" Ted demanded. "Are they all right?" He knew from the serious look on the officer's face and mass destruction of the scene that it was probable that loss of life must have occurred. The line of work his son was in had apparently resulted in someone making an attempt on his life. It was too soon to know who was in the charred Mercedes, but he assumed that the whole family must have perished.

"We don't know," the officer said, with compassion for the elderly couple. "All we know is that there are people in the car. I'm sorry," he consoled. "There's nothing to be done here. Please...let one of my men escort you home."

Alice was beyond reason, weeping and falling to the ground in hysteria. Ted knew that he must remain strong, for his wife if nothing else. Together, he and the officer carried his distraught wife to a waiting police car. A policewoman drove them to the nearest hospital, where they administered a sedative to Alice.

It wasn't until much later that Christian's parents finally learned that their son was not in the automobile...that, somehow, he had survived.

* * * *

As the DEA caravan approached Arlington, a black semi pulling a silver trailer passed them in the middle lane. Murray glanced up at the cab of the truck as it passed his Bronco, but couldn't see the driver through the smoked glass window.

"Check the plates," he said to Grover, his passenger and the team's Center.

Grover quickly checked his clipboard. "That's our objective," he said, nodding to the truck. "Shall I alert the rest of the team?"

"No air transmission." Murray tapped his brakes quickly three times, then held his foot to the pedal for a moment, sending a prearranged signal to the vehicle behind him. That vehicle did the same, and the routine was repeated until the entire caravan was alerted to the identification of their objective.

Murray slowed his Bronco, dropping back a respectable distance from the semi, checking his rear-view mirror to be sure the truck didn't have other company. He nodded to himself, satisfied that they had no escort. Whatever armed guards they had were apparently contained within the truck itself. He knew the Colombians wouldn't bring several million dollars of drugs into hostile territory without a heavily armed escort.

The semi made its way towards the Arlington National Cemetery, giving no indication that it knew it was being followed.

"My God, they're heading straight for the cemetery," Murray said with a stunned expression as the truck turned off the highway onto the road designated for Arlington Cemetery.

"Does that present a problem?" Grover asked with a concerned look.

"Only that there's nothing there but rows and rows of headstones. There's no place to hide or sneak up on them without exposure. They'll be out in the open, highly visible, but then again, so will we."

Grover looked at Murray with a questioning appearance. *No use asking the obvious,* he thought. Murray had to have a plan of attack. If not, he knew the coach would develop one. Both he and the rest of the team had come to look upon their elder leader, "the old man" or "coach" as they affectionately called him behind his back, their mentor and, in some cases, their second father. Grover's father had deserted the family when he had been but a child, so Murray had become a genuine father figure to him.

As the truck entered the cemetery, Murray said, "We'll have to pull over here. We'll have to observe the situation from here for a few minutes before embarking on a line of attack." Grover watched the frustrated look on his face with concern as Murray retrieved his field glasses from the glove compartment. He looked into the rear-view mirror as the rest of the caravan pulled in close behind.

Murray watched as the large truck entered the cemetery and circled around the tomb of the Unknown Soldier before heading towards the far end of the cemetery. There, Murray spotted two black limos parked with men standing near their fronts. They were dressed in dark woolen overcoats. It was obvious to the trained eye that they carried weapons under their coats, which were worn not only for weapon cover, but warmth as well, as it was still winter in Washington.

The truck stopped several yards short of the two limos. A few moments passed before two men climbed out of the passenger side of the truck and surveyed the men in front of them. They scanned their surroundings carefully before walking toward the limos. The driver of the truck quickly walked around to the rear and lifted the roll-up door, exposing three men brandishing automatic weapons.

Grover looked at Murray with an anxious face. "What do we do, boss?"

Murray didn't answer, but his face indicated obvious concern. The rest of the team waited in their vehicles for instructions. Suddenly, Murray jumped from his Bronco and rushed to the rear, waving the rest of his team up.

"We have to abort our plan of attack," he said to his team once they had reached him. He nodded towards the cemetery. "Apparently, I didn't give them enough credit," he seemed to apologize. "We'll have to deploy and wait for an opening. If none occurs, we'll just have to hit them on open ground when they depart."

"We have company," one of the men said, nodding towards a black Jaguar approaching the cemetery.

Murray waited until the vehicle and its occupants had passed—an elderly man and woman dressed in black, obviously on their way to pay their respects to a lost son buried in the cemetery. The woman carefully cradled a bouquet of flowers in her arms.

"Clever bastards," he said, more to himself than to anyone else. "They know there will be a ton of civilians visiting the cemetery today. One would have to be a fool to start a fire fight with civilians around."

"We can hold off our attack until they leave," one of the men offered.

Murray shot him a sharp glance. "In which direction, Kos..." he caught himself before he said the man's name, almost breaking his own rule. "When they leave, they can go into Washington across the Memorial Bridge or go down the Jefferson Davis Highway or take the Washington Memorial Parkway or get on any one of the several other tributaries available to them within a moment's drive from here," he said, waving his arms in all directions. "Hell, we could all take a departure route and still miss 'em."

No one spoke, each man looking at the target, then studying their leader's face, awaiting instructions. They knew he would devise a plan. They would be told when he was ready. Only Murray knew that he not only didn't have a plan, but faced the possibility of bungling the entire job at this point. He scanned the scene with his binoculars again.

The men from the limo had placed several brief-cases on the hood of their vehicle. It had to be the money, Murray thought to himself, feeling his face flush with frustration. He had waited months to nail these bastards, and now he was so close he could taste it and all he could do was wait and hope for an opening.

"All right. Here's the plan," he said quickly. "When the limo leaves with the drugs, I want the Ends and Backs to follow them. Here's what you're going to do..." Murray drew an imaginary map on the hood of his Bronco with his forefinger, outlining the plan. When he had finished, he asked, "Any questions?"

"What if they spot us? Do we engage?"

Murray looked at the man with a look that a father might give a child asking to take the family car on a first date. "You will not be detected," he said emphatically. "Do I make myself clear?"

"Yes, sir. Crystal clear," the man said nervously, avoiding the eyes of his commander.

"Good. Now, you're to stay in visual contact with the cargo until you have instructions from me. At precisely 14:00 hours, I'll ring you at this frequency. Make your transmissions short and succinct. I don't want to alert anyone to our presence."

He looked at the four mens' faces, as if asking for questions. When there were none, he said, "All right. Move out."

After they had left, he looked at the remaining team. "Our job is to take command of the truck without endangering civilians. If we let these men get back to their base on water, we'll be forced to rely on external assistance and, as you know, our chance of catching them will be greatly diminished. Besides, if they play the closing part of this game like they've played it thus far, I'm sure they have an alternate exit out of the country. After all, their load is considerably lighter now. So, here's what we do…"

Murray was too busy revising his plan to keep watch on the drug transaction. Murray's team barely had time to get into position before one of the limos departed. Murray held up his forefinger, indicating that the drugs must be in that limo. The other limo waited with the truck, which puzzled him.

One of his team members was parked outside of the cemetery, while the other was inside, waiting on a side road just to the left of the main entrance. As the limo passed the first of Murray's vehicles, they noticed that it was being driven by one of the Colombians. They had apparently left the drugs in the truck and had simply traded vehicles.

As the vehicle passed Murray, he noted the change, too, but by this time the die was cast. It was too late to alter their plan. The limo exited the cemetery, with Murray following at a safe distance. The second team's vehicle which, by now, was parked outside the main gate, followed 50 feet behind Murray's group.

The limo crossed the Potomac River on the Arlington Memorial Bridge and turned left onto the Potomac Parkway, heading towards Georgetown, with the occupants none the wiser that they were being tailed. The driver of the lead vehicle radioed the limo's route to Murray.

Murray watched them for a moment, then said, "They're heading for the airport!" He turned to the other members of the team. "You guys stick with the truck and wait for me to contact you," he said hurriedly, jumping into his Bronco. "Come on, Grover, I'll drive!"

Grover shot Murray a glance, with a sly smile creeping over his lips. *Even the boss can get rattled at times,* he thought to himself, and he replayed the ill-spoken sentence back in his mind.

Murray sped down the nearly vacant freeway and had the trailing van in sight in a matter of moments. He was thankful that the freeway was empty, with everyone either in church or at home celebrating Easter. He passed the first van, giving the driver a hand signal consisting of a closed fist, indicating that they were to hold off doing any action pending further orders from him. The driver nodded, but his face indicated that he was a little uncomfortable with the sudden change of plans. It was unlike Murray to make sudden, unscheduled alterations, especially at a time like this, without clear, precise planning.

Murray's mind registered the driver's confusion. "What the hell," he said, turning on his headset. *The Colombians are too busy counting their money to be playing with the short-wave,* he thought. "Ends and Backs, this is Quarterback." He was back in form again. "Subject vehicle has the cash and is heading towards the airport. A diversion is going to be necessary. Here's the plan..."

As the limo exited the freeway, heading towards the airport, the lead vehicle passed the Colombians limo, followed by Murray. The third vehicle trailed a safe distance behind.

As they approached a lighted intersection, Murray pulled his Bronco up next to the lead team vehicle and made a one-finger salute to the driver, shouting obscenities at him.

The driver made a like sign back, rolled down his window and began shouting at Murray. They slowed to a stop at the intersection, which had a cement divider separating them from oncoming traffic. The limo, which was trailing behind, was now blocked behind the two vehicles.

Murray got out of his vehicle and ran over to the first truck, pounding on its hood, shouting obscenities at the driver, who seemed to return the insult but stayed in his truck.

By now, the Colombians were getting impatient with these two American drivers and began honking their horn, wanting to pass, as they had a plane to catch. The honking got the attention of both drivers, who walked back to the limo driver.

"Take your arguments off the road, if you don't mind," the Colombian said in perfect English, forcing a smile. "I have a plane to catch. Please move your vehicle."

Murray looked at the other driver in anger as he spoke to the Colombian. "You saw what happened, didn't you? He pulled right in front of me," he accused, pointing his finger at his team member. "He cut me off. Give me your name and telephone number so I can contact you as a witness," Murray said, reaching inside his jacket, where he had his weapon.

"I'm sorry, I didn't see anything that could be of any use to you," he said, obviously irritated as he leaned out of the window. "Anyway, I'm leaving the country, and..."

At that moment, Murray pulled the unsuspecting man halfway through the window and hit him on the head with the butt of his weapon, knocking him out. In the meantime, the team which had been trailing the limo had pulled over, and the driver was at the rear door of the limo, pulling the Colombians from the back seat. They had been preoccupied with the staged argument between Murray and his men in the lead vehicle.

In a blink of an eye, the Colombians were in custody and wearing handcuffs, without a shot being fired. Murray laid the four oversized eelskin briefcases on the hood of the limo, snapped open the lids and whistled.

"Will you look at all that dough?" he said. Must be 10 or 12 million here. Not bad for a morning's work. I want the Backs to take this to the DEA headquarters and log it into the safe. No samples," he said, smiling.

He looked at the two Ends, who were eager for more action. They knew they were marked for other duty, however, and Murray's words solidified their fears. "I need you boys to take charge of the Colombians and put them on ice until we can get them into Federal court in the morning."

They knew it was useless to argue. Someone had to take the prisoners in, and the general certainly wasn't going to do the captain's work and vice-versa.

"We're going to get to the other half of the transaction before it gets distributed," Murray explained.

"Shall we meet up with you later?" one of the men asked, disappointed that he had to be sent back with the money.

"No. By the time you men get the money to headquarters and these punks to jail," he nodded towards the Colombians, "we should have the operation mopped up. I'll meet you back at home base."

"You could use some backup, just in case," the man meekly protested.

Murray knew their desire to be in on the bust, but stood his ground firmly. "Sorry, boys," was his only response. The look of understanding was on his face, for whatever that was worth. They nodded in quiet resignation and turned to leave.

"Good job," Murray called after them.

One of the men waved his hand over his shoulder without turning back. Murray knew how they felt, but there was a job to be done, and everyone couldn't be in on all the action all the time. It was just the luck of the draw.

Chapter Seven

Alfredo Carleone sat alone in his den looking out of the stained glass window, his eyes scanning the 50 acres of his lush, landscaped estate. His brother's wives and their families were gathered in the garden sitting room watching the children hunt for Easter eggs. Their voices squealed with delight as they found each hidden treasure. Some of the plastic eggs were filled with candy, others with coins or small trinkets. The mothers clapped with joy, urging each child to "look under the bush," or "next to the flower beds," as the children scampered about the grounds.

Grandfather Francisco Carleone sat quietly in his cushioned rocking chair, rocking slowly back and forth as he watched the children. This was his time of life to just sit back and enjoy the family while his sons ran the family business.

Alfredo Carleone was now 46 years of age, and had taken over the family business four years ago when it had become apparent that his father no longer seemed capable of functioning intelligently. Signore Francisco had contracted a touch of Alzheimer's disease, which had now advanced to the degree that his mind periodically slipped into paranoia, so that he trusted no one, including members of his own family. He was sure that his eldest son was plotting against him, but no one would listen to him, so he resigned himself to sitting quietly and enjoying the children.

Alfredo was the eldest of Don Francisco's three sons. He had been a successful attorney with a small but lucrative criminal law practice, devoting the majority of his practice to protecting the family's business. Other avenues of his practice centered around the legal needs of friends of the family. Periodically, he took time out from his practice to work for the church on a pro bono basis. Donating free time to the church was good public relations, a lesson he had learned from his father. Doing work for the church was good publicity for the family, and the church appreciated his efforts as well. It didn't hurt his case, either, on those few times he was required to defend a client in front of one of the judges. It also made a good show to probing busybodies like the District Attorney, he rationalized, who were always on the hunt to nail members of the underground, especially members of Costra Nostra or "The Family".

He lived on his father's estate with his wife and two daughters. The grounds were surrounded by a 10-foot wrought iron fence with Leland cypress trees planted next to it. They had now grown to the height of thirty feet, making a solid barrier between the property and the street. Trained Great Danes constantly patrolled the perimeter wall, discouraging anyone from trying to peek through the trees, let alone gain access.

Being the eldest of three sons, historical family protocol dictated that one day the business would fall on his shoulders. Although he dreaded the day when his father would retire or, worse yet, die, he had long been looking forward to taking over the reigns. Practicing law had provided him with a good living and had given him status in the legal community, but taking control of the family's business was the driving force that really ran through his veins.

When the time had come, it had been a difficult task to remove his father as head of the family, but self-preservation, not only for the family's business but for its members as well, dictated that it had to be done. He vacillated between feeling like Benedict Arnold and the conquering hero. Fortunately, through years of training and experience in his law practice of keeping criminals and family members out of jail, Alfredo had acquired the fine skill of negotiation. He utilized this negotiating experience to convince his father that it was time to step down from the throne and let him, his eldest son, take over. "After all," he rationalized, "this is what you trained me for."

Unbeknownst to his father, he had been preparing for this role for years. When he was but a lad of twelve, his father had begun his instruction in the ways of the family, as was the family's custom. As he matured, the aging Carleone took Alfredo, then a young attorney, to business meetings on family matters, teaching him the techniques of discipline and control. Signore Francisco was not only respected, he was feared, a fact soon learned by the young Carleone. As time progressed, the father introduced him to the family bookkeeping and banking business. When Carleone had reached the age of 35, Signore Francisco brought him into the muscle part of the business—drugs, prostitution and gambling.

Alfredo had proved to be a quick study. As he learned, he converted the knowledge he acquired into his private computer until, after years of training, he knew more about the business than the bookkeeper and his father combined.

The drug business, the mainstay of the family wealth, was doing well—excellently, in fact. Cocaine had not only become the recreational mainstream drug for America's rich and famous, but the usage of it had filtered down to the masses. Now most yuppie parties were supplied with dishes of the white, powdery substance. Professional people were hooked by its deadly addiction on a daily basis, and even college and high school kids had become recreational users. In short, people of every walk of life who had the money were buying. And those who had no money resorted to crime and violence to feed their habit. Business couldn't be better.

The prostitution business had been lucrative enough to pay for operational costs, but just the idea of selling whores disgusted Alfredo. If it weren't for his younger brother Carlo, who took a personal interest in not only that end of the business but in the girls themselves, he would have chucked the enterprise at a moment's notice, lucrative or not. At least this way, he rationalized, Carlo would be occupied and out of his hair.

Carlo had one flaw that irritated his father to the point of distraction, however. He loved black women. For a godfather to have his son favor black women was a baby step away from being gay, as far as he was concerned. And if he had a gay son, his father would have either disowned him and disavowed his very existence, or had him killed. That was how strongly he felt about the subject.

Carlo's favorite hangout was the Liedo Bar, a bar owned by black people for black people. If you were white and had the balls to enter the premises, at the very least the cocktail waitress would refuse to wait on you. When you would resort to going to the bar to get your refreshments, more likely than not you would be jostled and eventually coerced into a scuffle by one or more of the larger patrons. In the unfortunate event a whitey or two tried to exercise their masculine superiority, they were usually found in someone's dumpster, stabbed to death or beaten within an inch of their life.

It didn't take long for the owner and patrons of the Liedo to learn that Carlo Carleone was a son of one of the Mafia families, however. "Even black people have enough sense not to mess with the Mafia," Carlo would jest with the barkeep, who didn't appreciate his sense of humor, but preferred his hands unbroken.

When news reached his father that Carlo was hanging around black women, he resorted to hiring two black men to rough Carlo up. "Maybe Carlo needs a beatin' to make him see the light," he told them. "Now, don't break him up none, ya hear? Just rough him up enough to scare him."

Little did his father know that being roughed up was just the ticket that Carlo needed to set an example of his own to make sure that that never happened again. By greasing a few palms with a lot of green, he was able to have a greedy black woman identify the two thugs who had roughed him up. The next morning, they were found behind the Liedo Bar with their hands tied behind them, each with a single bullet to the back of the head: execution, Mafia-style. From that day forward, no one at the Liedo ever bothered Carlo Carleone again.

Niccola was the youngest, and was smarter than his two brothers. He had a natural propensity for math, and soaked up the numbers business like a sponge soaks up water. Alfredo delegated that portion of the family business as his domain.

That left drugs. When his father reached the stage of his illness where he was cautious and suspicious of everyone, Alfredo had become impatient with his father's small-time drug dealing. Initially, the family had been dealing with secondary sources in this country. By and large, those sources were either distant relatives of the Colombians or had contacts that dealt directly with Colombians. The purchases were usually in smaller quantities, consisting of $50 thousand or up to a quarter of a million dollars at a time.

Before Alfredo took over, in addition to dealing in cocaine, the old man had also been importing marijuana from Mexico. The risk of selling marijuana was the same as from selling cocaine, yet the profit was considerably less. Considering the bulk of marijuana and marketability to the generally less affluent younger crowd, Alfredo opted to discontinue that portion of the business and concentrate on cocaine.

He soon learned that a kilo of pure cocaine purchased by his source from the Colombians would automatically be cut 50 percent by adding lactose or some other neutral substance to the drug. Their suppliers would then sell the cut cocaine, which they bought for something in the neighborhood of $25 thousand per kilo, to the Carleone family for $20 to $30 thousand when cut, or an average of $50 thousand per uncut kilo. In short, the middle man was making 100% profit on the turn around, with no risk.

Alfredo figured that it was time to make direct contact with someone in the Cartel in Colombia, and eliminate the middle man. The problem would then become a simple matter of source. One couldn't simply fly to South America and take out an ad in the local newspaper seeking a cocaine supplier.

"Nick! Come in here for a moment."

He could hear when his younger brother dropped the pool cue onto the table top. Nick hated having his game interrupted.

"Yeah, bro. What is it? You out of Havanas?" he joked.

"When is our next buy?" Alfredo asked, not responding to his brother's humor.

"Next month," Nick said, taking a seat in the tufted leather chair opposite his brother. He automatically put his feet on the desk, more to irritate his brother than anything.

"Off!" Alfredo demanded with a sharp wave of his hand.

Nick smiled. He loved getting his brother's goat. "Why? You want to cancel or buy more?" he inquired, removing one of the Havanas from his brother's ivory case. He rolled it under his nose as he smelled the aroma. He didn't smoke, but liked to fill his lungs with the smell of the imported cigar.

"How much we buying this time?"

"Ten keys. Why?"

"That's $250 thousand!"

"Gee, you're quick with the numbers," his brother chided him. "Especially when your dealing with the 10s." He smirked as he replaced the Havana.

"Shut up. If I want a smartass answer, I'll call your playboy brother. How long we been using this source?"

"Danny? I don't know. Quite a few years now, I guess. Since before Father left the business. Why? He's reliable. You been hearing things?" he asked, his small frame straightening in the chair. He had tossed in the father reference just to remind his brother that he was still irritated at the way he had dethroned their father. It was no secret that he hadn't agreed with his brother when it came to his father's lack of ability to run the business, nor did he agree with his brother's philosophy of stepping up the volume of business. Before Alfredo had taken over, the family had made more money than they and their children and their children's children would ever spend.

"No. I just want to set up a meeting with the man. I think our relationship has about run its course. It's time we began dealing direct."

"Now you're talking my language!" Nick said. "I was wonderin' when you would come around to this. I've never liked that guy, anyway."

Alfredo looked at his brother, wondering if he was giving him the business or really agreed. He could never tell, with Nick's sense of humor. "If you were wonderin' why we weren't dealing direct, how come you didn't say something before now, stupid?"

"Hey. You're da boss," he mimicked, stupidly. "I'm just da flunky, remembah?"

"Get outta here and get hold of this jerk. Set up a meeting. The sooner, the better."

* * * *

The meeting was scheduled for 10:00 the next evening in the high school's parking lot. Alfredo and Niccola arrived early and waited in a black Jaguar sedan near the tennis courts, where the lights were the dimmest.

"It's 10:15," Alfredo barked impatiently. "Where is that scumbag? He better show!"

"Relax, bro. You're gettin' uptight for nothin'," Nick said. "He'll be here!"

"Better be, or I'll kick your..."

Just then a pair of headlights turned off the

street and came towards them.

"There. What did I tell ya? That's him in the black Isuzu pickup."

"Jeez. Can't the guy at least buy American?"

"Sure, Al. American," Nick said, waving his hand around the interior of the Jag.

"Here he comes. Let me do the talking."

Danny was a smallish, Latino-looking man, wearing a black leather jacket that seemed a size too large. *Probably to compensate for his size,* Alfredo thought as he approached the Jaguar.

"Hi. My name's Danny," he said, extending his hand to Alfredo. "Nicky there said you wanted to meet."

"Nicky?" Alfredo whispered to his younger brother with a look of disdain, not taking the man's hand.

Nick shrugged his shoulders.

"We still on for the shipment that's coming in next month?"

"That's what I want to talk to you about. There's been a change of plans, Danny," Alfredo said coldly as he and Nick exited the Jaguar. Nick sat on its front fender.

"Off!" Alfredo barked, glaring at his brother.

"What kind of a change?" The look on Danny's face changed perceptibly. "I got a lot of dough tied up in this deal." His voice went up an octave. "I had to borrow from some heavy dudes to make this buy. If I don't deliver..." He looked nervous. "I don't swim too good in cement shoes, if you get my drift," he said, making a facial gesture.

"The drift I get, Danny, is that the cocaine that you been selling us for the last who-knows-how-many-years has been diluted by at least 50 percent. I'm here to tell you that we're not buying cut-rate merchandise anymore."

"But—"

"Maybe you can sell it on the street yourself. We're not buying."

Danny's heart rate doubled as beads of perspiration began forming on his forehead. He smiled nervously. "Tell you what. I'll...I'll cut the price by 25 percent. What the hell, we've done enough business together, hey, Nicky?" he said, hitting Nick softly on his shoulder with the palm of his hand. "You can have it for 75 percent of the agreed price." His eyes danced nervously, showing his weakness.

"No deal, Danny."

"Nicky," he pleaded with outstretched hands to Niccola. Give me a little rope here."

"Sorry, Danny. I'm just an errand boy," Nick said, leaning against the Jag. "Mr. Carleone here is the man." He hoisted himself on the Jaguar's fender.

Alfredo shot Nick a sharp glance, but said nothing about him sitting on the Jag.

"All right. Tell you what," Danny said with a nervous twitch. "I'll...I'll give it to you for $200 grand...just this once."

"You're only paying $125 thousand, Danny." Alfredo looked hard at his adversary. He had him in a corner with nowhere to go, and they both knew it.

"You gotta let me make some profit," he pleaded.

"I do?"

"Hey. Come on, fellas. This is serious business, here. No fooling around. Okay?" He gestured with his hands and a weak smile.

"Who's fooling, Danny?" Alfredo pulled a six-inch switchblade from his pocket and snapped it open.

Danny stared at the knife as he stepped back

a pace. "Now, don't go gettin' mad," he said, holding out his outstretched hand.

"125," Alfredo said, firmly.

"125! It cost me that much plus shipping. I'd be losing 50 Gs!"

Alfredo smiled. "Well, it was nice meeting you, Danny. Let's go, Nick. It's getting late, and I don't want to be caught in this neighborhood late at night." He turned to open the door of the Jaguar.

"Wait! Wait. All right. Tell you what," Danny said with a resigned voice. "175. I'll sell five keys uncut for 175. I'll even eat my delivery charges. I won't be making a dime on the deal, but I've got to meet obligations. It cost me $50 grand to borrow the dough to make the buy. You gotta let me recoup that!"

"I guess you don't hear too good, Danny. I said 125. I'm not concerned about your financial obligations. That's your problem."

"Why you doin' this, man?" he said, mostly to Nick.

Nick shrugged his shoulder and got into the passenger side of the car.

"All right. All right. 175. Shit! You can't trust anyone anymore," he said boldly, forgetting that Alfredo had a knife.

"There's one more thing," Alfredo said, approaching Danny. He slipped the knife across his ear, severing the lower portion of the earlobe from his head.

Danny retreated in pain, holding his hand over his ear. Blood seeped through his fingers. There was a look of pain in his face but more than that, there was fear in his eyes...fear for his life.

"I want the name of your Colombian contact and how to get hold of him. From this day forward, we're going to be his sole purchaser," he said firmly. "You can find another source, can't you, Danny?" he said softly, moving closer to the man.

"Another source!" Danny screamed, temporarily forgetting about his ear.

Alfredo raised the knife to Danny's nose. Danny backed off, wide-eyed.

"All right, already! The source. You got it." He pulled a card from his wallet and gave Alfredo Carleone the contact code for getting in touch with one Molina Marquez, who was located in the city of Medellin, Colombia.

"This Molina Marquez. Is he reliable?"

"He's one of the up-and-coming power men in the Colombian Cartel. He's eager to expand and make a buck. He's ruthless, but reliable, so long as he isn't crossed." There was a note of warning in his voice.

"That shouldn't present a problem, do you think?" Alfredo chided Danny.

Danny turned to retreat to his pickup, holding his hand to his ear, whining softly.

"Oh, Danny?"

He stopped and made a half turn. "Yeah?"

"I wouldn't plan on selling around here anymore if I were you. I understand the competition is deadly. Cement shoes, if you get my drift."

Danny paused for a moment before getting into his pickup, then sped away, leaving a trail of rubber on the parking lot.

Chapter Eight

Alfredo Carleone placed a call to the business office of Molina Marquez Enterprises in the city of
Medellin, Colombia. He found Molina Marquez to
be an efficient and effective negotiator. "Yes. I'm
willing to sell you some of my commodity," Marquez
said. "My policy with new clients is to have 100
percent of the purchase money up front before
delivery. Upon receipt of—"

"The whole nine yards," Carleone interrupted,
complaining. "How do I know you won't just keep
the dough and stiff me?"

"How do I know you'll pay?" Marquez retorted
in a quiet but firm voice. "Until I get to know you
better, Mr. Carleone, payment will be due in advance. When I have confirmation that your funds
have been placed in my account, I will make the
product available to you. That is how I do business. If that is not acceptable, I thank you for the
call and wish you a pleasant day."

"Let's say that I buy five keys to begin with.
That's $125 thou, right?"

"Five kilos is $125 thousand, American. Cor-
rect."

"It's pure coke, right? None of this cut stuff
laced with sugar or whatever?"

"Mr. Carleone. What you will get from me is pure cocaine directly from my fields, processed in my own factory and shipped directly to you. We do not 'cut' the cocaine, as you put it. You get what you pay for. No more. No less."

"How do I obtain delivery? It's not like walking into a store and taking the bag home with me. I mean, you're half a world away."

"Once the product has been purchased, delivery is your problem. Until I have established a solid business relationship with you, I do not make delivery into the United States. There are too many officials waiting to confiscate the product, as well as the bearer. As you may well imagine, that could make for a strained and mistrusting business relationship. I'm sure you can find an independent reliable source that, for a few American dollars, would be willing to transport the goods to a destination of your choice. That way, there can be no accusation of non-delivery."

"There could be a problem of accountability, though," Carleone persisted.

"That is between you and your delivery contact, Mr. Carleone. You will receive from me precisely what you purchase," Marquez reiterated firmly.

Carleone knew that Dave wouldn't have made the fatal mistake of misleading him, so after further pleasantries he cut a deal with Molina. For delivery, he simply contracted a Mafia family in Miami that recommended a delivery service in the form of hungry but reliable crooks who had fast boats and small airplanes to make the pick-up and delivery for him.

Alfredo would now have pure cocaine to sell. He would cut the cocaine by 50 percent, equating his purchase of the 50 percent-pure snow that he had been buying from Danny. He then cut it two more times, until the original product was now one-eighth of its original strength. He knew he could resell his cocaine to the street vendors at the cut-price of $25 thousand a kilo. That meant that he would have turned his investment of $25 thousand into $200 thousand per kilo. It was no small wonder that he took the next logical step of organizing his own army of street people, further cutting into the street people's profit.

Taking that last step would enable him to step up into the ranks of the largest import dealers in Miami. He put his younger brother Niccola in charge of the street people.

Niccola, he found, had a propensity for breaking arms and legs whenever one of the low-life street thugs crossed him—and that happened more frequently than he would care to admit. His reputation of being a tough drug dealer, not one to mess with, quickly sped through the streets after a body or two was conspicuously displayed impaled on a dumpster, in an alley, or the victim was discovered with a plastic sack over his head, his eyes staring into space with a look of horror plainly implanted on his face.

It was with this grander scope in mind that he set up his first mega-deal with the Colombians, buying nearly 400 kilos of pure cocaine for $10 million. Taking delivery on Easter was a stroke of genius, he thought. He knew everyone would be asleep at the switch, enjoying the holiday, going to church, or getting drunk.

The buy had not only drained the family's cash coffers, but Alfredo Carleone had to put the bite on one of his more wealthy associates for a short-term loan of $2.5 million. The majority of their cash had been laundered through real estate. He didn't want to take the time to liquidate to acquire the rest of the cash, nor was it prudent to do so, as he knew no intelligent investor would buy a hotel that was running full on paper when, in reality, there was no one home most of the time.

As he sat at his desk looking out of his office window, he lit a Havana with a $5 bill, more for show for his younger brother than anything. He dropped the remains of the flaming bill into the large glass ashtray that occupied a central spot on his desk. Taking a long, satisfying drag on the cigar, he twisted it in his mouth, enjoying the rasping of his mustache on the brown tobacco covering. He exhaled slowly, with a satisfied smile, putting his feet on his desk and leaning back in the chair with his hands clasped behind his head.

"Not a bad day," he said, blowing a smoke ring. "We bag Murray and spit in the DEA's face at the same time by taking a flawless delivery of one of the largest buys in the history of Colombia's finest, all in one fell stroke. When the cocaine is cut and distributed to dealers and our own street people, we should net in excess of $50 million. Not bad, eh, Niccola?" he said to his younger brother. He blew another smoke ring, then laughed.

"Yeah, bro. That Murray fella never knew what hit him." Niccola laughed, putting his feet on Alfredo's desk. "I wish I hadda been there to see. Boom!" he said, imitating the explosion by throwing his hands in the air, then laughing.

"Hey! Off with the feet! Just because you blow up a car doesn't give ya squattin' rights." Alfredo knew that a pat on the back was one thing, but lack of respect couldn't be tolerated, even from his brother. He was on top now, and there was no stopping him. He had just moved up a major notch in the world of finance, and there would be 100 guys just waiting to knock him off, maybe even including his own brother, he thought as he studied Niccola's face.

Alfredo suddenly jumped out of his chair. "Gino. Check on the boys at the drop, will ya?" he yelled through the open door. "Never hurts to be too careful," he said to Niccola with a wink.

* * * *

"Quarterback to Defense," came the clear message over the team's headsets.

They had followed the silver and black truck to an industrial area on the outskirts of Georgetown, where it had pulled into a two-storey, windowless building. Since their arrival, only a single automobile had arrived—a black Mercedes with tinted windows. The driver had entered the side door of the building, and had left a few moments later with two of the men, leaving four armed men to guard the drugs.

When Murray arrived, he was apprised of the situation. "Things couldn't have worked out better," he said with a smile, rubbing his hands together. He was a bit cold, but ready for action.

It had now been several hours since Murray had left his family, but he had concentrated so intensely on the task at hand that he had no time to even think of his promise to meet Jana and the kids at church, let alone make dinner with his folks. Both he and Jana had known at the time that he got the call that his promise to make church and dinner was more of a token of goodwill than a promise meant to be kept, he rationalized. There had been too many broken dates for either one to put much stock in rigid time frames at this stage of the game.

"Here's the plan," he said, again using the hood of his Bronco as an imaginary blackboard. "The Guards," he nodded to two of his men, "will approach the building from the rear by going up the street one block north of the building, then cutting through the adjoining properties by foot, until you've reached the outside, northern perimeter. The Tackles will do likewise," he said, looking at the men, "securing the east and west side of the site. Center and myself will go up the middle. When you're in position we'll create a diversion. As soon as the opposition is clear, take 'em out."

He saw the look of confusion at his words "take 'em out," so he clarified his position. "If they can be taken without firepower, that's our first option. If there is no choice, waste them. Our objective is the drugs, not the men. They're only soldiers who won't talk even if captured. Questions?"

He surveyed the serious faces of his men. "If not, let the game begin. We'll hit our objective in precisely...15 minutes," he said, tapping the crystal of his watch.

"Set your watches...now."

The men quickly dispersed, leaving Murray and Grover behind.

To fill the time before making the hit, Murray mussed up his hair and rubbed mud from the roadside onto his face and clothes. "Jana's going to kill me for this," he muttered to himself.

Grover followed Murray's lead and did the same to his clothes and face.

* * * *

"Hey, boss," Gino said, poking his head into Alfredo's office. "The boys said everything is quiet. Just a few drunks milling around outside. They're complaining that they're bored. They say that at least they ought to have a TV or some dames and booze."

"You tell them to shut up and sit tight. We'll have someone over to relieve 'em in a couple hours. They can sit tight that long. Tell them if they're bored they can shove their thumbs up each other's asses for entertainment." He laughed.

"You got it, boss."

"And Gino?"

"Yeah?"

"Tell 'em to get rid of the bums. I don't want no one millin' around. I ain't taking no chances on drawing attention to the place. All I need is a couple flatfoots nosing around because the drunks are causing a disturbance."

"I'll tell 'em."

* * * *

Five minutes before the attack was to begin, Murray picked up an empty discarded whisky bottle, threw his arms around Grover and began staggering in the direction of the building singing *99 Bottles of Beer on the Wall* as loud as he could, with Grover harmonizing. Onward, towards the building they staggered, taking periodic simulated sips from the empty bottle.

When they were at the entrance door, Murray banged on it with an open palm, demanding to use the bathroom. The two men laughed and broke into another stanza.

A moment later, the metal door swung open. Murray was looking down the barrel of an automatic weapon held by a young Italian. He was dressed in a three-piece pinstriped olive-colored suit with a tan London Fog overcoat, making the small man appear much larger than he actually was. His counterpart stood behind him, peering over his shoulder to see who was there. Two larger men who were chewing on cigars peered over their shoulders.

"You're on private property, bum! Get off before I ventilate your ass!" he said, pushing the weapon against Murray's dirty coat.

"I need a bathroom," Murray said, while holding his crotch as he danced nervously. "I gotta go," he slurred, then belched.

"So piss on the building. Just get out of my sight, you slug," the Italian said, pushing Murray's shoulder.

That was the opening he wanted. In the blink of an eye, Murray had his hand over the Italian's hand, pressing it hard to his body. With the swiftness of a cobra, he brought his other hand up hard under the man's elbow. There was a loud crack, as his arm snapped. He simultaneously brought his knee into the man's groin, bringing him to his knees. A knee to his chin finished him off.

Within the same split second, Grover had his automatic weapon jammed in the other man's mouth, while the Guards and Tackles rushed in to overpower the two larger men. Murray looked at his team with obvious satisfaction. He nodded towards the interior of the building. "Sweep," he said quietly, gesturing with his right arm, just in case there were other men inside they didn't know about. The balance of the team rushed into the building in an instant, securing the inside.

"Clear!" each man yelled as he swept the rooms.

One of the men opened the back door of the truck, then whistled. "Will you take a look at this? There must be $10 million of pure Colombian here...enough to get everyone north of the Mason-Dixon line stoned."

"Let's get out of here," Murray said nervously.

"I don't want any uninvited visitors dropping in for a snort. Tackle One, take charge of the truck. Guard, ride shotgun. I want a car in front and one in back. We'll follow a hundred yards behind just in case. Let's move."

Within 30 minutes from the time they had scheduled the sweep on the building, they were on the road again: truck, cocaine and prisoners.

* * * *

Once they got back to the Federal Building, one of the men who had brought back the money met Murray's group with an anxious look. "Coach, headquarters wants to see you immediately."

"What? I haven't even filed my report, and there's problems already?" He removed his headset, handing it to Grover. "Take charge of the payload, will you, Grover? Have a couple of the guys take it over to storage and inventory the contents. Bring the receipt to Mr. Macaffe's office when you get done!" he yelled over his shoulder as he mounted the steps of the Federal Building. He walked down the empty halls to the inner office, where the attorney general, Robert Macaffe was waiting for him.

"Hell of a bag, Bob," Murray said as he extended his hand to the man dressed in a sports coat with an open shirt. "Happy Easter. This has to be the biggest haul in the history of..." The look on Macaffe's face told him the matter was grave, whatever it was.

"Sit down, Chris. I've got a serious matter to discuss with you." He never called him by his full name, Christian.

"Don't tell me something went wrong with the bust?" he said, rolling his eyes. "We planned for this for months."

"It's your family, Chris."

The blood visibly drained from Murray's face. "They've been in an accident?" he guessed. "Is everyone okay? Jana...is she all right? The kids...?"

"I'm sorry, Chris," Macaffe said, lowering his eyes as he laid a hand on Murray's shoulder.

Murray looked up at him in shock. "No! No! It's not true," he burst out. "It can't be!" He jerked the man's hand from his shoulder.

The cat was out of the bag. Now Macaffe had to tell him the whole ugly truth. "They were on their way to church, Chris. It was a bomb. It was set to go off the minute the ignition was engaged. They didn't know what hit them. They didn't suffer."

He tried to get it out in as few words as possible, as if it would soften the blow or make the pain any less.

Murray quickly paced the office, the palm of his hand on his forehead, shaking his head violently. "It was me. It was meant for me," he said, collapsing in the chair, sobbing. "I should have been there. I should have been the one. Why Jana? Why the kids? Everyone...all gone..." his voice trailed off as he charged blindly out of the office.

"Chris! Christian! Wait!" Macaffe called. The attorney general watched helplessly as the man ran out of the building, blindly crashing into anything in his way. His men, who knew nothing of the tragedy, watched as their boss, the man they called Coach, the man to whom they looked for strength and guidance, crashed onto the hood of his Bronco, banging his fists until their indentations could be seen on the metal.

It was then that they knew some horrible tragedy must have hit their beloved leader...a tragedy that would come to affect their lives forever.

* * * *

A man wearing silver-coated glasses so dark one couldn't see his eyes entered the back door of Macaffe's office. He had dark, greasy hair that lay flat with a lock dangling over one of the lenses. He wore a waist-length black leather jacket, black pants and dirty brown cowboy boots.

"Too bad about Murray," he said without emotion. "Think this changes things? I'd hate to have gone through all this trouble and expense to have the plan fold now that we're just getting started. I mean, it's not like we haven't collected a bundle, what with this latest bust, but..."

Macaffe shot him a sharp glance. "You're a cold bastard, you know that, Green?" his voice was tempered with anger and dislike for the man sitting across from him.

"Hey, business is business, sport. We all knew there were risks. This is just one we hadn't planned on."

Macaffe shook his head in disgust, but said nothing.

"There must be at least ten mil on this bust alone. That's a handsome hunk of change."

"Look, Green," Macaffe said, rising from his chair. There was a determined look in his eyes.

Green held up his hand. "Don't even think about it. We're both in this up to our double chins. Better start looking for a replacement for Murray, just in case he doesn't pan out." He gave Macaffe a hard look as he threw a copy of a newspaper on his desk. "Today's contribution. Seems the heat has been turned up a notch. We lose this battle, and the boys back home aren't going to be too happy." Having said that, he left.

Macaffe studied the paper. The front page was

headlined WILD GUNMAN GOES ON SHOOTING RAMPAGE. The article referred to a shooting at a McDonald's which was thought to be drug related. Five people had been killed, three of whom were children. 14 more were injured, 10 of whom were children.

An adjoining column referred to a domestic shooting. A husband had shot his estranged wife and three children after holding them hostage at a Howard Johnson's motel for fifteen hours, then had shot himself in the head. The estranged wife and children were dead, and he was in intensive care in a coma at the hospital.

Beneath these two items was a picture of 40 or so mothers carrying placards in front of the governor's office. They read, "WAG—Women Against Guns" and "BAW—Ban all Weapons and Down with the NRA Repeal gun rights!"

* * * *

Even though he was consumed with his own insurmountable grief, Christian Murray knew that his parents must have thought that he, too, had been killed in the bombing.

His mother answered the phone when Christian called from his cellular phone. When she heard his voice, she nearly passed out. Fortunately, his father was standing nearby, and was able to support his shaken wife and take the phone.

Christian talked to his father just long enough to assure him that he was alive and as well as he could be under the circumstances. Unable to maintain his composure, he hung up, leaving his parents shaken, but grateful he was alive.

Chapter Nine

The day of the funeral it was cold and raining. In attendance were grieving friends, fellow workers and, of course, Ted and Alice Murray and Jana's folks, Howard and Kathy Dolmann, 86 and 88 years old, respectively.

Ted and Alice Murray, though elderly, had chosen to stand next to their son rather than sit. Jana's parents sat on metal folding chairs while a light rain fell on the sobbing crowd. They held each other's hands, their heads touching, numbed by the irony that their daughter, the innocent wife of a powerful government worker, and their only grandchildren had been brutally murdered. They had come from a small town in Iowa where the only violence was the annual slaughter of chickens and pigs.

Jana had been their only child. Losing her this way was destined to take a terrible physical and psychological toll on their lives. In the days that would follow, they would come to realize that life as they knew it no longer held any attraction for them. They would sit for mindless hours at a time, staring blankly into space, not talking, their minds replaying moments of Jana's childhood on the farm where she had grown up.

Christian had one brother, an accountant by trade. By stature and appearance, he was a smaller version of his older brother. He looked up to his big brother with pride. On any given day he would have traded places with Christian in a heartbeat. Today, he just wished he could relieve the big guy of some of the pain he knew must be eating at him as he sat staring at the three brushed-brass coffins sitting next to the covered mounds of freshly dug earth.

As he sat there, staring blankly, Christian Murray had two forces fighting within his soul. The most prevalent one was mourning the senseless loss of his family. *Why my family?* he thought. *Why not me?* He would never forgive himself for living while his family had died in his place. No amount of logic would deter the pain and anger he felt for the job that had put his family in danger.

The other turmoil he felt was the desire to find the bastards who were responsible for this deed and avenge the senseless deaths. The bomb technique had Mafia written all over it. He knew he probably would never know who specifically had killed his family, not in the sense that he could submit proof to a court so they could render a judgment against them. They were too smart for that. Yet, he had ways. He hadn't spent his life fighting the scum of the earth without learning something of their trade or their calling cards— even their techniques.

This day, sitting with the remains of his family before him, Christian Murray vowed that those responsible would pay, if it was the last thing he did. He would find them, even if it meant lowering himself to their level. From here on in, it was no holds barred.

When the services were over, the people filed

by and shook his hand and hugged him, offering him their condolences, asking if there was anything they could do.

When they offered to come by the house to be with him, Christian shook his head and quietly said, "No thanks. I prefer to be alone. Thanks, anyway."

They understood and honored his wishes. It hurt his parents not to be with him in this, his hour of grief, but they understood.

By previous agreement, none of his Team were to attend the funeral. It would have been counterproductive to make a showing of the team he had so carefully hand-picked and whose identity he had meticulously kept secret. It was hard for them to stay away, but they, too, honored their leader's request for solitude.

After everyone had left, only Christian Murray remained. He walked over to Jana's coffin, laid his hand on it and said, "I'm so sorry that I wasn't there to take the pain instead of you. I'm sorry for everything: the missed dinners, the parties and anniversaries, but most of all, I'm sorry that I had to be the target that was responsible for the taking of your life. You know, if I had it in my power, I would trade places with you in a heartbeat." He wiped his eyes with the back of his hand. "I know you're in good hands now, and I know that you're watching over me. Wait for me if you can. I won't be long, I promise. I'll love you always, Jana."

Tears were streaming down his face as he laid his hands on Kalvan's coffin and thought of all the games he had missed. The last image he had of him was Kal standing proudly in his blue blazer, so grown-up, so manly. "I'm sorry I wasn't there enough for you, guy. You were the greatest. I was just too busy to stop and watch. I hope you'll forgive me," he said as he lightly patted the coffin.

"We had so much together, and I know I blew it. I love you, son. I'm sorry," he said again softly.

As he went to Kara, his hand hesitated, touching the metal as if it were hot. He had never told her this, but she was his favorite. He would have done anything for her. *Anything but keep her out of harm's way,* he thought angrily as he clenched his fist in anger.

The pain he felt towards the loss of his beautiful daughter was too great, and he could say nothing as he just stood there, tears falling freely down his cheeks. His legs weakened. He fell to his knees on the fresh earth. His head rested on the cold metal of the coffin. *She will never know the wonderment of womanhood,* he thought as he closed his eyes against the pain. *She will never know how it would feel to love a man or have a child. She had been cheated out of the pleasure and excitement of life.* He lifted himself from the dirt. The weight of his body felt enormous, as if he weighed five hundred pounds. Every movement was an effort.

The guilt and pain he felt was overwhelming. As he turned to leave, he noticed a lone figure across the road, standing tall in the rain, bareheaded, his hands folded in front of him. His head was bowed reverently. It was Grover.

Their eyes met momentarily, but neither made a motion of acknowledgment. Murray could sense the compassion that his Team leader felt. Although he shouldn't have been there, Murray took comfort in his presence.

Christian Murray climbed into his Bronco and slowly drove off into the cold, dismal rainy day. He had no recollection of the road, nor did his eyes register anything along the way home. He drove back to a house without a soul, without a family. The house was no longer a home. It was cold and empty, like a coffin itself, void of life except for himself. He sank into his overstuffed chair without bothering to even take off his overcoat. He closed his eyes and sank into a dark, forbidding oblivion.

* * * *

While the sounds of gaiety permeated the Carleone house and odors of the fresh-baked ham filled the air, Carlo and Niccola, Alfredo's younger brothers, huddled over the gaming table in the den, wondering what their brother's next move might be. They knew he was extremely upset at the death of Christian Murray's family. They also knew he was livid that Murray himself was still alive.

Even considering the infamous family wars of the '20s and early '30s that the Carleone's had been involved in during their climb to success, the one thing their father had always espoused was that the family was sacred, even the families of his enemies. To accidentally burn a family in the process of eliminating an adversary was not endorsed but tolerable. To eliminate the family, be it accidental or not, without destroying the target, was unforgivable.

Niccola and Carlo played a quiet game of 21 while they awaited their brother's invitation to join him. Alfredo had given the rest of the men the day off. The familiar group of cigar and cigarette smoking, automatic weapon-packing men dressed in dark pinstriped suits were conspicuously absent.

Finally, the doors of the atrium opened and Alfredo faced his brothers. "Niccola! Carlo!" came the staccato call.

They knew from the sound of his voice that he was displeased. In the few short years since Alfredo had taken over the family business, he had ruled with an iron hand, giving no leniency for error. He abhorred ignorance and wouldn't tolerate sloppiness.

"Christian Murray lives!" were his first words. They knew that, and he knew that they knew, but it was the introduction to a scathing tongue-lashing which they knew would follow.

"Because of your bumbling stupidity, not only did we miss the opportunity to get Murray and the DEA permanently off our backs, but instead, you can be sure that now he'll be after us with a vengeance!"

"There's no way he can know that it was us who did his family," Carlo said. "He might be pissed, but he won't know who to be pissed at." He laughed at Niccola, jabbing him in the ribs with his elbow. Niccola, the more ambitious and serious of the two, didn't respond to his older brother's ill-timed humor.

"You moron! Who do you think has been trying to put us out of business all these years? Who's constantly been the thorn in his side? Why do you think he formed his group of overgrown athletes that he calls his Team? To put us down! Do you think he's after jay-walkers and pimps?" He stood behind his desk, leaning as far forward towards his hapless brother as he could without falling.

The look of anger was unmistakable as his eyes pierced Carlo's unintelligent face. He was lazy, and if there was a shortcut to doing a job, he would find it.

"Sorry," was his only reply, as he looked at Niccola with a silly grin as if he had been caught by the teacher while throwing a spitball across the room.

Alfredo simply shook his head and addressed

Niccola, for the most part ignoring Carlo. If Carlo hadn't been his brother, he would have eliminated him long ago, but family was family.

"All right. Here's what we have to do," he said, talking quietly so the brothers had to lean close to hear what he had to say.

* * * *

No one had heard from Christian Murray since the day of the funeral. Everyone assumed that he was going through the grieving process and didn't want to interfere with his privacy. Ten days had passed, however, and there had not been a single word. Even Bob Macaffe tried to call him at home and had left a message on his recorder, but there had been no response. Knowing that Grover was one of Murray's favorite team members, Macaffe had asked if he would mind going by the house to check up on him, "Sort of off the cuff," he said.

* * * *

"Hey! Coach! You in there?" Grover hollered through the door after knocking several times. Murray's Bronco was parked in front of the house, just where it had been when he had returned home from the funeral. The broken windows had been boarded up, but, aside from that, the house was unchanged since the blast had shattered the front of the house.

Concerned that perhaps he was ill or, worse yet, had done something to himself, Grover took it upon himself to break into the house. Normal training with Murray's Team included the skill of quietly entering a locked structure without alerting its occupants or leaving any obvious trace that an intruder had entered the premises.

Once inside, Grover softly called, "Coach! You in here? It's me, Grover, I mean, the Center coming to see how you are."

Identifying himself was more of an act of self-preservation than an inquiry to see if Murray was home. He knew if Murray caught an intruder in his house, especially after the murder of his family, he would disable first and ask questions later. In this instance, disabling meant rendering one helpless—probably unconscious.

Grover had no desire to be knocked silly. "Boss? You here?"

He went down the hall, sidestepping the glass on the floor, stopping momentarily to look at a picture of the President of the United States presenting Christian Murray with an award. The brushed-brass plaque beneath the picture read:

DRUG ENFORCEMENT ADMINISTRATION
UNITED STATES DEPARTMENT OF JUSTICE
PRESENTS THIS CERTIFICATE OF APPRECIATION
TO CHRISTIAN H. MURRAY
FOR OUTSTANDING CONTRIBUTIONS
IN THE FIELD OF DRUG LAW ENFORCEMENT

Grover entered the living room and found Christian Murray slumped into a large, overstuffed chair, his arms resting on the arms of the chair and his head drooped motionless, as if he were dead.

Grover's first reaction was to rush to his side and shake him to see if he was alive. His eyes were partially open, but non-responsive. The shock of seeing him in that position, motionless, led Grover to the conclusion that Murray had either died of a self-afflicted wound or had simply willed himself dead.

Nonetheless, Grover cautiously put two fingers to the side of Murray's throat, checking to see if there was a pulse.

He detected a slight movement through the veins of Murray's neck. Instinctively, he reached for the phone to call an ambulance. He punched 911, then hung up before the phone could ring.

He looked at Murray and thought for moment. If the situation were reversed, in order to protect the Team, Murray would make every effort to keep the situation contained without alerting a public agency. He dialed the interior number of the Secretary of Defense, which rang directly through to Bob Macaffe's office.

"Leader," came the only response at the other end of the red phone on Macaffe's desk.

"Center Grover here. Situation is grave. Immediate assistance requested."

"Hold," came the monotone response.

A few moments passed, and Bob Macaffe came back onto the line. "Grover?"

"Check. The Coach is alive, but critical. He needs immediate medical assistance." Although Grover tried to remain calm, there was a sense of urgency to his voice.

"Has he been compromised?"

"Not to my knowledge, although I haven't checked him thoroughly," he quickly added. It was possible that he could have been drugged with a needle, and Grover wouldn't have known. Nothing around the house seemed broken or disturbed, however. He knew if Murray had been overpowered, even in a weakened condition, it wouldn't have been without a fight. "He seems to be dehydrated and probably hasn't eaten in days," he added.

"You haven't compromised the situation, have you?"

Grover was insulted that Macaffe would even suggest that he had called an outside source first, even though that had been his first instinctual response.

"No," came the simple answer.

"Secure the premises. I'll send a security team over right away." Macaffe hung up the phone, and Grover was left to watch over the Coach, his surrogate father.

Murray's eyes were sunk deep within his skull, creating deep, dark lines under them. His skin had turned a pale ashen-white. Even his dark brown hair seemed to have turned pasty gray.

Grover covered him with a blanket, then began making a search of the premises to see if he could detect any indication that the house had been broken into. Maybe there was a bug hidden somewhere which had transmitted his conversation, he thought as he quickly checked the phone, then searched under lamp shades, over doors and anyplace he could think of where a bug might be concealed. Maybe Murray had been drugged, and the perpetrator had left a clue somewhere. He searched everywhere, finding nothing.

Soon, a gray station wagon pulled up to the front door. A team of four men quickly entered the house. They stopped short with a look of shock painted on their faces. "What the hell happened here?" one asked as he looked around the glass-littered room. "Looks like he had his own private war."

They were quick and efficient as they examined Murray before putting him onto a portable gurney and loading him into the back of the station wagon.

Two men stayed to go over the premises while the other two took Murray away. Assuming that

he would help secure the house, Grover volunteered that he had already covered the living room
area but had found nothing.

"You're free to go now, sport," one of the men
said with a condescending tone as he looked at
his partner with a smirk. "We'll take it from here."

Again, Grover was insulted, but he knew the
procedure. He nodded and left without comment.

Chapter Ten

Nick reached Alfredo's office. He was out of breath from running, but there was a broad smile on his face. "Alfredo! Great news. One of my informants who works at Saint Mary's Hospital said a man matching Christian Murray's description was checked into intensive care yesterday."

"What makes you think it's Murray, and why would he be in a hospital?"

"Apparently, according to my source, he was checked in under an assumed name, a Robert Ackermann, supposedly suffering from severe malnutrition. The guy came in with a barrage of security. They have him in a private ICU with a guard standing outside."

"Check it out. If indeed it is Murray, it should be a cinch to snuff him in a hospital. Do you have an inside plant available?"

"For a price."

"The price is immaterial. Once he's successful, you'll have to take care of him. I don't want any loose ends. Does that present a problem?" he asked, looking at his younger brother.

"It's just a snitch. No big deal."

"Good. I'll leave it in your hands."

Nick turned to leave. "And Nick?"

Nick paused without looking back. He knew what his brother was going to say. "I know, no screw-ups," he said, waving over his shoulder without turning back.

* * * *

A uniformed guard stood at the door, devouring the approaching nurse with his eyes, taking no care to disguise his admiration as she approached Murray's room. She had long blonde hair that hung just below her shoulders, which swung to and fro as she walked. He couldn't help noticing that her skirt was a shade short and the second button of the blouse of her white uniform exposed a portion of a healthy, robust chest.

She cast a knowing look at him as she entered the room, pausing momentarily to say in a deep, sultry voice, "I'm going to bathe the patient. Be sure no one comes in, big boy." She glanced behind her just in time to catch the officer's eyes scanning the lower regions of her body.

She winked with a smile, then closed the door quietly. Once inside the room, she quickly removed a small vial from the pocket of her uniform. She chose one of the IVs which was dripping glucose into the patient's arm. She filled a hypodermic needle with the clear solution contained within the vial, then injected the liquid into the glucose mixture.

A moment later, the monitor on the wall, which registered, among other things, the rhythms of the patient's heart, sang out a loud, high-pitched scream as the red line went flat. The nurse flung the needle and empty vial under the mattress, then ran for the door.

"Officer! Hurry! Get a doctor! The patient's gone

into cardiac arrest!" she screamed hysterically to the guard.

The policeman ran towards the nurse's station while the nurse exited the stairwell at the end of the corridor. Moments later, a doctor and several nurses burst into the room and tried to revive the patient. The doctor tried external manual heart manipulation. When that failed to revive the patient, he administered a shot of Lidocaine directly into the heart. When that failed, a defibrillator was applied as a last-ditch effort to bring him around.

"Clear," came the loud voice of the doctor as he applied the two defibrillator plates to the patient's chest. The body jumped automatically as the muscles retracted, then relaxed, reacting to the electrical current. No response. "Clear," came the command again. Again, no response. A nurse checked his pulse, then slowly removed the stethoscope from her neck. She shook her head hopelessly. He was dead.

Resigned to the fact that they had no further options, the doctor shook his head and covered the man's face with the sheet. "He's gone. We've lost him," was all he said as he inscribed the time and date of death on his chart before signing it.

* * * *

"How did it go?" Niccola Carleone asked as the young woman approached him in the alley, removing her blonde wig and throwing it into the dumpster.

"Smooth as silk. Who was that dude, anyway? Got my ten Gs?" she asked without waiting for an answer, fluffing her short black hair with her fingertips.

"Sure. Right here," he said as he removed a

black .38 with a silencer attached from his vest holster.

"Wha... What's this? I did just as you..."

Niccola Carleone shot her twice, once through the heart and then once between the eyes as she fell to the ground. "Too bad. She was a nice kid," he said as he walked calmly down the alley to his car, adjusting his hat in the process.

* * * *

"I thought you said the room was secure," Bob Macaffe bellowed to the man standing nervously in front of his desk.

"We had no way of knowing that the Mob had a mole stationed in the hospital," the man offered, shifting nervously.

"Fine. So now a man's dead. All because you 'didn't know.' You didn't do your job." Macaffe glared. "It's that simple. The life of the department's most valuable man is placed in your care and all you can offer is 'We didn't know.'"

"Sorry," was all the man could say as he shifted his weight nervously. He had put his best men on the job and he'd had the door covered 24 hours a day. How was he to know that a nurse with fake ID would slip by? By the same token, he knew it was his job to be prepared for the unexpected. That was why he was there.

Macaffe shuffled some papers on his desk. "So, who did they get?"

"A transient off the street that was brought in drunk and had been beaten the night before. He was about the same size as Murray, so they shaved him and cleaned him up and put him in the room reserved for Murray. Poor bastard's probably better off now, anyway," he rationalized, shrugging his shoulders.

Macaffe didn't respond. "After this episode, I trust you've beefed up the watch on Murray?"

"I guarantee you, a bedbug couldn't get on that floor, let alone in the room, without having a half-dozen men ready to squash him. I'd bet my life on it."

"You just did," Macaffe said, without looking up. "I want a report on his condition every six hours. If there's any improvement or deterioration, I want to be informed instantly." He looked up at the man with fierce eyes. They were cold and unforgiving.

"Yes, sir. I understand, sir. Last I heard, he was resting comfortably and his condition was stable and improving."

"That will be all," Macaffe said, still looking at the man as if his eyes were burning through to his very soul.

"Yes, sir," he said nervously, backing into the door.

When the man had left, Macaffe punched a button on the intercom. "Marcie. Get me Grover. I want to be notified as soon as he arrives."

"Yes, sir." She knew that meant even if he was in a meeting or was otherwise indisposed.

* * * *

"So, Murray has been taken care of?" Alfredo asked his younger brother, who had just put his feet up on Alfredo's desk.

"A piece of cake. Went off without a hitch."

"And your plant? I take it you covered your ass."

He nodded his head reluctantly. "I took care of it, although I must admit that I did so with great regret. Not only was she reliable, but she was a great lay." He snickered to himself.

"A woman?" Alfredo retorted. "You left this job to a woman?" His voice rose.

"She was a trained nurse!" he retorted with equal vehemence. "She knew the ropes," he shot back at his older brother as he made a facial gesture displaying his anger for his judgment being questioned. "Besides, she got the job done, didn't she? Who'd expect a nurse to snuff her own patient? I thought it was brilliant, myself," he said, polishing his nails on his chest.

"How do you know that she got the job done?" he asked, staring hard at his brother. "Did you verify that he was dead before you eliminated her? Or were you too busy zipping your pants?"

"That's not fair," Niccola shot back. "She said the job was done, and if she said it was done, it was done!"

"And, of course, you verified that Murray was dead?"

"Well, no. Not exactly. How was I to do that? By now the place is probably crawling with cops!"

"Not exactly," Alfredo parroted his brother's words. "And I suppose that 'not exactly' you didn't verify that the man she snuffed was Murray?"

"It was his room. Who else could it have been?"

"You moron. It could have been a store mannequin for all you know. Shit! How stupid do you think those people are? Do you think they're just going to let some broad waltz in and snuff the most important man in the company without a clue?" he asked sarcastically.

Niccola just sat in his chair looking at his older brother's angry face without comment. He knew Alfredo was right. It had been too easy. The job had been completed, of that he was certain, but on who, he couldn't tell for sure.

"Get over there and find out who bit it, if any-one," Alfredo barked. "And take Carlo with you. Maybe you can teach him something in the proc-ess." He slammed the door of his desk, as much for effect as to demonstrate his anger.

Niccola rose to leave.

"If you missed him, don't come back until the job is complete!" Alfredo yelled as Niccola closed the door. "I'm surrounded by idiots," he said, look-ing up to the ceiling with raised arms, as if talking to God.

* * * *

"You wanted to see me, chief?"

"Come in, Grover."

Macaffe had a concerned look as he paused, looking into Grover's eyes before speaking. "We've been compromised, Grover. Someone made a move on Murray today. I want you to..."

"He's not...?"

"No. They got a drunk transient that we had sitting in for him, but the fact that they tried and would have succeeded had we not been a step ahead of them is what disturbs me."

"Who's they?" Grover inquired, edging his chair closer to Macaffe's desk.

"That's what I want you to find out. Use all the manpower you need, but try to confine them to the inner circle."

"The Team," Grover said, more to himself than confirming Macaffe's instructions.

"I don't want to lose control here: no press, no outside influences."

"I'll get on it right away." He rose to go, then paused at the door. "How is the Coach?"

"I'm told that he's resting well and has stabilized. As soon as you have something, you let me know, Grover. I don't care if it's day or night. I want to know."

* * * *

There were several police cars parked around the entrance of the hospital as Niccola and Carlo slowly drove by the entrance. "Go around to the back," Nick said. "We'll try the rear entrance."

Nick glanced down the alley as they rounded the corner. A black city coroner's wagon was parked near where the dead nurse lay, while several policemen appeared to be searching the surrounding area for clues. The forensic team had arrived, and they were taking pictures of the body.

"I'll miss that bitch," Nick said bitterly. "There was no need to kill the broad," he said, shaking his head in disgust. "Over there," he nodded to Carlo as they approached the emergency entrance.

"You wait here," he instructed Carlo. "Back in and keep the motor running. I may—"

"Al said for you to bring me along," Carlo whined. "I want to get in on the action, too. Don't leave me h—"

"Shut the fuck up! You don't have a clue what's going on in there, and if I have to act fast I don't want some slow-movin' rock hanging on my leg. Now, you do as I say and stay here with the car running," he said angrily, hitting his brother hard on his shoulder. "And keep your eyes on the door and the radio off. If I come running out that door, you better be ready to floor this tub and get us the hell out of here!"

"But, Al said—"

Nick pointed his finger at his brother with a stern, threatening look, but said nothing. He didn't have to. The look said it all.

"Aw. All right. But I'm tellin' Al when we get back," Carlo whined. "He said I could go."

Nick walked into the entrance, looking around to see if anyone was watching as he entered the stairwell. He carefully made his way up the stairs, peeking around the exit door of each floor until he got to the fourth floor. There were cops everywhere. They were standing by the nurse's station, interviewing nurses and doctors, coming out of rooms and just generally milling about.

Nick waited until some of the uniformed men left, then, when the hallway was clear, eased his way down the corridor, glancing into each windowed room as he went. The room next to the front stairs contained a body with the sheet pulled over the patient's head, indicating that he had passed away. Nick slipped into the room, closing the door carefully behind himself.

He quickly went to the bed where the patient lay and pulled the sheet from his face. At that moment, a voice of authority demanded to know what he was doing there.

Nick turned to face a uniformed policeman. "I'm, ah, someone said that my brother had passed away and I, ah..."

"Let's see some ID," the policeman demanded.

Nick reached around to his back pocket, pulled out his .38 with the silencer and shot the policeman twice in the chest. He fell back through the door as Nick brushed past him. He paused at the door only long enough to check the corridor, then raced for the stairwell. So far he was safe. No one had seen him.

The officer was temporarily stunned by the force of the shells hitting his flack jacket. A moment later, still lying on the floor, he recovered enough to alert the other officers. He relayed an account of what had happened and gave Nick's description over his short-wave.

Nick raced down the stairwell, taking three and four stairs at a time. He paused only for a moment as he reached the first floor, to listen to hear if he was being chased. The faint sound of footsteps echoing through the upper stairwell seemed to be at least two flights up.

Outside in the car, Carlo's eyes were darting from the entryway back to the ever-growing row of police cars that had suddenly pulled up in front of the hospital. As each car came to a halt, the officers within would scramble out, taking positions by the car with their weapons pointed at the entrance.

Carlo had no way of contacting his brother, nor of knowing what the status was inside the hospital. He could only hope that Nick would see the barricade of police before he came out.

Nick smiled to himself as he crashed through the stairwell door, still holding his weapon. It wasn't until he was outside that his eyes adjusted to the bright sunlight. He shielded his eyes from the sun. By that time, the officers had seen his weapon raised.

Seeing his weapon drawn, they thought he was going to fire on them. The police officers commenced firing, hitting him at least a dozen times. Niccola Carleone fell to the ground, dead.

Carlo slid down in his seat, shaking like a leaf, whimpering to himself as the police cautiously approached the body.

More policemen poured from the stairwell of the building and more arrived by car. While they were all preoccupied with the body of Niccola, Carlo eased his car into drive and slowly exited the hospital parking lot, taking care to stop at each sign and not draw attention to himself.

Chapter Eleven

"He what?"

"Christian Murray just walked out of the hospital," the voice reported over the phone. "Sorry, boss. Short of tackling the man, there was nothing I could do to stop him."

"Well, how the hell did he get his clothes? What did the doctors say? Was he all right?" The Attorney General fired questions at the voice.

"They tell me he just pulled the IVs and got out of bed, demanding to know where his clothes were. When the nurse said he couldn't leave, he pushed her aside and said 'Watch me.' Apparently, he was leaving with or without his clothes, threatening to walk out in his hospital garment."

"I would have paid money to see that," the voice quipped. "Murray walking down the corridor with his bare ass hanging out. A picture like that would be worth money."

The Attorney General failed to respond to the man's humor, although the visual image of Murray walking on a public street with a backless garment did bring a smile to his face.

"Where did he go? He had no transportation."

"Last we saw of him was when he drove off in a Yellow Cab."

"Shit! I'm surrounded by morons," he said aloud, more to himself than to the voice. "Well, check the cab company and see—"

"Sir. You have a visitor," came the voice over Macaffe's intercom.

"Damn it, Marcie. Can't you see I'm on the phone?" he yelled at the box on his desk.

"It's Mr. Murray, sir. Christian Murray."

Macaffe hung up the phone without further conversation. "Send him in," he said coolly.

The clothes that Murray wore were the same ones that he had worn to his family's funeral, only they were badly soiled. They had obviously been worn several days without being removed prior to his discovery. He was unshaven and his hair had been simply swept back with his hand, his fingers acting as a comb. In short, he looked like a homeless person himself.

"What the hell do you think you're doing, Christian?" Macaffe asked angrily.

Murray knew whenever Macaffe used his full name, it was because he was angry.

Seeing Murray standing in front of him didn't really surprise Macaffe, however. He had always known that Murray had a strong, stubborn, self-styled streak running through his veins. That was one of the reasons he was head of the DEA. "Do you know the Mob is looking for you everywhere, overturning every rock to rub out your ass? If we hadn't hidden you under an assumed name in the security unit of the hospital, you wouldn't even be standing here. And what's the big idea of leaving the hospital before you're released? Have you flipped your lid?"

Murray just stood before Macaffe's desk without comment, looking intently at his boss. Macaffe had seen that cold, hard look in his eyes before, and it usually meant that Murray was back to pushing a large rock uphill.

"I'm sorry," Macaffe said, waving his hand towards the chair. "Have a seat. We've got a lot to discuss. I know you've been through a lot, Chris. I can't tell you how sorry I am about your family. We all—"

"I've been thinking a lot," Murray said, interrupting Macaffe, dismissing his attempt at sentimentality. "I've obviously blown my cover as head of the Team. By now every pimp, pusher and gun runner knows about me, and those with any intelligence probably has ID'd the team, too. I want to go undercover."

"Undercover? What do you think you've been doing for the past three years? No one outside of this room and your Team even knows of your existence...not even the President, for God's sake," he said, looking around out of habit to see if anyone was listening.

"Well, we both know that's history. If it was such a secret, how did my family get blown up? And your weak attempt at security at the hospital..." He shook his head. "I heard about that."

Macaffe started to say something, but Murray held up his hand to stop him. "And even after they were successful in killing my sit-in, whomever the poor soul was, they still tried to get me, even while the place was crawling with security. I either have to retire and sit around some fishing hole waiting for them to hunt me down again and blow me away, or..." he hesitated, looking at Macaffe.

"Or what?" he asked impatiently.

"Or go underground."

"How the hell do you go underground, when, by your own admission, everyone knows who you are? You'll be dead within a week, Chris," he said with frustration, mopping his brow with a white handkerchief.

"As I said, I've been thinking. We both know that the crooks have a leg up on us. They don't have ground rules dictating how they are to operate. If they want something, they simply take it. If they want someone eliminated, they either kill 'em or have them killed. If they get caught, they buy the jury and/or judges and hire the best legal advice available. If that fails, they threaten to kill the witnesses and everyone on the jury, plus their families, until they get off scot-free.

"Any way you cut it, with few exceptions, they have free reign of our judicial system. They have more firepower than we do and have no compulsion about using it. They have illegal drugs, prostitution and gambling money to buy what they need, not to mention what they steal or print themselves. They have an underground network that makes us look sick—the Mob, the Colombian drug lords and all the crooks in general. In short, we're simply out-manned, out-gunned, under-financed and strapped by our own legal system!"

This was a speech that every police chief and politician had either given or heard since Al Capone dominated the liquor trade during Prohibition. "So, what are you saying?" Macaffe asked, leaning forward in his chair, hoping to hear something new.

"I'm saying that the only way we're going to beat these assholes is to whip them at their own game."

Macaffe sat back in his chair, furrowing his brow with a puzzled look. "I don't follow."

"I want to create an underground counter-force...one equivalent to our counterpart—the mob and drug dealers—using my Team as the nucleus of the operation. We'll operate by using the same ground rules as they do, only we'll be better trained, more disciplined and more sophisticated. And we'll be focused. They won't have a clue as to who they're dealing with or what hit them."

"Let me understand what I think you're saying," Macaffe said, turning his chair around so he was facing the wall, his back to Murray. "You're suggesting that you take your team underground and work outside the law?" He turned back to face Murray.

"I've got it all laid out in my head, Bob," Murray said, leaning towards Macaffe. "We'll hit them with every new technology available. We'll do to them what they've been doing to us. Only instead of destroying the booty, or turning it into the system, where it gets stored, destroyed or lost in some bureaucratic red tape, we'll use it against them to fight the war. I figure if I maneuver the situation just right, we'll have them fighting each other. They won't know whose finger is on the trigger."

Macaffe shook his head. "Whoa. You're going too fast for me."

Murray's eyes blazed with excitement as he paced the room, gesturing as he spoke. "It can't fail, Bob. Don't you see? It's perfect."

"All I can see is myself behind bars in Federal Place. Have you thought of what happens to you and your band of misfits when you get caught breaking the law, by the law?"

"You'll just have to cover us, Bob," Murray said with a smile. "We'll be a secret division accountable only to you, just like we are now. The only difference is we'll be underground."

Macaffe sat back in his chair looking up at the ceiling with his hands folded, his fingers touching his lips. "I don't know, Chris. It makes me nervous. How can I get funding for a venture like this?

How am I going to explain this to the FBI or CIA or, God forbid, the President if they ever unearth this...and eventually they will," he said, looking Murray in the eye. "It's inevitable.

"Rest assured, somewhere down the line, someone's bound to slip up. You'll cross swords with some other law enforcement agency, or one of your men will be hurt or killed and there will be an investigation. Then, bang, the shit will hit the fan," he said nervously. "I'm not ready to retire. Not yet, at least, Chris. Sorry."

"Don't be such a pussy. Creating the Team was your idea to begin with. All I've done is embellish the concept. Think of the dent we could make in organized crime if we didn't have to cross every 'T' and dot every 'I'. Come on. Give it a try. Life is too short not to take chances. Where would this country be if Patrick Henry hadn't decided to piss off the Queen of England?"

He could see that Macaffe was thinking. He loved that man. He played by the rules, but, by the same token, he hated losing, especially to crooks.

"Tell you what," Murray said, sitting down again and looking Macaffe in the eye. "I'll get the Team to train on their own dime. When we make our first hit, we'll make our own payroll and deliver all the overage to you as usual, just like the last bust. Everything will be documented," he added quickly, making sure that the thought of pilfering didn't cross Macaffe's mind, not that it ever would. "It won't cost you a cent. No senate appropriations. No house approval."

"They don't know shit as it is," Macaffe said, rubbing the back of his neck like he always did when he was nervous.

Murray ignored his comment. "If we don't succeed in busting our balls, we don't get paid. It's that simple. Now, how can you lose with a deal like that?"

Macaffe sat silent for a long time, looking intently at Murray. Murray knew he had him hooked. There was a thin line of larceny dancing through the Attorney General's veins. That's one of the reasons he liked the man so well. He didn't let protocol interfere with success.

"You didn't get to be the attorney general by not being creative," Murray good-naturedly taunted his friend. "Take a chance. That's how we get things done around here. Calculated risks. We owe it to Jana and the kids," he concluded soberly.

"Tell you what," Macaffe said slowly. "Get your men together and see if they're willing to take the risk. Make damn sure they understand the down side of the plan. They have to know that if their asses get hung out to dry, I don't even know your name."

He hesitated for a moment, letting the thought sink in. "If you get past them, I'll want a detailed schematic plan of how you plan to proceed, including targets, method of hitting them, how you plan to handle the drugs, weapons, security, etc. If I like what I see, we'll take it to the next step." He rose to shake Murray's hand. "And welcome back, Chris."

* * * *

The Attorney General had called a press conference, which took place at the bottom steps of the courthouse with Christian Murray and Bob Macaffe facing the building. The press had been told that a brash, bold policy was about to be implemented by the head of the Drug Enforcement

Administration, Christian M. Murray, and that he would lay out the skeleton of his plan for the press.

All major television, radio, newspapers and news magazines were present to record the occasion.

Bob Macaffe walked up to the microphone. "I called this meeting because I want to introduce Christian Murray, who most of you know heads up the Drug Enforcement Administration of this country, otherwise known as the DEA. He has been assigned to create and spearhead a special task force which he'll tell you about. He'll also have access to the most sophisticated surveillance equipment our country can devise. We intend to eradicate the despicable blotch of violent drug activity from our society, once and for all.

"Too long have our children been exposed to drugs. It's spread to the street corners of our cities and in front of your houses and even in the halls of schools. Children have been known to resort to carrying weapons just to protect themselves from the violence that this cancer has brought upon our society. It will be Mr. Murray's task to cut this cancer from our country."

Having set the tone of the director of DEA's speech, he said, "Ladies and gentlemen, I give you Christian Murray."

There was polite applause from onlookers, those few politicians in attendance and the out-of-town press. Local press never applauded news conferences.

Women from the Woman Against Guns, WAG, carried signs on wooden sticks, raising them in the air while they chanted, "Outlaw guns. Down with the NRA."

"This is an appropriate place," Murray began as he nodded his gratitude towards Bob Macaffe, "to announce this government's intention to wage an all-out war against organized crime, drugs in particular...the Mafia and the Colombian Cartel even more specifically." He paused to let the first sentence sink in. "And I want you ladies who are here representing the WAG to know that I applaud your cause," he said, looking directly at their group. "There is no place for automatic weapons in the hands of the American public."

The women yelled approval while pumping their signs.

A man dressed in a black leather jacket wearing silver-coated sunglasses and greasy hair stood at the rear of the crowd and scowled at Murray's words.

The cameras clicked, television crews stood with microphones on extended booms, and dignitaries who were in attendance had their pictures taken so they could tell their constituents that they had been there supporting the anti-drug movement.

Murray was dressed conservatively, in a dark blue suit with a red tie. He didn't smile as he gave his inspiring, short speech to the crowd, after which he opened the forum to questions.

"Mr. Murray. What makes you think that you'll be successful in eliminating illegal drugs when your predecessors, ranging all the way back to J. Edgar Hoover and Robert Kennedy, have failed?" the reporter from the Washington Post asked.

"The attorney general, Mr. Robert Macaffe, has agreed to make technology and support available that heretofore none of my predecessors have had, with the possible exception of Elliot Ness during the Prohibition days."

"What do you mean by tools? Weapons? Manpower?" the man followed up. "Even if you get them into court, between their unlimited funds, their smart attorneys and our legal system, they'll be out on the street before the ink is dry on the paperwork. How do you plan on changing that?"

"For obvious reasons, I'm unable to elaborate on our game plan at this time. Yes, Miss Henry?" he said, pointing to the young woman representing the *New York Times*. She was dressed in a business suit with a small, colorful scarf tied around her neck.

"Mr. Murray. After your family was killed, purportedly by organized crime, don't you feel that maybe you're too emotionally involved to be effective? I mean, isn't this liable to turn into some sort of a personal vendetta?"

"The death of my family has nothing to do with how I will perform my duties. The level of my performance will be the same as if my family not been the target of the very violence that plagues our society today. The only difference," he said somewhat wistfully, "is that now I'll have unlimited hours to devote to my job."

Some of the crowd laughed nervously.

Wanda Henry persisted. She had gained her job with the *New York Times* by being persistent to the point of embarrassment, and she got results. Incumbent candidates usually avoided interviews with her unless they had an impeccable track record and an even more impeccable background. Wanda Henry could make or break the back of any candidate's election. She was especially harsh on chiefs of staff and heads of office, like Bob Macaffe and Christian Murray.

"But, Mr. Murray, isn't this going to give you license to retaliate against—" she persisted before Murray interrupted her.

"Miss Henry, you can be assured that I am not

embarking upon a personal vendetta," he said, looking at her firmly. He was not running for political office and was answerable only to the Attorney General, thus he didn't have to pussyfoot around with her. "As my job requires, I will fight to eliminate those who have inflicted their cancer on society, and today I pledge to fight them to the death.

"Thank you. That will be all for now." Before leaving the platform, he looked straight at Wanda Henry as if challenging her.

Christian Murray turned to walk to a black limousine which had been parked behind him on the street. A chauffeur awaited with an open door.

"That will conclude our statement for today," Bob Macaffe said, taking the microphones as he watched Murray enter the limo, waving away reporters, who all wanted to have one more question answered.

The cameras focused on his limo as he climbed in and shut the door. The driver rolled up the smoked glass windows and started the engine. In that instant there was a loud explosion.

The hood and trunk of the limo flew 10 feet into the air. All four of the tires simultaneously blew. Black smoke bellowed from under the hood and trunk, followed by deep red flames.

Women screamed as the crowd fell back from the shock of the explosion. Some of the reporters were knocked to the ground, as they had been standing close to the limo when it exploded. Miraculously, none of the bystanders were hurt.

Within moments, there was a circle of motorcycle policemen surrounding the vehicle, keeping people back. The sound of a siren could be heard in the background.

A fire truck arrived, and the fire was put out

by covering the entire vehicle with a white foam. A firemen tried to pry open the back door of the limo, but the fire seemed to have sealed it shut.

"No one is going to survive that blast and heat," the fire chief said to one of the policemen. "Let's get this mess out of here."

After the limo had cooled down, a wrecking truck pulled in front, hooked up and towed it away. All the while, cameras were clicking, television commentators were giving graphic descriptions of what had happened, and the radio announcers had a field day. They had attended what was supposed to be a dull, routine news conference and had captured an explosion and the subsequent death of an important dignitary, live. This was the best news coverage since the Kennedy assassination.

The politicians and other dignitaries seemed to have suddenly disappeared from sight without comment, as if they feared that they could be the next target.

Once the limo had been towed away and the last picture had been taken, the reporters turned their attention to the attorney general, Mr. Robert Macaffe, who was sitting on the curb being assisted by an aide. He was visibly shaken and appeared to be in the early stages of shock.

"Mr. Macaffe! How does this change your plans?"

"Mr. Macaffe! How do you feel about your newly appointed task force head being blown up in front of your face?"

"Mr. Macaffe! This seems to be a clear message from organized crime, showing their complete disregard for law and order. What steps do you intend to take now?"

Macaffe held up his hand to stop the questions. "We have all just witnessed a terrible tragedy. I am not prepared to make any comments at this time beyond my obvious shock at what just took place. If this is a message from organized crime, they had better run for cover, because my answer will soon be on its way!"

Robert Macaffe, obviously angry and in shock, turned to walk up the courthouse steps, followed by some of the reporters. They were headed off, however, by the secret service agents who had been assigned to protect the Attorney General.

Standing behind the reporters was Mr. Green. He was studying the reaction of the crowd, especially the reporters. There was an uneasy look about him as he slowly walked away shaking his head.

* * * *

Alfredo Carleone sat at his desk staring off into space, a shocked look on his face. His eyes focused on Carlo, secretly wishing that he had been gunned down in place of Niccola. He wondered how he would tell his father that his second son had been killed by the police as he tried to rub out Murray.

His eyes fell on the paper lying on his desk, with the heading: US Vs. Organized Crime. There was an inserted picture of Christian Murray alongside of a picture of Murray's limo going up in flames, with the shocked look of faces of onlookers present. Murray's last words, "I pledge to fight them to the death!" were boldly captioned above the picture, with an excerpt from his speech and a detailed account of the disaster printed below.

He smashed his hand on the photo, crushing it in his hands.

"Hell-of-a-deal," Carlo said, slapping the paper with the back of his hand, trying to cheer up his brother. "Someone knocks Murray off and we get credit. I love it!"

"You moron!" Alfredo said, glaring at his brother, barely restraining himself from bashing him. "We just buried our brother who got iced by the cops, and you think I give a shit about Murray?"

"I thought you would be pleased that the guy got hit," Carlo said apologetically.

"Get out of my sight! And shut the door behind you. I don't want to be disturbed. I've got a lot to think about."

Chapter Twelve

It had only been two months since the funeral of Murray's family, and now everyone was back at the graveyard again. They had barely recovered from the shock of his family's funeral, and now they had come to bury Christian Murray. The news of his death had been too much for his mother. She had collapsed and had to be rushed to the hospital. Her husband, Ted, stayed by her side until the funeral. While she was under sedation, he had stolen away to wish a final farewell to his first-born.

The entire Team was in attendance this time, as there seemed to be no need for secrecy beyond this point, they rationalized. They knew that Project Team would be terminated with the death of their leader. The concept had been Murray's idea from the start, and he had been the driving force behind its success.

The service was short, as short as it could have been and still do homage to the fallen warrior. The light rain fell and a brisk breeze brought the wind chill factor well below freezing, deterring anyone who might have wanted to linger. Only Grover stayed until everyone had departed, to have a few private moments alone with the man he had come to love and admire as his father.

Before he left, he observed a black Mercedes limousine parked on the adjoining road. He knew it contained members of the Mob. They had come to assure themselves that their arch-rival had been put to rest. He also observed a mysterious, lone figure standing under the aspen trees just at the crest of the hill. The man was dressed in a dark overcoat, a black hat and, even though it was raining, he wore sunglasses.

After watching the black Mercedes limo drive slowly away, Grover looked back at the aspen grove, but the figure he had seen before had disappeared in the mist.

* * * *

Five weeks had passed since Murray's funeral, and this was the first time since his death that the Team had been called together. In that short period, discipline had perceptibly deteriorated, and they looked as if they could care less about themselves.

"Anyone know what the meeting's about, Center?" one of the men asked Grover, accenting the word "Center" mockingly. No one responded. There was an air of restlessness amongst the group. Everyone knew that the future of the Team hung by a thread. They anticipated the reason for the meeting was to disband the group and reassign the men to different units.

"I, for one, don't intend to have some shavetail college graduate giving me orders," Tackle said. "I had all of that bullshit I needed in the army. Get a guy just out of college and fresh out of OCS Academy, and he thinks he knows it all."

"Until the first round of live ammo heads his

way," one of the Defense said with a laugh.

"Then it's duck and head for the nearest fox-hole."

"And yell for the sergeant," one of the Ends howled.

"If they break us up, I'm outta here!" Tackle said sarcastically. There was a look of anger and frustration on his face. They were harboring an underlying feeling they didn't understand—a feeling of abandonment and betrayal.

Others nodded and mumbled in agreement.

Just then, the red light over the door flashed, indicating that someone had entered the outer corridor. Silence fell over the group as all eyes focused on the door. Each man braced himself for the message they knew was about to follow.

They expected Robert Macaffe, as he was the only other person they were aware of that knew of this place. Instead, an unknown figure entered the room, dressed in desert fatigues, wearing combat boots wearing a floppy desert-issue hat. He wore silver-coated dark glasses which partially masked his unshaven face. There was something familiar about his gait, however, as he stood at the head of the table surveying the group before him.

He removed his glasses and hat, then, without speaking, studied each man, one by one. His firm, yet somewhat familiar gaze elicited an uneasy feeling among them. When he spoke, there was a familiarity to his voice.

"Men. Welcome to Team Search and Destroy. I'll be your leader from here on in." He paused to search their faces for a response. He had neglected to give his name. As he removed his overcoat he told everyone to sit.

Only Grover remained standing, facing the man.

He leaned forward, his knuckles turning white under the weight of his large frame as they rested on the table top. He squinted as if trying to see through a fog. "Coach? Is that you, Coach?"

It wasn't until Grover spoke that the other men rose, one at a time, stretching to get a closer glimpse of the man. "It is! It's Christian Murray! Isn't it?"

The man was the same height, yet had a different look about him, some of which could be accounted for by the newly grown mustache and full beard. His eyes seemed to have a different set than they had remembered, however...sort of drawn or pinched, which altered his appearance. They also took on a different gleam than the men were used to seeing. His nose had been altered, too. It was less pronounced, and that noticeable hump over the bridge, where he had broken it in a raid with a bunch of Mexicans years back, was now missing. He was much slimmer, too, which could be easily be accounted for as a result of the stress he had been under, the men thought. The cheekbones seemed more pronounced—higher than they remembered.

None of the men were aware of Murray's brush with death at his home after he had buried his family. Only Grover knew of his physical condition and that he had been admitted to the hospital. Out of consideration for the man and for obvious security reasons, he hadn't mentioned it to anyone. As it turned out, not even Murray knew that Grover was the one who had found him.

After the initial silence that followed the shock of realizing that the man before them was indeed Murray, everyone had questions. They all talked at once, wanting to know why he wasn't dead. They had all seen him blown up in the limo. The entire nation had seen it. It had been recorded live on television. How had he escaped death? Was it all a set-up? Was he hurt? Why he had changed his appearance? Was it because of the accident?

Questions, questions and more questions.

Murray held up his hand, waiting for the excited men to quiet down. "I understand the confusion you have to be feeling, and, for some of you," he looked at Grover in particular, "maybe even anger. For that, I apologize. In due time, I'll discuss the detailed circumstances under which it appeared that I was blown up yet am now standing before you. For the time being, let it suffice to say that the Director and myself found it necessary to—how shall I say—make me disappear."

He studied the confused look on his men's faces. "From this day forward, the name of Christian Murray belongs to a deceased DEA agent. I will now be known simply as The Colombian, in deference to my heritage. Now, there is much work to be done."

He was all business as he spoke, talking in a quiet monotone. Then, as he continued laying out his plan, his voice took on an eagerness that swept through the men's imagination and carried them to heights they had only dared talk about in hushed circles over a beer and barbecue in someone's backyard.

"As you know, when operation Team was conceived, I hand-picked each and every one of you to be on my Team. My criteria were simple. You had to be dedicated, law enforcement-minded individuals, willing to put your life on hold for man and country. You all had basic skills that were learned in the service, be it as navy seals, marines, green berets, rangers or paratroopers. You were picked because you were special and had special skills."

He looked at the men he had come to love and admire as his own family. "In the past, I've asked you to perform some amazing tasks under equally difficult conditions—and you've come through to the man. For that, I want to thank each and every one of you."

The men gave one other knowing looks that said, "I feel proud to be one of the Team. I feel special again."

"As you all know, recent events have arisen which have brought me to a crossroads, not only in my personal life, but as a professional law enforcement officer."

He paused for a moment, as if reflecting within himself. "Due to events in the recent past, my professional life has been forced to make a directional change. I was faced with a couple of choices, one of which was to retire and move to a warmer southern climate and spend my life fishing and learning Spanish, in which case I would be constantly looking over my shoulder, waiting for that one piece of lead that had "Murray" written on it." He looked at the intent faces of his men. "Or, I could go deep into the underground and operate within a system that only exists in our imagination."

The men looked at one another, entranced by their leader's words, but not quite grasping their meaning.

"In addition to the skills I previously mentioned, you were chosen because you have no immediate ties to what I refer to as the social world. You have no wives and, in most cases, no girlfriends. Your parents are deceased, and you have no siblings. In short, you have no family at all. We," he said, encompassing the group with his outstretched arms, "are your family! I mention this because now I'm going to be asking you to pledge yourself to a deeper commitment than you've ever dared imagine, personally as well as professionally."

He walked around the room talking, looking at each man as he spoke. "Because this requires commitment, I'm giving each of you the opportunity to leave this god-forsaken group of misfits to start your life over—like a normal human being."

A number of the men laughed, some knowingly, others nervously. Murray didn't.

"I don't want you to feel that you have an obligation to the Team over your personal life. Once you decide to remain on the Team, however, the Team will become your family...your only family. You will be asked to put all personal ties on hold—indefinitely."

Murray studied each man's face for a moment before continuing. "I want you to consider that I'm asking for a 110-percent commitment here. Your personal life as you now know it, limited as it may be, will be all but non-existent."

He was exaggerating, but needed to drive the point home. The one thing he couldn't afford was to have one of his men personally involved with some woman and have his judgment clouded at some critical point in some future operation that could endanger not only his life, but that of the team as well.

"In short, this is an open invitation for any of you to leave. This will be the first and last time this opportunity will present itself."

His eyes quickly scanned the men's faces. He could detect who was undeniably committed to the Team and those who would like to go but knew this was their only life. There were only one or two that he was unsure of.

"There isn't a man in this room who will fault you for leaving. As a matter of fact, in all probability, we'll envy you, because that will mean that you've decided to have a life. I, for one, can find no fault in that, having once had one myself."

The men looked at each other, each asking with their eyes if the others were still in. They had been such a cohesive group that the majority of them couldn't conceive of living a different life. Normal life as they knew it was dull and mundane.

Paul Kirkman shifted nervously in his chair for a moment, then hesitantly stood.

All eyes shifted from Murray to Kirkman.

"Paul?" was Murray's only response, but Kirkman knew he was asking for an explanation.

He shifted uneasily on his feet, not wanting to look his leader in the eye. He was 26 years old, aged well beyond his years. He had previously trained and served with the navy seals for three years. He had been awarded the Bronze medal for outstanding service and bravery for returning to a blown target, risking his life to save a fallen comrade who had been hit by enemy fire.

He had known that the rule was to leave anyone who was too wounded to walk. "Don't jeopardize the team for a man" was the standard command. At the last moment, he had rushed back into enemy fire to carry his fallen comrade out on his back, taking two rounds in the process, one in the shoulder and one in the lower back.

He could have been court-martialed for disobeying strict orders, but instead his commander chose to praise his bravery, knowing that the morale of his men was at stake. The men had praised him for his actions, as did their leader.

"I've been taking graduate courses in engineering at the university and I've..." Kirkman choked on his words as if he was confessing to a criminal act.

"You've found a young lady," Murray added, helping him.

"Better than a young man," one of the men added, laughing. The rest of the crew laughed, too, looking at Murray to see his response.

"I'm glad for you," Murray said with genuine warmth. "There's nothing like a good woman to come home to." He hesitated for a moment, choking back the emotion that suddenly surged deep within his chest. "And there's no feeling like holding your own flesh and blood in your own two hands for the first time. Don't you feel bad, Kirkman. You have our blessing. Go. Enjoy your life."

Having said that, his comrades stood and applauded Kirkman. They loved him to the man and would miss him.

Paul knew he would miss the Team, too, as he passed from man to man, first shaking each hand, then receiving a warm bearhug. When he got to Murray, they stood looking at one another, eye to eye.

"Enjoy your life, son. Have one for me." Murray hugged him, holding onto him for an extra-long moment, making him feel a little embarrassed.

Although they were steel-tough to the man, several suddenly had an ember in the eye or their sinus conditions began acting up as Kirkman walked out of the door for the last time.

"He's a hell of a man," Murray said, looking at his Team. "I admire him for standing up for what he believes...anyone else?"

He waited, looking down the table. No one moved.

"All right. Now, let me tell you what we're going to do. If, when I finish, there's anyone who doesn't feel that he can adhere to the rigorous demands of the job and, make no mistake, it will be demanding—feel free to depart. There will be no hard feelings."

No one moved. They felt the anticipation of a new venture and ached for the game to begin.

* * * *

Murray flew the team to Fort Ord, California, in the Black Hawk jet chopper Bob Macaffe had assigned to the operation. Fort Ord had been one of many army training posts ordered closed under President Clinton's 1993 military cutback.

The fort was ideal for Murray's needs. It was located just off Monterey Bay, ideal for water exercises—if one didn't mind sharks. The fort itself, although visible from the highway, was secure, with its one main gate located just off Highway One. Incoming traffic was monitored by the military police. There were rifle ranges, grenade practice areas and plenty of hills, and sand dunes for small troop maneuvers.

As all personnel had long since been vacated from the fort, there were dozens of vacant barracks, mess halls and warehouse buildings to be utilized as training facilities.

Murray picked D-11-3, one of the newer two-storey red brick barracks, to house the team. Instead of the traditional army bunk beds, each man was provided a regular full-sized bed. Murray commandeered the Captain's quarters, just outside the double swinging doors and down the hall from the main sleeping room. He also had his own private shower and latrine.

The quaint tourist areas of Sea Side, Monterey, Carmel and Big Sur were only minutes away, although Murray warned the men there would be precious little time for sight seeing or recreation.

The Team arrived at the fort and settled in. Training began the next morning, with a 20-mile run from the barracks down to and along the beach for 10 miles, returning back through sand dunes.

Once back on the parade grounds, they unwound with a half-hour of calisthenics before being fed a high-protein breakfast of steak, eggs, whole-wheat unbuttered toast, a handful of vitamins, and fresh-squeezed orange juice. This was to become their schedule until Murray thought they were fit and back to thinking and acting as a unit.

The balance of the mornings was spent on tactical maneuvers, assimilating hostile situations, using the desert and large vacant buildings as training facilities. In the afternoons, the Team hiked down to the rifle range, where they sharpened their skills with handguns, automatic weapons and self-defense training.

At the end of six weeks, Murray assembled the men in the barracks staff room. They had just finished simulating a drug bust in an industrial building. Each man was still dressed in combat boots and desert camouflage uniforms and carried a sidearm as well as their assigned automatic weapon. Each weapon was equipped with a silencer. Their closely shaven heads glistened from the workout, but Murray could tell from the brightness of their eyes and the color of their skin that they were not only in superb condition, but were anxious to step up to the next level of "combat", as Murray called it.

"I've been notified by Home Base that there's a drug deal going down in the neighborhood. It would appear that our friends, the Colombians, are up to their old tricks. Apparently, they've scheduled a transaction with the Mob in Silicon Valley, just an hour's drive up the road towards San Francisco. Our job will be to take charge and neutralize the situation."

There were high-fives and a lot of whooping from the men as Murray watched their enthusiasm with pride. They had worked hard and were eager for action. All this training had been great, but it was no panacea for the real thing.

"Our mission will be to simply eliminate the competition, take possession of the material at hand, and leave without a trace."

"When you say, 'eliminate the competition,' you mean..."

"Eliminate means just that. No one leaves the zone except the Team—period."

The men looked at one another with mixed emotions. This was the training they had been practicing for the past month and a half. It was about to become a reality. Some of them showed a slight hesitance about taking life without first giving their opponent a chance to surrender and be bound over to a court of law. Murray had previously informed them of the change of the rules of the game. They had known this going in. Now they were going to be put to the test.

"This is war on the soil of the Mother Country, men," Murray said with a stern voice, his eyes blazing. "I mean to fight for it just as if we were under siege in the jungles of Vietnam. We take no prisoners and leave no witnesses. The goal is total elimination of organized crime, fought on our soil. We're using their rules with our total domination. Are you up for it?"

The men nodded, affirmative. Some said, "Yeah, you bet."

"I can't hear you! I said, are you up for it?" His

voice carried the emotion of a football coach down 10-0 at half-time.

"Yeah!"

"Kick ass!"

"Kill the bastards!"

Murray stood tall in front of his group, his hands on his hips. "All right! That's better. Now, here's the layout."

He had drawn a scale map of the drug drop on the blackboard. He went over the method of attack. When he was finished with his presentation, he added, "This is what we've been practicing for, for the last six weeks. Any questions?" He examined each eager face. "Okay! Let's draw supplies and prepare for battle."

Grover passed out ammunition, flack jackets and grease paint for their faces. The excitement in the air was equal to that of a championship Rose Bowl game.

Chapter Thirteen

It was near midnight when a black Lincoln limousine silently rounded the corner of the large vacant industrial building, extinguishing its lights before the turn was complete. The large steel-belted tires crunched softly on the gravel as it slowed to a stop short of the paved area. The driver surveyed the parking lot, which was vacant save for a single vehicle—another black limousine which was parked with only its parking lights on, facing the entrance of the property.

It had been raining all that day and well into the night, leaving everything wet and clean. The storm had temporarily rained itself out. The black asphalt surrounding the building glistened from the mercury lights bouncing off the wet surface.

The driver's eyes scanned the grounds, looking for movement...any movement. Nothing.

Silence permeated the air with anticipation.

The Lincoln slowly approached the building, its occupants surveying every nook and cranny of the cluttered "bone yard" where discarded machinery had been stored. They knew it would be easy for someone to hide behind the piled pallets, the 50-gallon oil drums or any one of the abandoned, broken machines which were stacked around the perimeter.

There was no movement, and no sound save the soft crunching of the limo's tires as it slowly inched its way towards the large twenty-foot door of the metal building.

The vehicle came to a stop in front of the building, facing the other parked limousine. The large metal door of the structure slowly creaked open, exposing the lit interior. The building seemed to be vacant, save for a fold-up conference table sitting in the center of the room with a number of chairs placed around it. A lone figure dressed in a dark blue pinstriped suit stood near the back wall with his arms folded on his chest, facing the door.

After several long moments, the back door of the limousine opened and two men quickly exited the vehicle, each carrying an AKA assault rifle. They walked sideways towards the entrance, back to back, their eyes nervously, expertly scanning the perimeter of the grounds, until they got to the large opening of the building. When they appeared to be satisfied that the area was safe and secured, one of the men nodded towards the limo.

A large bull of a man emerged. His head had been shaven clean. Large wrinkles formed at the base of his short, thick neck. The dark blue suit he wore seemed to strain at the seams as his body moved. He was as out of place wearing a suit as a cow wearing pants. He also surveyed the perimeter, through a pair of small, round, rimless dark glasses. He then held the door open, whereupon a small man of Italian extraction with a black, pencil-thin mustache, dressed in an immaculately tailored black suit, emerged. He was followed by a young man in his mid-twenties dressed in a black leather jacket, black pants and black hat. His closely cropped black hair was neatly slicked back with grooming grease. He carried a large burgundy eelskin briefcase. The three walked to the open door where their two associates stood, one on each side, wielding their AKA assault rifles. One faced inward while the other faced outward.

Once inside, the small mustached man took a seat at the table. The large bald man and the young man dressed in leather stood behind him, one on each side. Their eyes never stopped moving, expertly scanning the area from side to side.

After a few moments, three men of Colombian descent entered through the interior door, each carrying a black suitcase. The leather handles seemed to strain at the weight of the contents within. Although they were only in their mid-20's, their faces were hardened, devoid of emotion and showing the experience of their trade. They were flanked by two more men, each dressed in loose tan clothing and armed with AKA assault rifles as well. The Colombian men stood facing the two Italians, poised as if a shoot-out was imminent.

The men with the black suitcases set them on the table, opposite the man with the eelskin briefcase. Finally, the Italian spoke in perfect English.

"I assume that is the material to be purchased?" he said with a non-emotional, matter-of-fact voice, nodding towards the four large black suitcases.

The young Colombian nodded to the two men at his side, who then pushed the suitcases across the table.

"Open them, please," the Italian instructed.

The Colombian smiled knowingly to himself. With methodical deliberation, he unsnapped the latches on the cases, opened the lids, and turned them towards the man.

The cases were full of quart-sized Zip-lock bags containing a pure-white powdery substance. The

Italian lifted several bags, as if judging their weight, then randomly selected one packet from the middle of each case, setting them on one end of the table. He nodded to the man in the leather jacket, and watched as the young man quickly tested the contents of each bag, first by taste. Then the man drew a small sample from each bag, mixed it and a liquid chemical, then heated it with a small portable Bunsen burner.

After the process had been completed, he nodded to the Italian, who pushed his eelskin briefcase towards the Colombian.

"Open it, please," the Colombian said, with a twinkle in his eye.

With a look of disgust, the Italian briskly unsnapped the latches, opened the case and turned its contents towards the Colombian.

"Two million, as agreed?" he asked, looking across the table at the Italian.

The Italian instinctively turned his palms up like a card dealer, showing that he had nothing further up his sleeves. "Our business is finished," he stated, standing up.

The Latino nodded towards the two men at his side, one of whom returned the selected sample cases to the suitcases and latched the lid while the other stared at the men on the other side of the table. With the suitcases in hand, the Italian stepped back a pace, bending slightly at the waist like an oriental gentlemen, keeping his eyes on the Colombian. Then he turned to leave.

At that instant, a shrapnel grenade fell to the ground from above, landing between the four men with AKA's, exploding before they had time to react. They were killed instantly.

The men at the table instinctively ducked under the table, looking for the perpetrator. A moment later, bullets silently tore into their flesh from above, making a dull thud as each bullet found its mark. The massacre lasted only moments, felling all who were on the ground.

Four men who had positioned themselves on the rafters above were dressed in black, with lamp-black smeared on their faces. They had secured the premises without a shot being fired by their adversaries. The men descended from the steel ceiling rafters on ropes, dropping silently to the ground like jungle cats. Not a word was spoken as they picked up the four suitcases containing the cocaine and the two briefcase containing the money. They surveyed the premises, then departed through the large open door.

The front doors of both limousines were open, with their drivers limply hanging out of the doors. Their throats had been cut. Their open eyes stared blankly into space, seeing nothing. A light rain had began falling again, washing the blood from their bodies so that it formed red pools beneath their heads.

One of the men pulled out a small transmitter from his back pocket. "Hummingbird. The nectar has been gathered and is ready for pick-up."

Within a few moments, a small dark green jet helicopter circled overhead, then landed. The men quickly filed aboard, maintaining silence. Swiftly and silently they departed, leaving the grisly scene behind.

Inside the metal building, the Italian in the black leather jacket groaned as his eyes slowly opened and focused on the carnage around him. He lay on the cold cement floor for a few moments, assessing his wounds, listening for any sound that would alert him to further danger. Satisfied that the enemy had departed as swiftly as they had arrived, he attempted to pull himself up by hanging onto the overturned table, but fell back to the floor in excruciating pain. The bullets had torn into his shoulder muscles, shattering the collarbone and severing portions of his muscle. He was bleeding from the lower left side of his stomach. The shock from the shells ripping through his body was wearing off and the ensuing pain was beginning to intensify.

With his left hand, he tucked his limp right hand into his bloody shirt next to the stomach wound, trying to stem the flow of blood. Using his left hand to pull himself up, he crawled towards the limo.

It seemed an eternity before he reached the open door. With great effort he pulled the dead driver from the seat. Grabbing the steering wheel, summing up all the energy he had left in his body, he pulled himself onto the seat. Slipping the car phone from its cradle, he punched in a number.

"Yeah?" an irritated voice answered.

"It's Vido. Gimme Mr. DiGivanni. Emergency!" His breath was labored. The strength was seeping out of his body along with his vital fluids, but he held on.

"Vido. What's the urgency?" a sharp, impatient voice came over the phone.

"Mr. DiGivanni. We've been hit. Our boys, Mr. Capo, the Colombians. Everyone."

"What do you mean you've been hit? Is everyone dead?" the voice took on a shocked, disbelieving tone. "Who did this?" he demanded. "What happened?"

"I don't know." His voice trailed off for a moment. "They were at the drop when the deal went down," he said with labored words. "No one had a clue they were even here. They got everyone, even the Colombians. They...got away...with everything. The money...the snow...everything."

His voice was weak now, and he could hardly keep his eyes open. His hand slipped off the steering wheel and he slid back onto the wet pavement, still grasping the telephone.

"Who were these men?" the voice demanded. "Vido, speak to me. Who were these men? Where did they go?"

Vido did not answer. His soul had joined those of his friends as his eyes stared blankly into the wet darkness of the early morning.

* * * *

Dominic DiGivanni sat looking out of the lead-glass stained window into the darkness, his eyes staring blankly into space as his brain mulled over Vido's words. The governmental Drug Enforcement Administration had become stronger over the past few years. He knew it was only a matter of time until they infiltrated the Colombians. But this hit made no sense. The DEA would not have ambushed and killed the men then taken the drugs and money. It wasn't their style. No. Someone else had to be responsible for this, he thought angrily. But who?

DiGivanni had taken great pains and had invested a lot of money in maneuvering a mole on the federal staff. Since the death of Christian Murray several months ago, the thing that concerned him was there had been no covert activity, according to his informant. The DEA seemed to have gone into a holding pattern. As far as he knew, no one had been appointed to replace Murray. It appeared as if the DEA was still in shock.

DiGivanni had personally hand-picked his own

army of elite staff, so he was sure that no one had
infiltrated his organization. Yet it was obvious that
his worst fears had been realized. Someone had
either infiltrated the Colombians or his own security had been breached. Either way, the deal had
been compromised. He had lost several good men
and $2 million. Among those lost was Mr. Capo,
his younger brother. Sending him on each job had
been one of his security brainstorms. He had chosen the name Mr. Capo for his brother, Mario
DiGivanni, keeping his real identity secret from
anyone outside the family. This way, he figured if
there was a breach in security or a breakdown
within his army, he would know it first-hand and
be able to swiftly deal with the situation before
any damage had been done.

Mario was not only his younger brother, but
he was Dominic's best friend. The anger about his
death superseded the guilt and depression he
might have otherwise experienced. He had lost both
money and drugs. He had been defeated. Worst of
all, he had lost face.

DiGivanni slammed his fist down hard on his
desk as he vowed to find the perpetrator and deal
swiftly and harshly with him.

That $2 million worth of cocaine would have
brought $8 million into the family coffers by the
time they got through cutting and selling it on the
street.

He angrily slammed his fist on the desk again.
"Scalasia!" he screamed, turning his head towards
the living room, where his staff nervously awaited
instructions. They knew without being told that
something had gone amiss with the deal. There
was always the potential for betrayal—or even a
nervous trigger finger—to make a buy go bad. If
there was trouble, their job was clear: retaliation—

to whom or for what reason was unknown. They were prepared to do whatever Don DiGivanni instructed them to do.

A trim young man standing a hair under six foot, wearing a black leather jacket, his jet-black hair combed straight back and parted slightly on the left, walked briskly into the room. It was obvious to the trained eye that, aside from his size, he walked with confidence. Marco Scalasia was the only inside member of DiGivanni's army who was not related yet knew of Mario's secret identity.

"Close the door," DiGivanni said through clenched teeth. "There's trouble. We've been hit."

"Mario?" he hesitatingly inquired.

DiGivanni slowly nodded. "I want you to get over to the buy site and neutralize their identification," DiGivanni instructed him coldly. "I want no evidence that the men there were connected to this family."

Marco Scalasia looked into the eyes of his boss, searching for the pain he knew he must be feeling as a result from the loss of his brother. He saw only cold, calculating eyes, void of emotion.

Marco acknowledged Dominic's orders with a slight bow, then departed as quickly as he had come. Moments later, his 1,000 c.c. Honda could be heard screaming down the driveway and through the security gate as he sped towards the grisly site that awaited him.

He pulled his motorcycle to a stop at the entrance of the parking lot, viewing the grounds and the carnage for several moments before proceeding. He could see the two limos parked on the asphalt in front of the door of the metal building. The body of the Colombian lay stretched from the car seat onto the ground.

Satisfied that the area was safe, he sped towards the limos. He had killed many men himself, so dealing with the gruesome scene posed no problem.

After parking his bike behind the limo so it was not visible from the road, he left the motor running. If he had to make a hasty retreat, the moment it would take to start his machine could mean the difference between life and death.

Quickly, unemotionally, he went from body to body, men he had known and worked with for years, going through the pockets of each, relieving each of any personal articles that could identify them: watches, rings, wallets and pendants.

As he went about his work, he noted the expertness with which each man had been killed. The bullets had been dead on their mark, each hitting vital organs. There was no random fire, no unnecessary shots wasted. This had obviously been a professional hit. The perpetrators knew what they were doing and had wasted no time or ammunition in completing their mission.

He paused at the body of Mario, his eyes looking blankly in Marco's direction. Marco made a sign of the cross, said a silent prayer for his soul, then closed his eyes with the tips of his fingers before moving on.

He limited his initial search to the Italians, putting all valuables and ID into a leather pouch secured by a pull-string at the top. After he had finished with the Italians, he repeated the same procedure with the Colombians.

Any normal thug would have kept some of the money from the wallets or retained some of the jewelry, but Marco was no normal thug. He was a professional trustee of the family, adopted at the age of three when his family, whose father was a mentor of the DiGivanni army, had been executed

by another Mafia family over control of the lower
section of town. He had been raised by Dominic
DiGivanni as his own son and had been trained to
help control the lower stratification of the family's
business. He was eternally grateful for the
DiGivanni family's kindness towards him. He did
as he was told and prided himself on following orders to the letter.

After his work was done, he surveyed the scene
one last time, taking note of the ropes suspended
from the ceiling, hanging limply above the Colombian corpses, and the obvious damage that the
explosive had caused to the men. Satisfied that he
had successfully completed his mission, he stored
the collection of personal effects in the saddle bags
of the Honda, put on his helmet and sped away.

A light rain began to fall again. Soon the eastern sky would glow, preparing to greet a new day.

Chapter Fourteen

The contents of Marco's saddle bags lay on DiGivanni's desk: wallets with family pictures, watches, rings, gold chains and medallions—all mementos of personal lives. He picked up a chain which had a small, oval, gold Madonna medallion encased in mother of pearl dangling from it. He had given this to his brother the day Mario had received his first communion and celebrated his first penance at Saint John Vianney's church when he was seven years old.

Grasping the chain in his hand, Dominic clenched his fist to his head, his face a distorted grimace of pain. He angrily swept the items lying on the table to the floor. After a few moments, he wiped his cheeks with the back of his hand and grabbed the telephone from its cradle.

The phone rang several times before it was answered. "Quien habla?" the sleepy voice answered.

"This is Dominic DiGivanni," he said slowly with deliberate words. "Give me Francisco."

"He is retired," the voice said angrily. "Call tomorrow."

"This is tomorrow, you bean counter!" he said angrily. "This is Dominic DiGivanni!" He repeated himself forcefully, barely able to contain himself. "Now get him on the telephone pronto, before I have you shot!"

There was a long silence. Dominic could hear muffled voices on the other end of the line. Finally, a husky voice answered. "Francisco. What brings you to my attention this time of the morning, Dominic? Can it not wait until a man has had his morning cup of java?"

"No, this cannot wait, and I cannot discuss it over the phone. This is a matter of utmost urgency that requires our immediate collective attention. We need to meet—now."

There was a silence on the other end. Dominic again heard muffled voices. He was unable to ascertain what was being said, as they were speaking in Spanish and Francisco had his hand over the telephone.

"Twenty minutes. There is an all-night restaurant on the wharf near the Chart House."

"Twenty minutes," Dominic agreed.

* * * *

It was raining hard as the black Mercedes limo pulled up in front of the restaurant. Francisco had already arrived and was sitting in his white Lincoln, waiting.

As Dominic's limo parked, Marco stepped out, quickly surveyed the area, then held out his hand as if pointing the way for Dominic DiGivanni to emerge from the vehicle.

At the same instant, Francisco departed his vehicle, and the two men entered the brightly lit all-night diner. The sky was beginning to soften as the sun peeked its face over the mountain range, coloring the sky in bright hues of orange and purple. The air smelled clean and fresh thanks to the newly fallen rain.

"So, my friend, what's so important that we meet this way?" Francisco said coldly. He ordered coffee from the waitress, an elderly woman who looked tired and haggard, with bags under her eyes. It was obvious that she would rather be home in bed.

Marco's and Francisco's driver each sat at a separate small table which was situated between the entrance of the restaurant and the two men.

"Have you heard from your boys?" Dominic DiGivanni asked matter-of-factly.

"Boys? What boys?"

"Cut the crap, Francisco!" he said sharply. "You know damn well what boys. I'm not a fucking cop, so don't play dumb with me." His face showed signs of stress as his eyes pierced those of Francisco.

"I never discuss business before breakfast," Francisco said, with a stuffy, sophisticated tone, diverting his eyes to the black cup of coffee he held while warming his hands.

"Well, this morning, you're going to have shit for breakfast," Dominic snarled, hitting his fist on the table so hard the coffee spilled and the water glasses jumped.

Francisco quickly looked up, but said nothing.

Marco and the Colombian driver nervously stared at each other, then at their bosses, not sure what to expect next.

Leaning towards Francisco, Dominic slowly and deliberately said, "Your boys are dead and you're out a bushel of snow."

Francisco wore a look of disbelief as he studied Dominic's face. He said nothing as he tried to rearrange his facial appearance, which he knew must be giving him away.

Knowing that now he had his attention, Dominic continued. "They were hit while the deal was going down. Everyone was wasted, Francisco, including my own brother," he added through clenched teeth for dramatic effect. "We don't know who made the hit. One of my men was able to make contact before he checked out."

Dominic deliberately dumped the contents of a small leather pouch on the table in front of Francisco as he watched the expression on his face change from disbelief to awe. Wallets, rings, watches and gold chains rolled onto the table. Francisco tentatively looked at DiGivanni, then slowly pawed through the articles that lay before him.

"I had one of my men retrieve their personal effects before the law got wind of the situation. No use giving them any more to chew on than they already have. I assume the limo has fake papers?"

Francisco nodded slowly. He was still in shock. "The merchandise? All gone?" he asked, looking like a child who had just dropped his first ice cream cone. "The men? Dead?"

"Along with $2 million in unmarked bills. There had to have been a leak, Francisco. I know it's not in my organization. I personally hand-pick every man. You've got a leak. Find it! I want the informing bastard hung by his balls from the tallest tree so everyone can see! Then we go after those responsible for the murder of our men. When I get through with them, they will curse their mothers for the day they were born. No one crosses Dominic DiGivanni!" he said with a clenched fist in Francisco's face as he pushed his chair back to get up. "No one rests until the leak is found. Understand? I want reports. No one's going to do business until this is finished."

He motioned to Marco with his head. In a moment, he was gone. The limo's tires screamed out of the driveway.

Francisco sat motionless, too stunned to move, staring into vacant space. The cocaine had been of the highest quality, straight from his cousin's lab in the hills of Colombia, near the Medellin coca fields. The disaster couldn't have occurred at a worse time. Francisco was not a well-to-do man. He had just solidified a relationship with his distant cousin to provide him with drugs to get ahead in the world.

Francisco Regalado had been born in the same poor area of Medellin where Molina's father, and his father's father were born. The only way a poor family could survive in Colombia was by doing menial, unskilled work, or working in the coca fields for the drug lords, or resorting to unlawful activities, such as stealing.

His father had been a proud man who worked as a caretaker for a respectable family on an agricultural ranch. It was during this period of time that cocaine became popular with the America gringos, who had learned that by snorting or inhaling the white powder it had an immediate and unique effect on the brain. The cocaine high gave them a sensation of euphoria and dazzling clarity of thought. Typical first-time users often described it, "like 1,000 orgasms."

Farmers whose land had been used for agricultural crops had begun turning their land raising coca plants for the production of the drug cocaine. Soon they became rich and powerful, dominating everything and everyone in their region. Legitimate farmers were forced to either sell their land or go into competitive business with the group of powerful growers, who by now had become known as the Cartel.

Most small farmers neither had the stomach for such business nor wanted to get sucked into the vicious drug killings which had become a way of life for the Cartel.

The family Francisco Regalado's father had worked for had been forced to sell their land to the powerful members of the Cartel and retire. When Francisco's father married and had children, he was faced with the choice of how to make a living. For the poor man, making an adequate, honest living in Medellin sufficient to raise and educate a family was next to impossible, so he escaped from their village and moved to the seaport industrial town of Barranquilla. It was there that Francisco grew into manhood.

When he became of age, all he was able to find was manual, unskilled work in factories and on fishing boats. The pay was barely enough to maintain the status quo, never allowing him to get ahead. One day, while out on a commercial fishing boat, fishing for tuna, he overheard a conversation between two of the men, who were planning on migrating to America. They had heard that there, good, fertile land was available for the taking. The Americans called it "homesteading".

This was the opportunity Francisco had been looking for. He was nearing the age of 30 and still had nothing to show for his life. With a portion of the meager savings he had accumulated, he was able to bribe his way into a job on one of the fishing boats bound for the west coast of the United States, where they had planned on fishing the waters for salmon. Once there, Francisco thought, he would somehow make it to shore and homestead a piece of land. He would live in America and finally be rich!

When they arrived off the coast of the United

States, the fishing boat stayed far enough off shore so as not to be caught by the shore patrol for fishing in their waters. It wasn't until the end of the ninth day of fishing that the ship had drifted close enough to the continent that the men could see land. The eyes of Francisco and his two friends gleamed as they realized that the time had come for them to leave their ship.

They made their getaway in the middle of the night by stealing one of the ship's life rafts, reaching shore by daylight. They landed near the fishing village of Fort Bragg, California. Fearful of being caught, they avoided contact with the populace. They traveled south on the coastal highway, catching a ride when possible, finally reaching the city of San Francisco two days later.

It didn't take long for them to find people who spoke their native tongue. They found steady jobs working at the fishing docks, making more money than they had seen in all their lives.

Within time, Francisco learned English and saved enough money to purchase a small attached house that the Americans called a condominium. He bought his first automobile, an old Ford pickup. In the evenings, he enrolled in a night school in order to become more proficient in English. His goal was to eventually enroll in San Francisco State University's night school and earn a degree.

It was there that he met his wife-to-be, Gloria. She was a secretary for a law firm. She, too, was going to night school, studying to be a paralegal, which required extensive university training. They fell in love and six months later, were married.

Gloria was of Brazilian descent, although she had never been to that country. She was fascinated with Francisco's Colombian background and thought it would be nice if they could establish contact with their South American families. Perhaps they could one day save up enough money to travel back to their respective countries and renew family ties.

Within three years of meeting Francisco, Gloria had become a paralegal, and Francisco had a thriving wholesale vegetable business. They figured with the money they had saved, if they flew coach and stayed with family and friends and watched their spending, they would have enough to make the trip back to their blood-country.

It was agreed that Gloria would fly to Brazil to visit her grandparents. Francisco's parents had since died, so he thought he would fly into Medellin, Colombia, where he had cousins. They arranged to meet later, midway between their two families, at Bogota, the capital of Colombia, and enjoy a second honeymoon.

Francisco had never flown before, and when the plane approached the airport of Medellin, he thought his life was about to come to a fiery end. As the plane prepared for landing, it negotiated the countryside of imposing hillsides on either side. The noise of the landing gear finally indicated that they were about to land, but Francisco could see no flat land in sight. He was sure that they were going to crash against some mountain. The plane rocked between valleys and hills, making sharp turns as if avoiding a collision, until finally leveling out and coming to a bumpy landing at Medellin Airport.

After collecting his luggage, Francisco hailed a cab to town. When the driver asked him his destination, without thinking he instructed the driver to take him to the residence of Molina Marquez. It was only after he had said his cousin's name that he realized that the chance of the driver knowing his cousin, let alone his address, was highly remote. Much to his surprise, the cabby gave him a startled look.

"Don Molina Marquez?" he asked.

"Molina Marquez," Francisco replied quizzically. "He is my cousin whom I have not seen since I was a boy. I am here from America to visit him," he said proudly.

The cabby shook his head, straightened his cap and drove Francisco to a grand villa nestled into the rocky hills above Medellin. They arrived at an iron gate manned by two armed guards.

Francisco looked past the guards up to the magnificent villa. Molina must have a very important job to work at such a place, he thought to himself, knowing that the villa must belong to one of the wealthy drug lords.

"What do you want?" one of the guards demanded, looking first at the driver, then at the passenger dressed in an inexpensive American coat and jacket.

"He wants to see his cousin, Don Molina Marquez," the driver said.

The gatekeeper looked at Francisco through the open window. "What's your name?" His voice lost a bit of its edge, but the authority was still there.

"Francisco. Francisco Regalado. I'm his second—"

"Wait here," the gatekeeper said, picking up the phone inside the gatehouse.

Francisco could see the man talking for quite a long time, looking at Francisco periodically. Finally, he came back to the cab. "Out," he demanded, gesturing to Francisco with his automatic weapon.

"Leave your belongings. If the Don wants you

to have them delivered to the house, we'll bring them up. But first, I must search you."

Francisco looked dismayed, but submitted to the search. The whole time, the other gatekeeper kept his automatic weapon trained on Francisco and the cab driver. He remembered how security conscious the drug lords had been when he was just a boy. *Normal precautions,* he thought. Actually, he was more than a little surprised that he was even being admitted. *Then again,* it crossed his mind, *there may be more than one Molina Marquez.*

When it was clear that Francisco carried no weapon, the guard instructed the cab driver to set the luggage next to the gatehouse and leave.

Francisco thanked the driver and started to pay for his fare with the scarce amount of money he had left in his pocket. "No charge," the cabby said, holding up his hand. "The ride is on me. Any friend of Don Molina Marquez is a friend of mine."

Francisco smiled weakly and put his money back into his pocket. Now he was sure he had the wrong Molina, but it was too late to turn back.

The guard led him into the main entrance of the villa. *Perhaps Molina is a house servant,* he thought. *Maybe even a butler.* No sooner had he entered the house than Molina appeared. It had been many years since he had seen his cousin, but the boyhood features which had turned into manhood had not changed that much.

They greeted one another like the long-lost cousins they were. "This house, it is so large," Francisco said, turning a full circle, his eyes large with amazement.

"You like it, cousin?" Molina asked as he studied his face. "Come. Let us sit on the verandah and you can tell me what has brought you to Medellin."

As they sat on the verandah sipping fresh-squeezed orange juice, Molina proudly relayed the sequence of events that had delivered him from Comuna Nororiental after the massacre of his family by Pizano. Francisco remembered the massacre of his cousin's family, but had lost contact with Molina after he had left the village when his parents were killed. He was amazed by the rest of Molina's story.

After he had finished his tale and the conversation began to lag, Molina offered to show his cousin around the villa. Francisco was astonished at the enormity of his cousin's house. Although Molina Marquez seemed genuinely glad to see Francisco, he soon discovered that they had little in common save childhood memories.

Once Francisco comprehended the enormity of his cousin's wealth and power in the drug world, he saw an opportunity to use his lineage to a greater advantage. "Cousin, we grew up poor together, and, while I moved to the fishing village, you stayed here in Medellin and made your fortune in the coca fields," he said, looking around, encompassing the room with his hands.

"I feel so poor and inadequate compared to you," he said, somewhat shamefully. "I reside in the magnificent city of San Francisco, which is located in the state of California in America. I have seen the need for your product among the wealthy. Although I do not have the money to purchase large amounts—my money is tied up in modest investments, you know—I feel that I could be of immeasurable assistance to you in selling your cocaine to the Americans."

"Francisco, I only sell to major purchasers who buy directly from me here in Medellin. It is not necessary for me to take the risk of going to

America, where the capitalists look upon our cocaine as illegal. Everything I grow is automatically sold to the Italians in Miami in Florida. They have an organization similar to our Cartel. It is known as the Mafia. You may have heard of it?"

"No, Molina. I have not. But perhaps I could deal with them for you," he was quick to add. "I could be your personal representative." There was a short period of silence as Francisco realized that Molina wasn't buying his line. He glanced down at his imitation-leather shoes and the sleeves of his cheap coat, then said with humility, "I need to make more money, cousin." He couldn't bring himself to look Molina in the eye. "My business barely makes enough for me to come and visit you here in Colombia, Molina. Do you think...for old time's sake...?"

Molina Marquez felt bad about the plight of his cousin. He couldn't ignore the undeniable fact that Francisco was blood. He paced the room for a while with his hands behind his back, thinking. Finally, he said, "Tell you what, Francisco. Because you are family, I will break an unbreakable rule and allow you a credit for two kilos of cocaine. The value of such is $50 thousand, American. You should be able to convert that amount into $200 or $300 thousand if you work at it. And, if you're not familiar with the cocaine market—and I assume you're not—I'll lay out the procedure for you, the way the Americans do it." Molina could see the gratitude in his cousin's eyes. It made him feel good to help someone from the old days. "Finally," he added, "I am not currently dealing with the Mafia on the West Coast, so that should give you an automatic opening while not creating a conflict of interest, should you decide that's the route you wish to travel."

Francisco nearly choked on his drink. He had never dreamed of having that much money in all his life, let alone possessing such a sum all at once.

"You will take possession of the merchandise in San Francisco," Molina explained. "It will arrive via a fishing scow by the name of The Tuna in ten days. The captain's name will be Manuel Vasquez. When you see him, give him this note," he said, handing Francisco a handwritten note to which he had simply initialed his name.

"But, cousin Molina, I do not have the immediate funds to pay for the shipment, as I previously..."

Molina held up his hand. "You will pay me thirty days after you receive the goods. I have written the account number of an American bank on this card," he said, handing Francisco a small business card made of transparent rice paper which had Molina's name embossed in gold lettering. "That should give you ample time to cut the cocaine, package it and establish contacts to either move it piecemeal or sell it all at once. You will soon learn that the larger profit will be derived by the greatest amount of work. That is selling it in small quantities to individuals for the greatest amount of money."

Francisco Regalado couldn't stop caressing his cousin's hand in loving affection.

"You must forgive me now, cousin," Molina said, rising from his chair abruptly. "I have many important matters to attend to. I have enjoyed your visit. Perhaps we can see one another again soon. Emilio will see you to your luggage and take you wherever you wish."

Molina had made it clear that the meeting had come to a conclusion, leaving Francisco standing in the middle of the large office, holding his half-consumed drink with a confused look.

Molina stopped short of the door of his office and turned to face his guest. "Oh, and Francisco?"

"Yes, cousin Molina?"

"Be on time with the payment. You are blood and I have entrusted you with a large sum of money. Do not mistake my generosity for weakness. I'm a businessman. You need to know that I deal harshly with those who break their bond with me. If you need to have your memory jogged, remember what used to happen in Communa Nororiental when the patrons caught someone stealing even a coca leaf."

The memory of the slaughter of Molina's family was still vividly clear in Francisco's mind. He nodded meekly.

"Business is business, cousin," Molina said firmly over his shoulder as he left the room.

* * * *

Francisco had made good on his promise to pay back the $50 thousand, making himself $50 thousand in the process. He had been so anxious to sell the coke that he had only cut his supply in half by adding lactose as Molina had suggested. The unusually pure drug sold almost immediately. He then reinvested his capital with his cousin, doubling his profit each time.

By now, he had purchased enough drugs with the intent of making a million dollars by just acting as a middle man. He just had to cut the cocaine once prior to making a deal with DiGivanni's brother. He had promised his cousin that he would deliver the balance of the money as soon as the drugs were delivered to the DiGivanni family and he had been paid.

As their relationship of mutual trust developed, Molina had delivered the cocaine via The Tuna with only half of the fee paid. The balance of the money was now due. Without the $2 million from Dominic, he knew his life span was limited, cousin or not. He had no foreseeable source to come up with the rest of the money.

Maybe Cousin Molina would understand, he thought, trying to rationalize, knowing he was kidding himself. His hands shook as he gathered up the personal belongings of his men from the table.

He looked outside the cafe as the light rain sparkled like diamonds in the reflection of the rising sun. His eyes saw only disaster, however, as the tired waitress cleaned up his table in preparation to go home.

Francisco felt that impending doom was inevitable.

* * * *

The time was 2:20 in the afternoon. The temperature had peaked at 102 degrees as the sun baked the asphalt of the abandoned naval air strip. Waves of heat rose from the asphalt, creating surrealistic images of waving buildings and impressionistic patches of moving water.

A large tumbleweed rolled lazily across the airstrip, blown by the only relief from the heat, a soft afternoon breeze cascading down from the hills. A jackrabbit stood on his hind legs next to a large abandoned hangar, intently listening to the change in air vibrations, assessing the potential danger in scampering across the open pavement.

A small Commanche circled overhead, then approached the landing strip. It touched down, then taxied towards the open hangar. The rabbit retreated across the runway, back into a hole in the ground near the base of a large, dying sagebrush.

The air became quiet again as the Commanche's propeller chugged to silence once the ignition was turned off.

The jackrabbit's head emerged to survey his surroundings. Then he stood on his hind legs, stretching to see the intruder. A tumbleweed silently rolled in front of the Commanche.

The occupants waited in the plane while the pilot surveyed the area with his binoculars. After several moments, a cloud of dust arose from the distance. Through the heat rising off the asphalt, the object looked like a white jitterbug approaching, as it appeared to weave and dance from side to side. As it got closer to the hangar, the form of a white limousine emerged.

It pulled into the large hangar, made a circle, then parked inside under the shade of the building. It sat silently for several moments, its silver, shiny windows shielding its occupants from prying eyes.

Soon, a large black man emerged from the automobile, carrying an AKA assault weapon. He walked the perimeter of the limousine, glancing at the Commanche from time to time. When he felt sure that the area was secure, he nodded towards the limo. Three other black men emerged, two of them, despite the searing temperature, wearing black leather jackets. The man in the middle, a slightly built black man wearing a tailored pinstriped black suit sporting a close-cropped goatee, carried a large black briefcase chained to his wrist.

They went to a large wooden spool, which at one time had apparently been used to hold wiring or cable of some sort and had been placed in the center of the building as a table. The driver drove the limo out onto the tarmac, parked it, then returned to stand guard outside the door. The three men with assault rifles covered the perimeter while the man with the briefcase faced the Commanche.

Soon the doors of the Commanche opened and five Colombians emerged. Two of the men were each carrying a large briefcase, while two more men walked behind them displaying their fire power. With the exception of the man bringing up the rear, they all wore light-colored slacks and short-sleeved print shirts. The man following the four was dressed in a cream-colored cotton suit, wearing a Panama hat with a colorful headband.

As they approached the middle of the hangar, each party looked his counterpart in the eye as if trying to read his thoughts. The black men in leather jackets, despite the shade, were perspiring profusely. The Colombian smiled as one of the men nodded towards them, saying quietly to his comrades, "Pinches negros."

One of the Blacks heard him and swung his weapon towards him, but the man dressed in the black pinstriped suit held his hand up in protest, calming him.

"Thee dinero. You have hit?" the man in the Panama suit said in halting English as he nodded towards the black case.

"$3.5 mil, as promised," the Black in the pinstriped suit said. "You got the coke?"

"100 percent pure Colombian." He nodded to his men, who placed the cases on the wooden spool and opened them. Each case was filled with small, clear packets containing a pure white substance.

The Black holding the briefcase was about to open it when, suddenly, the center of the wooden spool blew open, emitting a deep reddish-yellow substance. With the aid of the breeze, the smoke quickly engulfed the entire area.

The men gasped and grabbed at their necks and tried to cover their faces, but within moments they all lay dead on the floor. Their faces had grotesque, distorted looks, as if they had suffocated and had seen an alien monster at the same time.

Having viewed the grisly scene from the plane, the pilot of the Commanche started his engines and quickly turned his plane into the wind, preparing to take off. At the same time, the Colombian limo driver dropped his automatic weapon and sped across the asphalt in the direction of his car.

Within moments the Comanche's wheels were about to lift off. Then, from above and behind, a fast-approaching small jet helicopter fired a missile at the plane. On impact the Commanche exploded, scattering hand-sized pieces of the plane and its contents in every direction.

The jackrabbit stood on his hind legs, then scampered down a hole as a second missile hit the limousine. The force of the explosion catapulted it 20 feet into the air, dispersing pieces over the runway and into the desert.

The area became silent again, save for an occasional thud as pieces of metal hit the ground. Small fires burst from some of the flammable pieces, extinguishing themselves as they burned out.

The dark green jet helicopter landed next to the hangar. Remnants of the reddish-orange smoke still hung in the air. Six men dressed in desert camouflage coveralls and crash helmets with smoke-colored gas masks jumped from the helicopter as it touched down. They raced into the hangar. While two men gathered the briefcases, cutting the chain from the wrist of the black man holding the money, the third methodically fired a round into the head of each man with his silencer-equipped weapon. All that could be heard was a pop and a thud as each round left the chamber and hit its victim. The remaining two men stood guard, facing the compound.

Within moments after they had landed, the men had accomplished their mission and were in the jet helicopter and on their way back to home base.

Chapter Fifteen

Joseph Mann had been born and raised in a small town in eastern Oregon with a population of two hundred and eighty-one people. There were eight other kids in his freshman class in high school. He had already reached the height of six-foot-six, the tallest boy, not only in the school but in the entire county's all-white population.

What he lacked in scholarly skills, he made up in athletics, especially basketball. He rarely studied, just scraping by on average grades. By the time he was a senior, his reputation as a two-time all-conference basketball player had spread throughout the athletic community of the state of Oregon.

He had planned on going on to college upon graduation. Although many of the larger universities would have liked to have him on their teams, his scholastic grades were too low for their consideration. He was offered three athletic scholarships, however: one from the Eastern Oregon School of Education, one from Pacific Lutheran College in Washington, and one from a small junior college in San Jose that had scouted him and was in desperate need of a center. Tired of the small town atmosphere, he opted for California. He had visions of the white, sandy ocean beaches and blonde, sun-tanned women.

His father, Joe Mann Sr., was a hard-working laborer who was barely able to sustain himself, his wife and their remaining four children. Giving his eldest son money to continue his education was not only not in the cards, but he thought his son should have stayed home and worked next to him on the farm. "Goin' to college is for rich kids," he said when his son announced his decision to leave home. "I ain't had no education beyond the sixth grade, and I've done just fine, thank you. I know all you want to do is play ball, but thay's no future in that," he had told his son. "You might just as well know that up front. You got to get yourself a real job and get yourself a start in life. Find a woman before the good ones are all taken and settle down." Joe had five girls in his class, none of whom he would have considered marrying, even in desperate times.

The athletic department in California understood Joe's lack of financial backing. They knew if he were to play ball for them, he would have to devote time studying so he could remain eligible to play. The first semester they created a job for him, collecting tickets at football games. This gave the college justification to give him spending money for clothes and other necessities. Food and lodging were provided as part of the scholarship.

The athletic department enrolled him in basic, low-level, required courses for his physical education major. One of the elective classes he took was a beginner computer class, which consisted of basically typing on the keyboard. It wasn't long before Mann discovered that he had a flair for the machines, and he plunged into the science of programming.

He played basketball his freshman year, but didn't seem to have the discipline that was required to make the cut. Stripped of his scholarship and the cushy job the coach had found for him, he was now faced with the prospect of finding another form of employment if he was to continue his education.

The placement department found him a job parking cars at Devalle's Chuckwagon. His shift started at six, which gave him time to attend classes and even offered time to study his notes between parking cars. He was paid minimum wage, but earned a significant amount of money in tips. Eventually, the owner moved him inside the restaurant and gave him a chef's hat. He was given the job of standing at the end of the smorgasbord, cutting ham, roast beef and turkey for the customers.

One Saturday evening Dominic DiGivanni rented the restaurant for his family and friends to celebrate his daughter's 21st birthday. It was then that Joe met Virginia. At the height of six-foot-six plus wearing the chef's hat, Joe Mann struck an impressive figure at the end of the food table. He caught the eye of Virginia DiGivanni as he carved a generous portion of roast beef for her.

He had been given strict instructions by Mr. Devalle, the owner, to stay at his post until all the guests were fed, and no fooling around. Virginia had other plans. She had decided that this tall stranger was to be her personal birthday present. She began making her intentions known by making frequent trips to the head of the table for additional small portions of meat.

"You must have a powerful hunger." Joe smiled as he sliced another piece of turkey on her fourth trip to the table. He was so attracted by her dark

Italian eyes that he wasn't paying any attention when he sliced a small piece of his finger in the process.

"I like mine rare," she smiled. "But not quite that rare," she said, taking his bleeding finger in her hands.

He had barely sliced the skin from the surface, but it bled profusely, making the incision appear much worse than it was. She looked around to see if anyone was watching, then took his large finger and put it into her mouth, sucking on it.

"Does that make it better?" she asked, looking up at him seductively.

Joe was beginning to have sexual feelings that he was unable to hide. He tried to position himself behind the turkey so he wouldn't embarrass himself, but it was too late.

"I'll have some of that," she said, her eyes locked on his pants.

Joe was so nervous he didn't know what to say. He had never known a girl that acted so forward before...especially one as attractive as Virginia. "I...I'm working. I..." he stammered, unable to express himself.

Joe's apparent naiveté challenged Virginia all the more. "We came in the white limo," she interrupted with a sly smile. "I got the keys from the chauffeur," she said, dangling a pair of keys on a gold chain. "It's parked at the bottom of the hill behind the building. I told the driver that I had a slight headache and might want to lie down for a little while. I'll meet you there in 10 minutes. Don't disappoint me." She smiled, turning to leave. "It is my birthday, and Papa said I could have whatever I want. We wouldn't want to disappoint him, now, would we?" She winked as she took her plate back to the head of the table, next to her father. "Be there, ya hear?"

Joe Mann and Virginia DiGivanni saw each other frequently after that day. Their relationship seemed to blossom to the point that Mr. DiGivanni feared that things were getting out of hand. After a few months, Virginia started hinting at moving in with Joe. DiGivanni knew that once the sexual infatuation wore off, Mann would have nothing to offer his daughter. Besides, he was neither Italian nor Catholic.

One day after school, DiGivanni visited Joe. When the meeting was concluded, he had convinced Joe that he should discontinue seeing his daughter and move out of town. The meeting had cost DiGivanni the price of Joe Mann's education, plus room and board, plus walk-around spending money. He would have paid double that amount to save his daughter the embarrassment down the line, but Joe didn't know that. Had Joe not agreed to the arrangement, he would have had Joe killed, but Joe didn't know that, either.

DiGivanni kept tabs on Joe Mann, knowing that one day his investment would pay off. That day came when Joe graduated from college. He had demonstrated knowledge and skills in the computer field that were sought by several firms, including the government. Before he made a choice, he sought the advice of DiGivanni.

DiGivanni saw the potential of having a man working in computers for the government—a man on the inside. Again, he cut a deal with Mann. As an inducement to be his man inside, he bought him a three-bedroom, two-bath house and a white BMW. Joe Mann was now indebted to DiGivanni beyond his wildest imagination.

Mann went to work for the government. He was instructed to keep his eyes open at all times for potential business dealings that could be advantageous "for competitive business", as DiGivanni put it. In order for DiGivanni to test his loyalty, he had Mann acquire non-vital, general information for him that he knew he could verify from other contacts that he had within the government.

One of the skills that Mann possessed was his uncanny ability to break computer codes. Soon DiGivanni had him probing deeper and deeper into the government's business, but lacking security clearance, he was only able to penetrate into lower levels of intelligence. Even at that, Mann loved the mystery and challenge of possessing the knowledge unlocked from within people's computers. Although Mann never questioned the motives behind DiGivanni's thirst for government documents, DiGivanni tried to assure him that his indiscretions would not be unlawful. Yet he periodically cautioned him that he was to speak to no one about their arrangement.

With the passage of time, Mann was promoted through the ranks, gaining higher security clearances along the way and becoming a more trusted governmental employee. This enabled him to have access to more computer files and data banks. Through constant practice, he also acquired skills which gave him access to higher-level programs.

Experimenting with codes by trial and error late one evening after everyone had gone home, he accidentally accessed a file by punching in the code name Gunshot 1994. Inside that file were names and dates with bank deposits and their account numbers. No particular bank was referenced, but the numbers were either incomplete, were foreign bank numbers or were specially coded. Either way, significant amounts of money had been recorded.

One of those dates coincided with the hit on DiGivanni and Francisco. The two separate accounts had dollar amounts that coincidentally added up to exactly to $2 million, each as to one-half of the total dollar amount. One file had the heading Project: Green-Macaffe. The other was NRA: Presidential Election Contributions. The same amount had been taken from DiGivanni's men.

Joe Mann had no idea of the significance of these dates and amounts of money, but he gave the data to DiGivanni anyway, as previously agreed.

Chapter Sixteen

Manuel La Torre crouched behind the 50-gallon cylindrical cement planter filled with purple-and-white sweet alyssum. He held up his hand, motioning for the three men behind him to halt. La Torre was the senior agent of the California division of ATF, or Alcohol, Tobacco and Firearms service, based in San Francisco. They had been tracking this particular gang's activities for the past fourteen months, and now all their work was going to pay off. They were about to make the largest cocaine bust in California's history.

Two of the men they had been watching paced the perimeter of Olive Park while a third stood guard over a large suitcase, purportedly full of money, which sat on the wooden picnic table. The small park was vacant of people. Two more men stood by a tan Lincoln Town Car, smoking cigarettes, nervously glancing from side to side and then down the road. They looked to be of Italian extraction—members of the Mafia, Manuel had come to discover.

Finally, a white Mercedes approached the park, stopping short of the Lincoln. It waited for a few moments, then slowly approached, parking 20 feet from the Lincoln, away from La Torre's men. They waited for 10 minutes before disembarking. Two men exited the rear of the Mercedes, each armed with automatic weapons. They quickly walked into the park where they stood next to a large pine tree as if seeking cover.

At that moment the Italians followed suit by standing at the base of one of the large pine trees.

"What the hell?" Manuel whispered, looking back at his partner George Machella.

Machella shrugged his shoulders. "Cautious bunch," he whispered back to La Torre.

At that moment the front door of the Mercedes opened and a small man with a pencil mustache dressed impeccably in an expensive Italian suit walked towards the picnic table. He was accompanied by a large, bullish man carrying an eel-skin briefcase. They went immediately to the picnic table, and set the briefcase on it.

The Italian opened the briefcase, made a motion with a nod of his head, indicating that his partner should give the man their suitcase, presumably full of money.

The bullish man took the case, opened it and showed it to Pencil Mustache, who nodded. He then closed the briefcase.

"What the hell's going on?" La Torre whispered. "Are they so stupid that they don't even count the money or test the coke?"

He nervously scratched the side of his face.

"I don't like it, boss," Machella whispered, moving closer to La Torre. "Something's fishy. I say we shoot the bastards where they stand."

La Torre shot him a sharp glance. He knew Machella was kidding, but not that much. If he had his druthers, Machella would have shot every one of the drug-dealing bastards where they stood, on every bust. They had spent too much time setting up busts and arresting the perpetrators, only to discover at trial that the defendant's smart-ass attorney had found some flaw with the arrest procedure or the officers had said or done something at the time of arrest that left a margin of error.

During the course of the trial the defendant's attorney would succeed in confusing the jurors by cross-examining the arresting officers separately until there were enough insignificant, conflicting flaws in their testimony to create reasonable doubt. Officer A said the defendant had been wearing a black tie, while officer B testified that he hadn't even had a tie. Officer A testified that the defendant had been standing in the middle of the park when the arrest had been made, and officer B said the defendant had been guarding the money. Officer A said the defendant had said one thing, and Officer B said he said another thing. They were small conflicts in testimony, but conflicts nonetheless.

In summation, the lawyer would emphasize to the jury all of the small discrepancies he had meticulously uncovered, accompanied with obvious facial gestures and body language. "I'm sure that these officers are good, honest cops, but let's face it," he would say, rolling his eyes and raising his hands, "they can't even agree on what the defendant was wearing, where he was standing or what was said." He would enumerate a half-dozen other inconsistencies that he had uncovered. "How can you convict my client for a crime when the arresting officers can't even agree with each other on their own testimony? And they were there together!" he would argue.

In the end, the jury usually felt that there was indeed enough conflicting testimony to establish reasonable doubt. The result was the defendants usually got off scot-free and the lawyers got a suit-case full of money. The arresting officers would walk out of the courtroom shaking their heads in disgust, ready to either turn in their badges or next time shoot first and ask questions later.

"Let's shoot the bastards and go home," Machella repeated. He was getting nervous.

Both sides now had possession of the other's suitcase and were ready to depart. Meanwhile, each pair of men continued standing behind the trees.

"As soon as they move into the clear, we nail 'em," La Torre said. Like Machella, he had an uneasy feeling about this bust, but they had come too far to turn around.

"They ain't moving from behind the trees, boss," one of the men whispered anxiously as his eyes shifted nervously from the departing figures with the drugs and money, then back again to the pine trees, where the other men seemed to be holding their ground. "They're gonna get away, boss!"

La Torre could see the men poised behind the trees as if they were going to shoot one another, yet no one made a move to follow the drugs and money.

"All right. Let's get 'em. If the guys behind the trees don't throw down their weapons on demand, shoot to kill. Questions?" he asked, turning around.

His men raised their weapons, holding them head-high in both hands, ready to attack.

"All right, let's hit 'em." His voice went from a whisper to a loud yell as he led the charge into the clearing. "Freeze! Hands up! Alcohol, Tobacco and Firearms!" he announced. "You're under arrest. Throw down your weapons!"

Suddenly, there was a barrage of bullets whip-ping through the air from both directions, knocking bark off the trees, hitting the wooden picnic tables and searing off branches from overhead. The fire fight lasted for what seemed an eternity, but in reality was over in a matter of minutes.

When the shooting stopped, the night became silent once again. The drug dealers spoke softly to one another in Italian. "Jose? You okay?"

"Yeah, you?"

They spoke to one another, the tones of their voices becoming more confident and louder with the addition of each new voice. La Torre and his men all lay dead, ambushed by the two cars full of Italians who had learned of the impending bust earlier that day. They had canceled the real transaction with the Colombians and set up a fake meeting—all with their own men.

When the Colombians had learned of the ruse the Italians had set up they had asked to take part in the slaughter. The Italians refused, of course, not trusting their Colombian counterparts. The object: teach the DEA a lesson they wouldn't soon forget.

With the deaths of La Torre and his team, the department of Alcohol, Tobacco and Firearms had suffered a major setback. What they had always feared had now been confirmed, that there was a mole in their organization who had caused the deaths of some of their best men. Somehow the mole had gained access to information that only those with a high-level security clearance could have known. Towards the end of his investigation, just before the bust, fearing that there was a mole within the company, La Torre had even resorted to sending private, secret messages within the organization on handwritten notes. Computers and telephones had become too easy to bug.

With these deaths the search for the mole would intensify.

In the wake of Manuel La Torre's death, he left a wife and a 21-year-old divorced daughter, Terry Jane Escobar, to mourn for him.

The families of the Alcohol, Tobacco and Firearms personnel who had died in the line of duty that fateful day had gotten together and decided against having a funeral, opting instead for a memorial service to honor their dead. The memorial service took place on Sunday morning and was held in the garden of the state capital in Sacramento. A soft breeze drifted through the crowd of mourners, carrying the subtle scent of flowers and freshly cut grass as members of the ATF division, their families and friends gave short, tearful accolades to their fallen comrades and loved ones.

Terry Jane—or TJ, as she liked to be called—was left with an especially large void in her life. At the young age of nine she had demonstrated a strong propensity towards the game of tennis. After a year of private lessons, her tennis coach had urged her father to enroll her in a high-intensity program of daily private lessons. She improved and began attending tennis camps around the country. Soon she was good enough to participate in tennis tournaments, which not only deprived her of her childhood, but of a quality relationship with her family. When she wasn't in school she was on the tennis court.

The training paid off. At the age of 14 she had realized her dream of becoming a national tennis contender. She and Tracy Austin competed for the last position of the Wimbledon matches. In the end, it was Tracy who won the playoff match on the last game of the last set. The letdown of not being able to play in Wimbledon not only demoralized her, but seemed to form a psychological barrier that prevented her from being a contender at any national match from that day forward.

After a long layoff and considerable counseling from her coaches, coupled with constant nagging by her mother, she took up the game again. She played in local and state tournaments, where she won trophy after trophy. After she graduated from high school her father urged her to devote the next two years to the sport, confident that she could become a contender again. As a carrot, he tried to convince her that her tennis skills combined with her natural ability could earn her enough money to set herself up for life.

She had lost her taste for competition, however, and opted to teach instead. She contracted herself out to national and international tennis clubs which catered to the rich and famous. She was beautiful, and her striking build and charming personality made her a commodity in demand, especially by young men on holiday, including those who were on holiday away from their wives.

It was while she was teaching tennis at Club Med in Mexico that she met Stephen Escobar. He was a tall, dark and handsome, clean-shaven, successful oil man from Brazil with a charming personality. He carried himself like a prince and dressed and acted the part. He spoke perfect English with just a slight accent, enough to be enchanting.

He swept TJ off her feet the first day they met. She didn't have a chance. They were married 20 days later. She learned too late that Escobar was a womanizer. He swept women off their feet everywhere he went. "I was blind, dumb and gullible," she would say with a laugh. "Thinking that I was the only one that he fell for. A man as handsome as that, and rich and single to boot? I should have known it was too easy."

The marriage lasted a total of 180 days. "That's two mistakes I've made in my life. The third is bound to be just around the corner," she added.

Now, her father was gone—executed by drug dealers. She had missed her childhood and a normal child's relationship with her father. All the years without her father had now been evaporated by senseless violence.

After the services were over she singled out her father's boss, Thomas Edwards, Chief of the West Coast Alcohol, Tobacco and Firearms Division.

"I'm so sorry for the death of your father," he said, putting his arm around her slender shoulder, consoling her like a daughter. "He was a good man. We'll miss him. Are you going to be all r—"

"I want to take his place," she blurted, interrupting his consoling speech.

He stopped to face her, looking into her beautiful green eyes. "You don't know what you're saying," he said with a guarded tone of sarcasm.

She knew that look. He was looking at this young, hysterical woman whom he thought of as just a child, a helpless tennis player at best. *A woman looking to do a man's job*, she thought. What he didn't know was that she was determined to get revenge.

"This work is not what you think. It's demanding and dangerous. And you have no training, no qualifications. Look what happened to your father, heaven help him. And he was a trained professional, cautious and meticulous to a fault. Yet, look what happened to him. Can you imagine what chance you would have out there? A fragile young thing such as yourself," he said with a smirk. "Don't worry, we'll find the men who did this," he said, squeezing her shoulders. "We'll find them, and you can rest assured, they will be punished."

His eyes were saying, "Go home, little girl, and play tennis with your rich friends." His words said, "leave the man's work to the men."

For the first time, she resented the man that her father worked for, but she understood the male mentality. "I can be of use. I know it," she insisted, holding back the resentment she felt. "I know I can't replace my father. I don't expect to have a gun or a badge and go out and arrest bad guys, I know that. But there must be something that I can do. I know there is. Give me a chance, Mr. Edwards. Please?" Her eyes were pleading, as was her voice.

Edwards looked at her pleading face and recognized the determination that had brought her within a game of Wimbledon. "Let me think about it," he said, patting her on the shoulder.

"Don't dismiss me, Mr. Edwards," she said firmly, looking at him with stern eyes. She was determined to do this and wasn't going to let him treat her like a child. "I'll surprise you. You'll see," she asserted confidently.

He hesitated for a moment. "All right," he said, with a note of resignation. "Tell you what. You be in my office first thing Monday, and I'll introduce you to our coordinator, Miss Walton. Perhaps she could find some useful thing for you to do within the department."

She grabbed his hand, jumping up and down with excitement. "You won't regret this, Mr. Edwards. I promise."

He looked at her and saw the young woman that she was, wondering if he might have made a judgmental error. *Caroline will soon weed her out,* he thought to himself as he watched her walk away with a renewed bounce. *It's always easier for a woman to deal with another woman,* he thought, dismissing her from his mind.

* * * *

"Miss Walton? There's a Miss Escobar here to see you—Terry Jane Escobar. Says she has an appointment, but I don't see her name on the calendar."

"Terry Jane Escobar. Oh, yes. Manuel La Torre's daughter. Send her in."

TJ was dressed in a simple white knee-length, cotton dress and sandals without nylons. She wore little makeup, just enough to accent her cheekbones, and a slight amount of blush that made her pouty lips alluring. *This woman would never get lost in a crowd,* Caroline thought as she watched the confident, well-tanned woman approach her desk.

"Thomas tells me you want to work for the company, Miss Escobar," she said, smiling as she extended her hand.

"TJ, please," was the reply. "Everyone calls me that."

"Is there a Mr. Escobar?" Caroline asked, putting pen to paper to make notes, full-well knowing from the notes in the father's file, which she also had on her desk, that TJ had been divorced.

"No. Well, yes, but we're no longer together," TJ stammered.

"Divorced or separated?" Preliminary questions meant to test her honesty.

"Divorced."

"So, tell me, Miss—er—TJ, what is it that you had in mind in working for the company?"

Chapter Seventeen

A coded message came over Christian Murray's fax that read, "The fox is hungry. Solo at eight tomorrow." It was a message from the attorney general, Robert Macaffe, which meant that he wanted to meet Murray alone at 8:00 the following evening. That meant that Murray had to catch an early morning flight out of SFO to Washington.

"What's up, Coach? You look deep in thought."

Murray looked up at the concerned face of Grover.

"I'll be out of town all day tomorrow. You're going to be in charge. I've got to go to town for some groceries."

In other words, duty calls. Don't ask, Grover thought to himself as he nodded.

* * * *

"You rang?" Murray inquired as he walked into the security office of Robert Macaffe wearing acid-washed blue jeans and a black flight jacket. "You don't wear suits anymore," he commented, as he noted Macaffe's eyes looking him over.

"Hadn't heard from you for a while, Chris," Bob said, ignoring the comment. "Thought it was time we had a sit-down and talk a bit."

He threw a handful of newspapers on the desk for Murray to see. The headlines read: "Colombians and Mafia killed in drug deal gone bad," "Colombians and Mob gassed in Mysterious Fashion," "Unidentified gang members executed."

"Your handiwork, I assume?"

"Looks like the work of a pro," Murray said, sliding the papers back towards Macaffe.

"In each incident, there were no drugs or money found. It's as if some mysterious force ravaged the poor bastards and then disappeared."

"No witnesses?"

"None."

"What a shame."

"Except for these," he said, sliding a Zip-lock bag containing an empty army-green gas canister towards Murray. "And these." Another Zip-lock bag containing several empty shells. "Government issue," Macaffe said.

"You can get this stuff in army surplus stores, you know," Christian pointed out, glancing at the bags but not touching them.

"Don't be flip with me, Murray. You know as well as I do that these aren't from any army surplus, or any other store for that matter." He looked at Murray sternly. "So far there haven't been any repercussions because everyone thinks the crooks are bumping each other off."

"Thought that was the plan."

Macaffe slid a copy of the Washington Post across the desk to him. "The President isn't too happy about all this shoot-'em-up, kill-'em news."

The heading of the column that Macaffe had circled in yellow read, "President expected to beef up gun control in Crime Bill."

"Sounds like he's on the right track. He should

be pleased that the dummies are wiping each other out, and not civilians."

"I'm sure he is, but that's not an opinion available for public consumption. He's not real pleased about the heat he's been getting from his constituents, either," Macaffe said, sliding forward another paper with a picture circled. He watched Murray's eyes scan the picture of a group of women carrying placards reading "WAG, Women Against Drugs" and "Ban guns."

"So? A few bored women are taking time out from TV and eating chocolates to prime their cause. I happen to agree with 'em. What's the big deal?" Murray grunted.

"It isn't just a few bored women, as you so aptly put it," Macaffe slapped the papers in irritation. "This is the nucleus of a giant wave floating across our land. The women of this country comprise in excess of 60 percent of the vote. We keep seeing headlines like these," he glared at Murray for emphasis, "and heads will roll!"

Murray studied his face for a moment. He had never known his boss to get this excited about anything political before, especially concerning the political ambitions of the President.

"You're supposed to eliminate crime, not cause it," Macaffe ground out.

Murray just shrugged his shoulders. "If wiping out the Mob and the Colombians in one fell swoop isn't eliminating crime, I don't know what is."

He's taking this all too lightly, Macaffe thought, frustrated. "There's an election coming up in another eighteen months, and the President is trying to get his crime bill passed." He removed a file from his desk containing a number of press clippings. "The public is getting fed up with the crime in this country," he said, tossing a handful of clippings on his desk. "This is just a sampling. A bunch of kids get shot at McDonald's," he pushed one towards Murray, "A disgruntled employee shoots fifteen people, killing five", "Random shooting at a school", "Ex-husband kills estranged wife and his kids, then commits suicide". The list goes on." He thumbed through the clippings.

"If the people of this country don't see some change in violent crime, it's likely to become a one-term presidency. Are you beginning to see the point?"

"I take it there's a message in this speech?" Murray challenged.

"The idea is to keep crime out of the news, not to create more news with more dead bodies." Macaffe rubbed the back of his neck vigorously. "The idea is to eliminate the type of crime that propagates the usage of guns—like gangland, drug-dealing mass murders," he said, facing Murray with a glare. "The idea is to make things look good for the commanding chief, and we look good in return."

"I thought that was what we were doing, Bob. But now that you bring it up, I've been thinking, and I've decided to make a directional change in our—"

"It's not just drugs," Macaffe interrupted. "We're concerned with our image abroad. A week doesn't go by when a tourist isn't getting mugged or killed on our streets." He took another file, which was full of clippings. "A German couple is murdered visiting Disneyland," he read aloud, throwing a clipping on the table. "A Japanese exchange student is murdered." Another clipping. "An elderly couple from Norway is mugged and the husband is killed. Here's another German couple killed. A bus full of Chinese on tour is held up and robbed at gunpoint. Take your pick." He flung the clippings on his desk in disgust.

"Bob," Chris tired to calm him down, "you can't single-handedly take the weight of the world on your shoulders. You start taking your job personally, you're going to end up having a heart attack."

"I know," Macaffe relented. "It's just that... It's frustrating." He stood up and paced the floor behind his desk. "There's more at stake here than you think." His eyes were glassy, unfocused. "There are things...things that I can't begin to tell you about."

"The media just likes to sensationalize bad news," Murray reasoned, "You know that. That's what sells papers. No one ever heard of selling good news. Look at this way, Bob. We've made several successful hits. We've been grabbing drug money and have taken a ton of drugs out of circulation in the process. I agree that more needs to be done." Murray paused for breath. "That's what I started to tell you earlier, before you got wound up tighter than a ten-dollar watch.

"You know as well as I that our little group of in-house terrorists has been more successful in the short time we've been in operation than any task force since Prohibition." Murray stood up behind his chair, looking hard at his boss.

"But, successful as we've been, I just get the feeling that all we've done is piss off the bad guys and drive them further underground." He scowled, running his hand through his hair. "I had planned on making a deeper dent in the drug market, but I'm concerned that all we've done is slow down the play a bit, which may have inadvertently raised the price of coke a dollar or two."

Murray sighed wistfully. "At the very least, I

had hoped we would have started a drug war. Let the bastards think they're ripping each other off and let them kill each other."

"That's what I'm talking about," Macaffe retorted, throwing his hands in the air in desperation. "Haven't you been listening? An open gang war is the one thing we don't need right now!" he spat as he continued pacing. "Things don't seem to be working out as we had planned," he complained, more to himself than to Murray.

"Watch your blood pressure, Bob. I'm just pushing your buttons," Murray grinned. "But you have to admit, we've held true to course, and to that end we've been successful."

"I know you must be making a dent in someone's pocket," Macaffe conceded. "And, from the looks of your reports, I've gotta believe that the Mob must be hurtin'. Hell, you've taken in an excess of $40 million from those dudes—not to mention the same amount of coke from the Colombians. They have to be feeling the pain."

"You know as well as I that forty million dollars for the Mob is a month's take on the streets." Murray shook his head. "As for the Colombians, they can raise and make coke faster than the Mob can sell it, which is a damn sight faster than we can cut them down. No. We're missin' something in this picture, Bob. We need to send a message that will be heard around the world that says, 'Stay off our turf or suffer the consequences!'"

"I take it you've got a plan in mind?" Macaffe asked skeptically.

"I'm workin' on an idea," Murray hedged. "But it's still rough. I'll keep you posted," he added in a tone indicating he wasn't ready to talk about it.

Macaffe grunted, "You're turning into a cowboy, Murray. And, frankly, that makes me nervous." There was a wrinkle in his brow, and Murray knew whenever Bob Macaffe referred to him by his last name it either indicated displeasure or a form of discipline.

"You've got my reports." He defended vehemently, waving his hand towards Macaffe's desk. "So I assume you can't be too unhappy?"

"Yeah. I know you're bustin' heads and taking names—" Macaffe started tiredly.

"Not to mention money." Murray put in. "By your own admission, we're collecting more money than the Internal Revenue Service during tax time. That should make someone uptown happy."

Macaffe looked at Murray and nodded, picking up the newspapers, clearing his desk, as if dismissing the topic from further discussion.

"Well, you take good care of yourself," Murray offered, rising from his seat. "I'd hate to see all that dough lost in some bank, gathering interest for the rest of time." He smiled.

"It'll be put to good use, of that you can be sure," Macaffe assured with conviction. "I doubt we'll have it spent before you're finished."

"Finished?" Murray stopped. He peered at Macaffe intently. "You know something you're not telling me?"

Macaffe knew he had hit a nerve. "You know as well as I that it's only a matter of time before the lid comes off your little operation," he pointed out. "Sooner or later you're bound to get shot, caught by some law enforcement agency, or videotaped by a passerby. You can't go on being lucky forever."

He added wistfully, "Sometimes I wish I hadn't let you talk me into this harebrained scheme of yours. Life would be a lot simpler."

"You worry too much," Murray shot back. "Besides, don't forget—I'm legally dead. You can't prosecute a dead man," he joked.

Macaffe got a strange look in his eye. "Make light of it if you like, but mark my words—"

"I know," Murray finished for him, "Don't get caught, dead or not."

Macaffe shook his head in frustration, as if he were a father who was lecturing to the deaf ear of his teenager.

* * * *

As Christian Murray exited, Mr. Green entered the back door of Macaffe's office. "At least you could wait until he's out of the building," Macaffe reprimanded as Green occupied the seat across from his desk.

"Don't get your pantyhose in a ripple," Green quipped. "He said his piece and now he's gone." He took a cigarette out of his pocket and lit it.

"Don't smoke in my office, if you don't mind," Macaffe huffed. "It's a filthy habit and irritates my sinuses."

Green blew a smoke ring into the air, ignoring the request. "I'm concerned about your man, Murray," he said, then formed another ring of smoke.

"My man!" Macaffe sputtered.

"You're his boss," Green pointed out. He shrugged his shoulders. "At first, I thought this grab-and-run plan would work, and so far it has." He drew a long puff, then blew smoke towards Macaffe, who brushed it away while making a face. "But now he's starting to sound like a loose cannon. I get nervous when I don't know what he's hatching." Green addressed the ceiling. "If his grab-and-kill scheme succeeds in escalating the conflict between the Mafia and the Colombians," his flat gaze returned to Macaffe, "and the public continues putting heat on the politicians, this whole damn mess could blow up in our faces."

"Let's not panic just yet," Macaffe reasoned. "Murray hasn't let the company down so far."

"It's not 'The Company' I'm concerned with," Green emphasized, pointing at Macaffe.

"Let's see what direction he's going first," Macaffe offered, ignoring the obvious threat.

"You're his boss. Be sure he doesn't forget it," Green suggested.

"I don't need you to remind me of my job," Macaffe bit out.

"Do you need to be reminded who pays your bills?" Green sneered.

Macaffe stared at Mr. Green, his stomach knotting. "I thought I told you to never speak of these matters within the confines of this building," he admonished.

"Relax," Green assured him. "No one's going to bug the attorney general's office." Green paused as he blew another smoke ring directly at Macaffe. "I trust that I need not remind you of what's at stake here," he said ominously. "The six-by-nine club is one organization we never want to join, if you get my drift."

"I don't need reminding," Macaffe returned.

"Did you transfer the money?"

"Yesterday. The Cayman bank is $40 mil and change fatter."

"Good," Green nodded his satisfaction. "At least Murray's doing something useful. Wait about a week, then divide and transfer half the funds into the two Swiss accounts. No need to make things easy to track."

"Twenty-five percent in each of the minor accounts?"

"Unless you want to settle for less." Green eyed him contemptuously.

Macaffe looked at him, but offered no response.

"Well, I'm off," Green said cheerfully, rising from his chair. He extended his hand to Macaffe, who hesitantly shook it.

Macaffe waited until Green had closed the door, then angrily snapped a yellow pencil in his hands. "What have I gotten myself into?" he said aloud as he leaned back in his chair, closing his eyes tightly while gritting his teeth. There was a distorted, pained look on his face.

* * * *

The success of Murray's team, coupled with their sudden disregard for the human lives they had been taking, albeit drug-related, had begun to reflect an air of arrogance on the men that bothered Murray. He was painfully aware that arrogance could breed carelessness, which was just a baby-step away from mistakes and disaster.

Authoritative discipline seemed to have all but disappeared. The men had their feet on the table and were laughing and basically ignoring Murray as he entered the room. Some were cleaning their assault weapons, while others practiced aiming at imaginary figures. Murray stood at the head of the conference table, patiently waiting for order to restore itself. One by one, the men became aware of his presence and stopped talking.

When the room was finally quiet, he finally spoke. His voice was quiet, but his words stung. "When we first started our crusade against criminals, operating outside the law, so to speak, I was satisfied with our results. I was confident that we'd been successful in our endeavor to stem the tide of crime, but now I can see that three things have happened. One, I'm no longer convinced that wiping out a single drug transaction, regardless of the size, is making any significant dent in the big picture.

"Secondly, and for this I take full responsibility, I've come to be concerned about your moral fiber. While I freely admit it was and still is the game plan to eliminate the bad guys, I've begun to question the wisdom of my judgment. This issue will have to be addressed down the line, however, when I've had time to think it through more thoroughly.

"Last, but not least, in conjunction with the aforementioned moral fiber issue, I've begun to notice a significant breakdown of discipline." He paused momentarily, looking harshly at his men. "And that spells disaster!"

The blood was beginning to flow to the surface of his face, betraying his anger. The tone of his voice started to be more vehement.

"It is the last item that I wish to address at this meeting. You've become lax in technique and lazy about procedure."

He paced the room, his hands locked behind his back. "I'm as much to blame for the state of affairs as you, so beginning at 11:00 hours today, we're going to commence a new phase of training. We'll form in front of the barracks with full field packs and weapons, after which time we'll take a 10-mile hike to the beach. Once there, we'll utilize the firing range for two hours, then return through the desert. Any questions?"

There were groans among the men as they looked at one another, but none complained. They knew the Coach was right. They had fallen into complacency and admittedly had become ill-disciplined.

"As to the first item, I've decided to make a directional change in our offense procedure. Instead of attacking individual transactions, which, in light of our recent success, are sure to become more difficult to pinpoint, I've decided to go for the head of the snake, eliminating the source of the problem."

"We gonna hit the Mob? Which family?" There was an air of electricity that immediately shot through the room. The wiping out of a Mafia family by a governmental agency had never, in the history of American crime, been done before.

"No," Murray denied, cocking one eyebrow. "But that's not a bad idea. My thought was to eliminate the source of the problem—the supplier."

"You mean the growers? The Colombians?"

"Precisely. How can the Mob sell coke if there isn't any coke to sell?"

"They'll always find ways of getting coke into the country," Grover said. "Look at how they get it now—boats, small planes, even individual carriers swallowing cellophane bags of the stuff."

"Stupid bastards." One of the Ends laughed. "One break in the bag, and they suffer a death worse than torture."

Murray ignored the comments. "We're going to demonstrate to the Cartel that it isn't healthy to sell cocaine to any American—criminal or not."

Murray had their attention. Next to a good fight, these guys loved a challenge. This was going to be both. Eliminating the Cartel was definitely challenging. Considering the way of life of the Colombians, harassing the Cartel meant taking on the whole country. The Cartel, for all intents and purposes, ran the country.

Chapter Eighteen

Try as he might, Molina Marquez had never been able to shake the undeniable fact that he came from Communa Nororiental and was uneducated, even if those facts existed only in his own mind. Although he had learned how to read before leaving school, and was competent in speaking English and proficient in mathematics—sufficient enough to satisfy his immediate needs—he attempted to make up for his lack of education by indulging in areas that he felt would overcome his shortcomings. This took the form of two sports: tennis and soccer.

Molina's exposure to tennis had been limited to viewing it on television and seeing elegant men and women of breeding playing at Medellin's exclusive athletic clubs. The fact that it was an international sport added to the attraction.

One day, while he was having lunch on the verandah of the exclusive members-only Medellin Swim and Racquet Club, he was so absorbed by a foursome of young couples playing on the court beneath the verandah that he decided then and there that he had to learn the sport.

He contracted to have a fenced-in clay tennis court built beside the villa, in addition to a 20x40-

foot swimming pool, which was accented with a lava rock water-fall and a free-form spa. He purchased several of the most expensive, oversized racquets on the market, bought an automatic ball machine and outfitted himself in the latest tennis gear. Now all he needed was to learn how to play the sport.

He wanted to be sure no one in Medellin knew that he was learning the game, so he contacted the National Tennis Association in Bogota to hire a pro to teach him. "I prefer an American," he told the woman who answered the phone. "They have mastered the art of the game. Everyone in America plays tennis, just as all Colombians play soccer." Besides, having a foreigner teach him prevented anyone from spreading rumors that they were teaching a member of the Cartel, a tidbit worth money, no doubt.

Two days later, he received a call informing him that they had in fact contacted a pro who was available and willing to fly to Medellin. They said that the teacher was presently employed as a pro at an exclusive swim and racquet club in Cabo San Lucas. The instructor had been contacted and had indicated a willingness to personally take Molina on as a client, all things being equal. "I own my own tennis facilities," he said, "and it will be imperative for the instructor to reside at the villa until his services are no longer required. Will that present a problem?"

"Your request will be forwarded. If there is a problem, you will be notified within the next twenty-four hours," she had said. "Unless you hear from us to the contrary, within that time frame you can expect your instructor to arrive at the Medellin airport on the 10:00 flight Saturday morning. The name of the person you will meet is TJ Escobar."

Molina thought it best to meet the pro himself, in person. That way, there would be no slip-up of someone finding out who the American visitor was or what his business was with Molina.

Molina arrived at the airport with time to spare, just in case the plane was early, an event that rarely took place in Medellin. He was dressed in a white cotton suit, wearing a white Panama hat with a red-flowered band. He wore a small red rosebud in his lapel.

He was standing by his white bullet-proof Rolls Royce at the airport when the commercial flight arrived. When the passengers deplaned there were businessmen with briefcases, visitors, tourists and several single people, but no American carrying tennis gear, or even one resembling a tennis pro.

"Mr. Marquez? Molina Marquez?" a feminine voice inquired as he stood resting his elbow on his knee on the front bumper of his car.

He turned to face a tall, slender woman wearing a multi-colored cotton dress. She had shoulder-length auburn hair, with a white sash around her head. She had gorgeous sea-green eyes which seemed to nearly dance from her sun-tanned skin.

What a beautiful woman, Molina thought as he looked her over before responding. "Yes, I'm Molina Marquez. Do I...know you?"

"I'm TJ Escobar," she said, extending her slender hand to Molina. "I believe you hired me to teach you tennis?"

"You're TJ Escobar?" he said, astonished, standing back to carefully examine her as if undressing her in his mind's eye. The look on his face was one of surprise.

"Yes. Is anything wrong?"

"No. It's just that...well, I was sort of expecting..." he stammered.

"A man?"

Molina hesitated for a moment. "Yes. A man," he responded tentatively.

"I'm sorry to disappoint you," she said with an air of light sarcasm. She knew it was not uncommon for powerful Colombians or any Latin, for that matter, to be used to treating women as nothing more than a sexual object or a house mouse to cook and clean for them. Even in her own trade, in her own country, she often encountered this male chauvinistic attitude towards her independence.

"Shall I schedule a return flight to Cabo?" she asked, without a hint of disappointment. If she was to be fired before beginning, it would be without giving Molina the satisfaction of seeing disappointment on her part.

"You're the tennis pro?" he reaffirmed, still finding it hard to believe. "The one from—"

"That's me," she cut him off. "You asked for the best, and that's what you got. I've given lessons to some of the world's top players." TJ defended herself matter-of-factly, without airs or arrogance. "Both men and women. But I'll understand if you feel that being taught by a female is less than—how shall we say—acceptable." She hesitated for a moment before continuing, and a self-satisfied smile crept at the corners of her mouth. "I've become accustomed to the Latin male mentality regarding women teaching men anything," she concluded, looking Molina straight in the eye, as if challenging him.

This was a new experience for Molina. He had never encountered a woman such as this, so bold and outspoken. It fascinated him. She was a challenge, like a beautiful, unbroken wild stallion. "Ah, no. Well..." he finally said after regaining his composure. "You're here now. No use wasting the trip," he lamely rationalized. He was more interested in her as a woman than as a tennis pro. "I'd hate to think that you came all this way, and at the very least, didn't stay for lunch," he concluded, extending his hand towards his car.

"Eating is not the reason I came," she countered firmly, standing her ground. "I need to know if you want me to stay—to teach tennis. If not, I have a class that I can continue teaching in Cabo tomorrow."

Molina knew he had to have her stay for the sheer beauty of herself, if for no other reason. Since his reign of power began, he had had his share of women, mostly loose women who slept with anyone in power or had an abundance of money. They were lookers, all right, but nothing one would want to necessarily be seen with in public, let alone take home.

The other group of acceptable women, single social climbers looking for security and wealth, had more or less held themselves at bay until Molina had secured his place on the Colombian power ladder. It was common knowledge that those who dealt in drugs had a tendency to either rise to power or to find themselves aerated with machine gun bullets, along with their families and friends. Thus Molina's contact with the finer women of Medellin had been limited.

"Please. Accept my apologies. Let my driver pick up your luggage and we'll proceed to the villa," he said, extending his hand towards the car door. "Please," he urged again as she seemed to hesitate.

TJ Escobar set the tone of their relationship the very next day, on the tennis court. She was showing him how to hold his racquet when he slipped his arm around her waist.

"Mr. Marquez..." she protested.

"Please! Call me Molina. Mr. Marquez is so formal. If we're to be in each other's company—"

"That's precisely the matter I wish to address," she cut in, gently but firmly removing his arm from around her small waist. "This is going to be a professional relationship. You have hired me to be your instructor, and that's what I intend to do while I'm here. Instruct. Tennis!" she emphasized with a firm look.

"I have a hard and fast rule, Mr. Marquez. I never get involved with my students. It's not only bad for their game, but without exception, getting involved usually ends up creating ill will between student and instructor. We don't want that, now do we?"

"No disrespect intended," Molina responded with a slight bow. "I was just being friendly."

There was a twinkle in his eye that contradicted his words. TJ made a mental note of the twinkle.

Molina turned out to be a quick study and a natural athlete. His love for the game and desire to excel inspired him to practice every morning and every evening with TJ. When they weren't on the court together, Molina would practice his strokes with the ball machine.

Despite the flame of desire burning to have TJ, Molina honored her request to keep their relationship at a professional level. By the end of four months, he had become a proficient player capable of holding his own with most "C" class club players.

Their relationship had progressed to the point that their eyes often locked during the day while they practiced. TJ modified her attitude towards Molina and allowed him to momentarily hold her hand and give her a hug at the beginning and end of each lesson. Eventually, that had progressed to an exchange of a light, friendly kiss.

Molina couldn't help himself. He had fallen helplessly in love with TJ Escobar.

"I feel that I have done all I can for your game," TJ said after practice one evening. "The rest is up to you. To continue paying me to teach you is wasted money."

"It's not the money I'm concerned with," he said as he fumbled with his racquet, looking her in the eye. "During these past months I've become the happiest man alive. I want you to stay in Medellin, TJ Escobar. I want you to do me the honor of becoming Mrs. Marquez."

TJ had known that Molina had feelings for her. Although she had tried to prevent it, she had also developed an attraction towards him. In fact, if the truth had been known, the past month he had dominated her thoughts every hour of the day. As she looked into his eyes, she longed for his lips...yearned for his body.

"I'm flattered and deeply honored that you would ask me," she began carefully.

"But..." he anticipated.

"But, you barely know me," she protested weakly. "We barely know each other. You know nothing of my life, nor I of yours."

"There is nothing to know beyond the fact that I have fallen helplessly in love with you."

"Look at you," she tried again, "You're rich. You're handsome. You're bright and healthy. You could have any woman you want. Why me?"

"You're the only woman who's honest and yet challenging to me," Molina growled. "All the rest—they're either after my money or just looking for a husband. You? You are neither."

"Is that a reason to want to marry someone?

'Cause they're honest and not after your money?"

"It's not that. You know that," he said taking her hands in his. "I've never said this to another woman before." He looked into her eyes. "I love you, TJ Escobar. Marry me? Please."

She held onto his hands, meeting his gaze. "I've done the marriage bit already, Molina, and it didn't work out." She related her experience with Stephen Escobar and the shortness of that union. "So you see," she finished. "I don't want to repeat myself."

"Don't judge me on a past mistake that you've made," he argued. "I love you and promise that I won't 'dump' you, as you put it."

"I'm sure that you have the best of intentions," she said. "You have to understand the situation from my point of view. I just can't afford another mistake like that. Life is too short."

Molina studied her face, as if trying to read her most inner thoughts. "I'll tell you what I'll do— to prove that my intentions are honorable." He squeezed her hands gently, taking a deep breath before he spoke. "I don't know if you know it or not, but I'm a very wealthy man."

"I assumed as much from what I can see." She smiled, glancing around at the magnificent grounds of the villa. "But that has no bearing on my decision," she explained patiently.

"All the more reason why it is important that you understand what I'm about to say. I wouldn't make this statement if it were not for the fact that I feel you have no interest in my wealth."

"Nothing could be further from my mind," she said firmly. "Money is not and has never been of much interest to me. I'll take tranquillity and happiness over money and conflict any day."

"So," he grinned with satisfaction, "there you have it!"

"Have what?" TJ queried.

"The money," Molina explained, "my wealth and power." He said with a flourish, "I am willing to sign a document stating that if we do not stay married, for any reason, half of everything that I own will automatically become yours."

"That is totally unnecessary, Molina!" TJ was startled.

"It is to me, because it's my way of demonstrating the fact that I am not nor will I ever be like your Mr. Stephen Escobar and marry you just for the fun of it. I want our union to be for life."

"Tell you what." She swallowed the lump in her throat. "Let me sleep on it. I'll give you your answer in the morning." She took his hand in hers and kissed him lightly on the lips, then ran away to her room, before he saw the tears of anguish that began streaming down her face.

* * * *

Molina was already sitting on the verandah overlooking the pool and tennis court, sipping a large glass of freshly squeezed orange juice when TJ strolled in. She was wearing a short white cotton dress that accentuated her golden tan. The morning sun filtered through the overhead trellis and birds sang.

Molina's pulse quickened as TJ passed by his chair. She paused behind him, resting her hand on his shoulder as she admired the view of the rugged hills. A soft smile formed on her lips as he rose to greet her. Neither spoke as their lips met, softly at first, then for the first time with a wave of passion.

The kiss seemed to last forever, yet not long enough. "Oh, how I love you," Molina whispered huskily in her ear. "Does this mean that you will marry me?" It was more of a statement than a question.

TJ held him at arm's length. There was a moment before she spoke as she searched his eyes. "I must be honest with you, Molina. I have come to admire you—yes, even love you, these past months. I've given your proposal a lot of thought." She studied his handsome face, then kissed him softly on the lips. It was more than just a friendly kiss. "What would you say if I suggested that we live together for a couple of months? If, after that period of time, you still want me, and I feel the same, we'll discuss the possibility of my staying on a more permanent basis." She smiled warmly. "That will give each of us time together to see how compatible we really are. Nothing brings out the worst in a person more than living together." She laughed, hugging him, holding him hard for the first time.

"We'll be so compatible, so ecstatic with one another that you'll want to get married next week," he said confidently, lifting her into the air. "I'm going to see to it that this is the most unforgettable period of your life." He grinned, hugging her so hard he raised her off her feet. Then he swung her in a circle while she squealed.

"Let's hope it's the most successful," she said with a seductive smile. "I hate failure."

"You couldn't fail if your life depended on it," he assured, carrying her into the house.

* * * *

Molina's second great passion was soccer. The game is taken very seriously in Colombia, and the city of Medellin is no exception. Soccer is the one facet of life for which both poor and rich, worker and president alike, equally share an affinity. When a local soccer match is scheduled, everyone gives the totality of their concentration to the game. Heaven help the official who makes a bad call against their team, especially if it's a game-deciding call. Given the attention that the game is paid by members of the Cartel, and the money that is at stake on wagers, any unfavorable call by an official could well be life-threatening.

Molina knew that the powerful drug lords loved the game and were known to bet heavily whenever there was a soccer match. When a block of owner's investment became available in the club Atletico Nacional de Medellin, he decided to buy it and become a major shareholder. This elevated his status amongst the Cartel and gave him access to the soccer players as well.

The Colombians had great aspirations of taking the World Cup soccer games, which were to be played in 1994 in the United States. Their desire to become world champions rested with their national hero and goalie: Pibe Valderrama.

All of Colombia knew that not only was the good name of Colombia at stake in the World Cup soccer games, but certain governmental officials had high hopes of eradicating the country's image as the world's largest cocaine theme park. Rene Higuita had even been quoted, saying that "The Colombia National Soccer team will be on a dual mission: to win the World Cup and to eradicate the country's image."

Chapter Nineteen

"I've got some interesting news relative to one of your busts," Macaffe said. He extended his hand to Murray as he entered his office. "You may recall that this was one of your first confrontations, just after your so-called demise, where the Mob was involved in a cocaine purchase from the Colombians."

"What was the modus operandi?" Murray asked as he removed his leather jacket and took a seat across from Macaffe.

"Some of the perpetrators were killed by a fragment grenade and the rest with automatic weapons. You do recall our meeting where I had the shell casings that I reamed you out about?"

Murray's face indicated recollection of the meeting without comment.

"Well," Macaffe went on, "Once the local authorities discovered the crime scene, they fingerprinted all of the victims. One of the Italians in particular was of great interest. Once I tell you who it was you'll be as confused as I was. Maybe you can help shed some light on the matter."

"Well, are you planning on telling me, or do I have to tune to in Paul Harvey and the 6:00 news to get the rest of the story?"

Ignoring the dry humor, Macaffe opened a file. "It turns out that one of the victims was one Mario DiGivanni."

Murray studied his face for a moment. "Dominic DiGivanni's brother? As in the Mob?"

"That's the one. His younger brother, 'The Enforcer', I believe he was affectionately called."

"Well," Murray said thoughtfully, "we bagged one of the big ones. Wonder why he personally went on a drug buy? The family usually likes to keep their dealings at an arm's length, just in case there's trouble. That way all they lose is money. In this instance, apparently, he lost a brother, too. You know that's got to cut deep."

Macaffe could see his mind working. "I know what you're thinking—that it was one of the Mob that had your family killed. As we've discussed, there's no proof."

"You've got to admit, though, it was their style. Get in their face, and they get your attention by killing you or your family, just to be sure the message is clear."

"If you're thinking Carleone hit your family because of the drug bust, you may recall that we hit him the same day that Jana and the kids were killed. There's no way that he could have known he was going to be hit. Think about it."

"I know that, Bob," Murray snorted disdainfully. "Call it intuition, but there's a connection here. I can feel it in my bones." He began pacing the room, rubbing his chin. "Isn't the old man still alive? Francisco?"

"Yeah, but he's retired. Word has it that he was forced to retire because of Alzheimer's disease. Why?"

"What about other offspring? Is Alfredo his only surviving son?"

"According to the file, there's one additional surviving son..." Macaffe consulted the folder, "...one Carlo Carleone." Macaffe glanced sharply at him. "Why do you ask?"

"Just thinking. Can I see that file? Maybe squeezing the old walnut will give us the break we're looking for."

"On drug trafficking or Jana's death?" Macaffe asked. "I know you, Chris. You're like a dog with a bone. Once you get an idea in your head, nothing can dislodge it. I want Jana's killers as much as you, but you're on thin ice here. You take on the Carleones because of a personal vendetta, and you'll not only blow your cover, you'll endanger the operation, and your men, as well. Is that what this is all about?" Macaffe's look intensified. "Just take a moment here and think about it. You're a smart man. Word gets out you're on the hunt, then we'll all have some explaining to do—senate investigating committee, the President, the works."

"Give me a little credit, will you, Bob?" He tossed the file back on Macaffe's desk. "You keep forgetting that I don't exist. I could walk up to Carleone's door and shoot the bastard where he stands. Who would believe anyone if they said it was me? Hell, I don't even look like me. Sometimes, in the morning, I look into the mirror and even confuse myself."

Macaffe was clearly uneasy, but made no comment.

"Relax, Bob. You're too uptight." Murray gestured. "Look at yourself in the mirror. You look like a constipated asshole trying to shit. Go fishing or take a trip up on the Hill and get yourself laid. There's plenty of little miniskirts who work in the congressional or senate offices dying for a chance to serve their constituents."

"I'm going to get out of here. Just listening to you makes me nervous. I'm beginning to wonder how I ever get sucked into this covert shit anyway," Macaffe complained.

Murray rose to leave. As he reached the door, Macaffe said, "Keep in touch, you hear? I don't like surprises."

"Watch the newspapers," was all Murray said as he closed the door after himself.

Macaffe shook his head and dialed a number on his black phone. "Macaffe here," he said quietly, looking around to see if anyone was listening. "Murray just left. I think he's going to hit Carleone."

"Carleone, as in Don Alfredo Carleone?"

"Yeah. That's the one. If it gets ugly, you may have to initiate Plan Exterminate."

"Just give him another drug bust to keep him busy. I'll round up some of the boys and take care of the matter myself. Since the Klan's all but been shut down, the boys have been hankerin' for a little action, anyway. This will be better than hangin' a nigger, and be more excitin', too. I'll make it look good in the eyes of the press, don't worry."

"You're not dealing with a scared, uneducated backwoods black," Macaffe warned. "These boys fight back. Be careful."

"Hell. These good ol' boys know how to barehand a six-foot rattler or snatch the stinger off a scorpion. Nabbin' some greaseball will be a cinch. Keep ya posted."

* * * *

"Joe. We need to meet for lunch today. You free—say at 12:30? I want you to meet me at Mark's hotdog stand in the park. Don't forget, and be on time! It's critical."

Dominic DiGivanni was sitting on a wooden bench, throwing peanuts to the pigeons, when Joe Mann strolled across the street. His six-foot-six-inch height, accentuated with his lumbering walk, made him stand out like a Zulu warrior in a Pygmy tribe.

"Sit down before anyone sees us," DiGivanni said nervously.

"How about a dog?" Joe asked. He was always hungry.

"Forget about your stomach for a minute, you clown. We've got some serious work to discuss. Remember that list of bank accounts you turned up?"

"Sure. Anything come of it?" he asked, suddenly concerned.

"No. It's just that I need more information—more details about whose accounts they are and where the funds came from. Do you follow?"

"I follow, but how can I find out who made the deposits? Wouldn't that be private banking business?"

"Tap into their computers. You can do that, can't you?"

Joe was quiet. DiGivanni could see that he was thinking. "I could try," he said, shrugging his shoulders. "I guess it's possible. Let me work on it. When do you need it?"

"Today!"

"Today will be difficult." He smiled. "Can I get my Polish now?"

"Shit!" DiGivanni rose to leave. "Call me as soon as you have something."

* * * *

"Want to buy me some lunch?" Joe asked DiGivanni a week later.

"You got something?" Dominic barked over the phone.

Joe started to inform him of his progress when DiGivanni broke in, "No, wait. Not on the phone. Meet me at noon tomorrow. I can't make it today."

"Mark's?"

DiGivanni made a face. He hated hotdogs, but it was a safe place to meet, outside, away from prying eyes and unwanted ears. "Yeah. Mark's."

Joe had just finished his first Polish when DiGivanni sat down. He made a face as Joe wadded up the paper. "How can you stand those things?"

"They're great." Joe grinned, wiping the mustard from his face. "Want me to get you one?"

"What have you got?" DiGivanni ignored the offer.

"All I could dig up was the bank where the deposits were made," he said, handing DiGivanni the list.

He looked down the list of banks and their addresses. The deposits had all been made to the same bank, but different branches, some in different states. "They seem to start in Virginia and work their way west," DiGivanni commented, running his finger down the list. "Anything else?"

"Just this." Joe handed DiGivanni a legal-sized envelope.

"What's this? More accounts?" Dominic grunted, scanning the paper.

"New accounts, old money. From the looks of things, they transferred the funds from US banks to an overseas account."

DiGivanni looked at the list, then compared it with the old list, which he had in his vest pocket. "It's the same money and same headings, all right. Looks like they're trying to hide the dough. Do you know where these accounts are?" He peered at Joe expectantly.

"All I know is that the banking numbers aren't US based. I did a quick check before I came, and if I was to make a guess, I would say they're using one of the offshore islands."

"Like the Cayman Islands," DiGivanni smirked, pleased with himself.

"Could be."

"Thanks, Joe. And good work. Here. Have a dog on me." He handed Joe an envelope containing $5 thousand in $100 bills.

"Wow! Thanks, Dad."

"Don't call me Dad!" DiGivanni barked. "I gotta go now. Talk to you later."

* * * *

DiGivanni sent fax transmissions to all the major Mafia families on the West Coast and in Virginia, where the largest deposit had been made. The fax simply stated that he had a mole planted within the federal system and that he had uncovered some major federal bank deposits. He went on to state that some of the deposits that had been made were coincidentally the same amounts and same dates as some of the recent drug busts which had resulted in family losses.

He requested that the heads of the families correspond back to him in the event they had experienced similar losses, and asked for the dates and amounts of such losses. If their losses coincided with information that he possessed, he promised to share his information with the responding family.

* * * *

The following day DiGivanni received a fax from Don Alfredo Carleone in Virginia. The fax read:

> Received your transmission. Lost $12 million to the Feds Easter of this year. If you have any knowledge pertaining to this transaction, I would greatly appreciate hearing from you. Would be willing to pay for information leading to possible recovery of lost funds. I'm sure you will agree we cannot allow anyone to interfere with business in this manner. As always, the source of your information will be protected. Look forward to return reply.
>
> Sincerely,
> Alfredo Carleone

Dominic DiGivanni quickly scanned the "Gunshot 1994" deposit list. There it was, the first banking day after Easter: a deposit of $6 million to Green-Macaffe, and a deposit of $6 million dollars to NRA and presidential election contributions.

He angrily slapped the paper with the back of his hand.

"Gotcha, you thieving bastards," he said with malice. "Now the only questions are what to do with you and how to get my money back."

* * * *

It had been 90 days since the $500 thousand that Francisco Regalado owed his cousin Molina Marquez was due. Molina had fronted him half of the money, $500 thousand, to purchase cocaine for that fateful drug deal that he had made with Dominic DiGivanni. When Francisco Regalado returned home from the market that evening, there was a message on his recorder that simply said, "Cousin, you have 24 hours to pay the $500 thousand American which is due. If I do not have proof that the money has been deposited into my account, as previously agreed, within that period of time, you can expect delivery of a new pair of shoes."

It was unmistakable whose voice it was that was on the tape. It was his cousin, Molina Marquez. He also knew the shoes he referred to were cement shoes which would be worn on a one-way trip to the bottom of the bay.

Without waiting for his wife Gloria to return home from doing her daily research at the courthouse for the firm she worked for, he threw a few shirts, some socks and an extra pair of pants into a handbag and sprinted out the door. After bolting out of the elevator, he stopped short to survey the grounds.

There was laughter coming from the swimming pool, and he could hear someone on the tennis court. The only people in sight were a young couple walking up the sidewalk with a bag of groceries. Satisfied that he wasn't being observed, he walked briskly to his car, his eyes scanning in every direction and looking over his shoulder periodically.

He threw his bags into the passenger side and inserted the key. He was about to engage the ignition when he stopped. He had recalled seeing movies of cars being blown up by the Mob when they wanted to get someone. He grabbed his bag and quietly closed the door of the car, forgetting his keys, which still hung in the ignition.

Francisco headed away from Fisherman's Wharf, staying in the shadows of trees and large vehicles, hiding himself periodically as an automobile approached. It took the better part of 20 minutes to make it to a shopping center, where he ducked into the first establishment that had a pay phone.

Plunking a quarter in the phone, he dialed information. "The number for the Drug Enforcement Administration, please," he asked, then wrote the number down on his hand with a ballpoint pen.

Another quarter. "DEA," the soft female voice answered. "How can direct your call?"

"My name is Francisco Regalado," he said nervously, looking around the store for any suspicious faces. "I need protection."

"Protection from whom?" the voice asked, with a definite tone of concern.

"He's going to kill me. I need protection!" Francisco blurted.

"Mr. Regalado, please calm down. Who is going to kill you? Where are you now?"

"Molina. My cousin Molina from Medellin. I..."

All the operator needed to hear was the word "Medellin" and she knew where the call had to be routed. "Hold one moment, please."

"DEA," a strong male voice said. "Thompson here."

Francisco repeated his dilemma in more detail to the voice. "Hold for one minute," the man said.

Francisco was near panic by this time. Everyone that entered the store looked to be a gangster carrying a concealed weapon. He was about to hang up when the voice came on the line again.

"This is Mr. Thompson again, Mr. Regalado." This time his voice had a more sincere tone, more personable. "If you will tell me where you're located, I'll send a car to pick you up."

* * * *

"Mr. Macaffe, there's a Mr. Thompson from the San Francisco branch of DEA on the line. He says he has a man that he thinks may give you a direct line to one of the Medellin Cartel boys. Shall I put him through?"

Chapter Twenty

The Liedo Bar was jumping when Green and his three large friends walked in. There was a jazz band playing and the dance floor was full of young black people, ages ranging from the mid-20's to late thirties, jiving to the music. Carlo Carleone occupied a table back in a corner near the dance floor. He had his arms around two young black women who were snuggled next to him, one on each side. They were laughing and kissing, ignoring everything and everyone around them. From time to time Carlos would slip his hand down the front of the dress of one of the girls. She would laugh and gently pull it out, slapping it lightly as she looked around nervously to see if any of the other blacks were watching. Aside from Green and his men, Carlo was the only white man in the club.

All the tables were taken, save a table next to the dance floor. There were a half-dozen half-filled drinks sitting on the small table with a cigar smoldering in an ashtray. Green and his men sat down at the vacant table, pushing all the drinks to the far side of the table, dousing the cigar in one of the glasses.

All eyes were on the intruding four as the music stopped and the dancers spoke to one another in muffled tones.

"You sittin' in my seat, boy!" a large black man bellowed as he towered over Green's table.

"That so? Don't see your name on the table there, boy," one of Green's men said, with the emphasis on "boy".

"That's my seegar you just doused, too," the black bellowed. "You must be playing with a short deck, whitey. Now, why don't you get your porcelain-white ass outta here while you still in one piece?" He leaned down. "Unless you want me to cut you from ear to ear where you sit," he said through gritted teeth.

The man grabbed a handful of the black man's balls and squeezed and raised his hand at the same time, sending the black man sprawling back onto the dance floor, knocking down several people in the process.

As if in choreographed motion, everyone in the bar formed a circle around the men at the table, murmuring protests to each other. "Guess we gotta teach these boys a lesson," one of the blacks said, overturning a table as he charged towards Green's table.

In that second, Green and his three friends pulled back their coats and each man drew an automatic weapon in one hand and a sawed-off shotgun in the other.

"You boys don't know the name of the game," one said, kicking over their own table, sending it rolling towards the crowd of stunned blacks. The crowd was momentarily shocked into silence as Green's men started randomly shooting fixtures, mirrors and ceiling tiles with their sawed-off shotguns, splattering debris over the people while holding their automatic weapons on the crowd. The bartender made a move to retrieve something from under the counter and was instantly dropped by a shotgun blast by one of Green's men.

That started the crowd screaming for the door, knocking each other down in the process. Only Carlo remained sitting quietly at his table, his two black women having previously departed.

"And how about you?" Green asked, putting his automatic weapon under Carlo's chin.

"Do you know who I am?" Carlo asked, with a quiet air of arrogance.

"I think so. You're Carlo Carleone, the nigger lover. We've got a special treat for you, boy. When we get through with you, not even one of those black whores will want to touch you. On your feet!"

* * * *

Macaffe got in touch with Murray and relayed the conversation that Thompson had had with Francisco Regalado. "I want you to get right over there and interview him," Macaffe said. "You never know, you could get lucky. He may be the key into the Cartel that you're looking for."

* * * *

Christian Murray met Thompson and introduced himself as Tom Miller, sent directly from the head office of DEA in Washington to deal with Francisco Regalado, the man said to have a direct contact with the Colombian cartel.

Thompson led Murray to the interrogation room where Regalado was being held. "Mr. Regalado, this is Mr. Tom Miller," Thompson said, admitting him into the interrogating room. "He's here, straight from the top. Washington sent him down just to work with you on this one. He's in charge of dealing with the Cartel drug imports into this country. You got a story, Washington says he's the man to tell it to."

He nodded to Murray with a wink. "Here's his file, Mr. Miller," he said, then left the room.

Murray took the file, then shook Francisco's hand. "Why don't we go into one of the vacant offices?" he said, leading Francisco in that direction. "You'll will be much more comfortable there. We can talk undisturbed. Coffee?"

Once they were settled, Murray got right down to business. "So, Mr. Regalado," he said, reading the file. "It looks as if you haven't been in this country too long, and already you're into dealing cocaine. I see by Mr. Thompson's notes here that you were born in Medellin, Colombia. Why don't we start there? Tell me about Medellin."

Regalado shrugged his shoulders. "There's not much to tell. My family was poor, and we lived in the poorer section of town."

"And this is where you met this...Molina Marquez?" Murray urged, reading notes from the file.

"Yes. Well, his name was Juan at that time."

"Juan. When did he change his name from Juan to Molina?"

Francisco relayed the events of the death of Molina's family and how he had taken on his father's name when they were killed.

"His family was killed by one of the Cartel? I don't get it. How is it you think he's now a member of the Cartel when you say he was born in the poor village?" Murray's interest in Regalado's story had just decreased markedly. This was either a man who had obviously been taken in by a cousin with an active imagination or who was fabricating a story to get protection from some drug dealer. Either way, he didn't see how there could be anything of value here.

Murray rose to go. "I'm a very busy man, Mr. Regalado. If someone is after you for an unpaid drug bill, as I believe you told Mr. Thompson, then you've already given us enough reason to protect you. We'll automatically do that by putting you in jail for selling drugs. If what you say is true, that you've been selling cocaine, by all rights we should deport you back to Medellin where you came from."

"No. Wait! You don't understand," Francisco panicked. His face was distorted as he looked around as if seeking a place to hide. "My life is in danger! He's going to kill me. You have to protect me," he pleaded. "I'll do anything."

"Including making up a story that your poverty stricken cousin is a member of the Medellin Cartel? Come now, Mr. Regalado. We Americans may appear to be slow and inefficient to you sophisticated drug dealers, but we're not as dumb as we appear. Even I know that one doesn't just rise up from the depths of despair and become one of the most powerful men in Colombia, especially in Medellin. It just isn't done."

"Please, Mr. Miller. You don't understand. I'll do anything. Just don't send me back to Colombia."

"That's not up to me. The courts and immigration department will decide what to do with you. In the meantime, you'll be safe and secure in jail, at least for the time being," Murray needled him.

He returned Francisco Regalado to the interrogation room, where an officer was waiting to take him back to jail.

Murray called Washington to report on Macaffe's golden find.

"Anything there?" Macaffe asked with interest.

"Just a scared drug dealer. He claims he owes

some drug dealer money and now he's afraid they're going to kill him for it."

"No! Do they do things like that?" Macaffe laughed.

"Not as often as I would like. Anyway, I don't think there's anything there. He had some cock-and-bull story about being a cousin of one Molina Marquez, a boy he knew when they lived in Medellin—in the poor section of the city, no less.

"Then this Molina, whose name was Juan—changed his name when the Cartel killed his family—he suddenly became rich and a member of the Cartel himself."

"Sounds a little off the wall to me. Is that he best he could come up with?"

"I say give the lying bastard to immigration and send him back to Colombia. Let his cousin have him. One less scumbag dealer to contend with. Anything else worthy of our attention?"

"That's about it. Sorry to get you down there, but it seemed like a good lead at the time," Macaffe apologized.

Murray started to hang up.

"Oh, wait!," Macaffe said. "There is one further development. I understand from the grapevine that Alfredo Carleone's brother has been kidnapped. We've got a special team on it, so stay away from that case for the time being."

"This has the odor of a Macaffe cover-up," Murray commented. "You sure you aren't cooking up something just to keep me off their asses?"

"Now, would I do a thing like that?"

"In a heartbeat."

"Well, for the time being, it's off limits for the reason previously stated. You've got your hands full with the 'new deal'".

* * * *

"Before I decide to give you my life in blissful matrimony, I need to know more about the man I'm marrying," TJ Escobar said to Molina as they sat on the verandah after playing tennis one morning. TJ was basking in the sun while Molina sat in the shade of a large umbrella drinking orange juice.

"What do you want to know? My life is an open book."

"Tell me more about your family. You said they were killed in an automobile accident when you were a child—your brother, sister and your parents. How is it you weren't with them at the time?"

"I was playing in a soccer tournament, you see. The games were scheduled to be played in Muzo, and the team left the day before so we could practice. As you may have noticed when you flew into Medellin, this is very hilly country."

"You can say that again. I've never been more frightened in all my life than the day I flew in."

"They were in an old automobile, driving around one of those sharp curves, when they were met head-on by an old truck carrying sheep. It was a terrible wreck. The car was smashed like an accordion," Molina lied. "The whole family was killed. I guess I was lucky," he said, looking somewhat somber.

"Poor baby," TJ sympathized. "It must have been an ugly experience."

"You cannot imagine."

"And your family left you all this?"

"No. Not exactly. Obtaining this villa was a combination of luck and opportunity," he hedged. "But that's a story for another day. How about some lunch?"

TJ pressed the point. "The fields that you drove

me by out in the country. What is it you raise there? You seem to have so many workers."

"I raise coca plants. The leaves are used for medicinal purposes."

"Is it necessary to have the fields so heavily guarded? I mean, way out in the country, away from civilization and all those men with guns and stuff."

"The one thing you will learn about Medellin is that although it is a beautiful place to live, it can also be a violent place, especially against those who have nothing to lose. So many people want to steal your crops. And there are those who envy my wealth and would like to see me fail. If I didn't protect what is mine, we could not live like this." He encompassed the house and all his acreage with a gesture. "You will hear stories that people make up about me," he warned, "but you must know in advance that they are just that, stories. Some people will do anything to get at me—jealous people."

TJ nodded. "And the guards at the gate? Is that for protection, too?"

"As I said, one cannot be too careful. I've had close friends killed because of lack of attention to their welfare. You are never to leave the grounds without either myself or one of the men accompanying you," he said sternly. "That is very important! I would never forgive myself if something were to happen to you." His voice was one of concern, yet he had a stern tone to emphasize the point.

"You scare me when you talk like that."

"It's just one of the facts of life in Colombia. This is not America. In Colombia, one must be cautious and protect what is theirs. It is nothing to be frightened of. One just needs to be watchful. Now then, about that lunch..."

* * * *

Molina J. Marquez and Terry Jane Escobar were married the following month. The ceremony took place on the grounds of the villa, next to the swimming pool and tennis courts. Molina was dressed in a white suit with a flaming red floral tie. Terry Jane wore a soft, flowing cotton dress with a plunging neck-line that showed off not only her exquisite tan, but a delicate portion of her chest. A strand of pearls given to her by Molina accented her golden skin.

All the dignitaries and people of wealth in Medellin were invited to attend the ceremony. Although they had not been introduced as such, TJ knew the members of the Cartel even when they were introduced as business associates by Molina. He was careful not to mention what their business was, nor did he elaborate on his relationship with them. For all outward appearances, he had no knowledge that his guests were members of the Cartel.

TJ played along with the ruse. She made it a point to remember the Cartel members' wives and families, however. Although they all seemed happy, it was obvious that the wives were subservient to the whims of their husbands. *A trait that will not come over me,* she mused to herself as she watched with interest. *One day, this may be all mine,* she thought to herself as she looked over the throng of guests. She knew it would be important to retain a certain degree of strength and respect, especially since she was a woman.

Although the prevailing mood was one of celebration and gaiety, there was an underlying tone of mass security, as the perimeter of the grounds was dotted with somber men in suits wielding automatic weapons. Their faces betrayed any attempt at frivolity as their eyes constantly surveyed not only the grounds and the guests, but each other, as each member of the Cartel had provided their own security. TJ refrained from asking her husband the obvious, knowing that the answer would be anything but factual.

The music was light and gay, provided by local musicians.

The wine was from the hills of Colombia and flowed freely. A pig and calf were barbecued on a rotating spit, and Molina's guests and his men were treated to the finest party they had ever attended.

Molina was proud as he displayed his new bride with honor. TJ surprised him by being a gracious host to his guests.

"Are you planning on going to the United States for the World Cup?"" one of the men from the Cartel asked Molina while TJ was holding onto his arm.

"I would love to, but you know how travel can be a problem when you go to the United States," he said with a guarded look.

"They will have no reason to detain you," the man assured Molina. "Our business is legal here in Colombia," he asserted, as if addressing a jury of his peers.

"I know that, and you know that, but do they?"

"Hugo Garcia made several trips to the States before his demise. You remember Garcia, don't you?" he asked, elbowing Molina.

Molina responded with a weak smile, not wanting to discuss the matter any further, lest his new wife start asking questions about topics which he had no desire to discuss.

"A trip to the States would be nice," TJ interjected. "You've never been to my country, have you?"

Molina shook his head. "Sadly, no."

"Well, then, we must go. Some of the World Cup soccer games are being held at Stanford University. That's just south of San Francisco, in California. We could take in the games and the city of San Francisco at the same time. You haven't eaten until you've eaten at Scoma's on Fisherman's Wharf. Their crab Louie is the best."

She shook his arm like a child. "What do you say? It would make a great honeymoon."

"All right. If you say so," he conceded with a smile. "I have a cousin in San Francisco that I need to clear up some unfinished business with, anyway. I could kill several birds with one stone," he said with a faraway look in his eye, mentally toying with the word "kill".

"Good. Then it's settled. When can we leave?"

"My, you are the ambitious one. Let's get through this day first," he said, taking her arm and leading her to another guest.

Chapter Twenty-one

Green and his men drove Carlo Carleone to a wooded area on the outskirts of town. Carlo was beginning to be frightened, although he couldn't believe that anyone would have the nerve to capture a member of the Carleone family, especially if they knew who they were dealing with. And he made sure they were aware of that fact.

"Do you know who you are fucking with?" he spat angrily when they shoved him into the back seat of the black sedan.

"Yeah. A nigger lover," one of the men said as they pushed him across the seat.

"When my brother finds out what you've done, you're gonna be mincemeat!" Carlo threatened.

"Sure wish you wouldn't scare a body like that," one of the men laughed, slapping Carlo along the side of the head.

"Oh, he'll find out all right," Green said. "When we're good and ready."

They didn't bother to tape his eyes, so Carlo could see where they were going. He could identify the men. In the one sense, he couldn't believe his good fortune, for he fully intended to get revenge when they were through toying with him. On the other hand, it became a source of concern because perhaps one reason they didn't blindfold him was because they didn't care. And if they didn't care, it was either because they were so stupid that they didn't know the difference, or they were going to kill him. He had to think it was the former. They were just a bunch of rednecks, out for a good time at his expense, he thought. Still, it bothered him.

As they drove off the main road and into the woods, Carlo's attitude changed from one of arrogance to nervous anticipation. "All right. Tell me what you clowns want and let me go. If it's money, just tell me how much and I'll try to get it for you." He was scared, but tried to mask his fear with arrogance.

No one responded to his comments.

"Cocaine! That's it. You want cocaine. I can see you're not users, so you must be dealers. How much you looking for? A key?"

"You got nothing I want," Green said as he motioned for the driver to pull into a group of aspen trees.

Carlo's hands had been tied behind his back, so when the car came to a halt the boys in the back seat simply opened the door and pushed him out, rolling him onto the ground.

He looked up as they stood around him like giant redwoods dwarfing a bush in the forest. Suddenly his eyes took on a different cast. He was in the middle of nowhere, with no one to hear or help him. For the first time in his life, he was genuinely scared.

"All right. You made your point. I won't see any more black women again. You have my word. Now, come on, guys, untie these ropes."

"You're right about one thing, jerk. You ain't gonna see any more blacks. Tie him to that tree over there, Joe. Let's see how far he can bend."

Carlo struggled to get free, but the men simply slapped him about his head and body until he stopped struggling. They stood him up facing a sturdy tree, then tied his feet to the base of the tree before bending a tall sapling over until the top nearly touched Carlo's head.

"That should do it," Green said. They then tied Carlo's hands to the top of the sapling. "Okay. Let her go!"

Carlo screamed as the sapling sprung back towards its upward position, stretching Carlo like a rubber band. He screamed in pain as his body was stretched to the limit.

"Let's make an adjustment here," Green said, raising the rope binding his feet up the tree a few feet until they were almost perpendicular to his body. Carlo now hung four feet off the ground in a horizontal position.

"I think this calls for a drink," one of the men said as he broke out a bottle of Jack Daniel's. He took a swig and passed it around. They all laughed as they took turns taunting Carlo by rocking the sapling, which in turn put more pressure on his frail body.

"Care for a swig?" Green said, splashing some of the bourbon over Carlo's face, some of which spilled down his throat, making him cough.

"Now then, how about a few answers?" Green said, twisting Carlo's face towards him by pulling on his hair. "Now that we've got your attention, let's talk about killing feds."

Carlo's eyes looked at Green. "You guys cops?"

Green laughed. "We're hunters, Carlo. And I figure we got ourselves a pig. Bring over some of those dry twigs there, Ben," he said, gesturing with his head. "It's a mite chilly. Don't want our guest here gettin' cold."

Carlo's eyes were as big as his head would ac-commodate as the man piled dry twigs under him.

"What are you guys trying to do?" he asked in a voice, twisting to see under himself. "All right! I'll tell you anything you want. I'm just a flunky. Al makes all the decisions. I just run the girls. I'm nobody," he sobbed.

"Are you telling me that brother Al is the mus-cle and all you do is finger the girls in this opera-tion?"

"Nick. My brother. He was the enforcer, but he got killed by the police a while back. The other guys do all the dirty work. I'm just a..."

He was sobbing so much at this point that Green decided to let him calm down.

"Listen. I can get you money, coke, even real estate if you want. We own lots of hotels. I'll get you one," Carlo said eagerly. "Just cut me down!"

"And how are you going to do all this if you're just a nigger-lovin' pussy-getter? Think your brother is going to trust you to get us anything? Once we let you go, all we'll get will be a bullet in the head, Mafia style. You're familiar with that tech-nique, aren't you?"

"I never killed anyone," Carlo sobbed. "I'm tell-ing you the truth."

"Who hit Christian Murray?"

Carlo stopped sobbing the moment he heard the name.

Green looked at the other men. "I thought so." He pulled Carlo's head towards him by his hair. "I want answers and I want them now. Who killed Murray and his family?"

"I don't know."

Green hit him hard on the kidneys, making him writhe in pain.

"I don't know," Carlo sobbed. "Al sent Nick to

the hospital to get Murray, but he failed. He got some drunk that they had substituted in his place. I don't know who killed him, honest to God. Al was all pissed because he knew we would get the blame."

Green knew he was telling the truth about Murray's faked death. "Murray's family?" Green pressed, hitting Carlo in the kidneys again.

"Nick! It was Nick. He was only supposed to get Murray, but he messed up and got the family instead. Al was pissed and made him try again when he learned that he was in the hospital. That's when the cops got him. That's all, I swear. I had nothing to do with it. I wouldn't hurt a fly."

* * * *

"Al! There's some chick on the phone. She says they got Carlo," the man said, holding his hand over the receiver of the cellular phone as he stuck his head into Alfredo Carleone's office.

Alfredo grabbed the phone. "This is Mr. Carleone, Carlo's brother. Who's this?"

The woman identified herself as one of Carlo's girls. He could tell by her voice that she was black. She relayed the circumstances where the four men had charged into the Liedo Bar and started a fight with the customers, then took Carlo by force. She had seen them drive away in a dark sedan, but couldn't get the license plate number, as it had been covered with mud.

"Stupid jerk! If I told him once I told him a dozen times, lay off the niggers. Sooner or later he's either going to get his throat or his pecker cut messin' with those women."

"Domini! Round up the boys and get over to the Liedo and see what you can find out. Don't come back until you've got my stupid brother."

* * * *

"Why don't we get this brother of yours on the phone?" Green said. "I'd like to talk to him." He flipped his pocket cellular phone open with a flick of his wrist. "The number, if you please?"

Carlo told him the number and Green punched it in. It rang twice before Alfredo Carleone answered.

"Yeah! What you got?" he asked, expecting to be speaking to one of his men.

"I got someone who wants to talk to you," Green said.

"Who's this?" Carleone demanded.

"Your next partner," Green said, jamming the phone next to Carlo's mouth.

"Al! They got me! You gotta get me outta here. They're going to kill me. They got me stretched on this—"

Green jerked the phone away from Carlo and hit him in the kidneys again, making him scream.

"You got the picture, big boy?"

"You're dead meat, whoever you are," Carleone growled through clenched teeth. "If I don't get my brother back within the hour, I'll hunt you down, and when I find you I'll cut you into tiny pieces and personally feed you to the fish."

"Didn't your mother ever tell you to be nice to strangers?" Green asked. "Now, I'll tell you what. You're going to meet me at midnight. You know the Liedo Bar? Be there at 12:00 sharp, and come alone."

He snapped the cellular phone shut. "Well, that should take care of the big fish. Now for the guppy."

"Tell me everything you know about your operation," he said to Carlo calmly. "And don't leave out a single detail."

"I thought you just made a deal with Al."

"I just told him to meet me. I didn't hear anything about a deal, did you guys?"

They looked at Carlo as if he was their next meal.

Carlo looked frightened, but said nothing.

"Nothing to say? Mark. Don't we have a gallon of gasoline in the trunk of the car? Would you be so kind as to retrieve it for me?"

"Wha—what are you going to do? I thought we had a deal," Carlo said, his lips trembling. He was trying to control himself, but was having difficulty maintaining any degree of composure.

"The only deal we have is that we're going to get answers outta you, or we'll have a weenie roast right here in the forest. And guess who's the weenie?"

Mark returned with a can of gasoline. Green swished the can around. "Hmm. Nearly full. This should be enough," he said, taking the top off the can.

"Now, wait a minute!" Carlo screamed as terror swept over his face.

Green poured a portion of the can over the top of Carlo's body while he screamed. "Anything! I'll tell you anything you want. Just cut me down and get that stuff away from me!"

Green poured the remaining amount of gas onto the pile of twigs beneath Carlo, then took out a cigar and lit it.

Carlo watched and screamed in horror as the flame from the discarded match seemed too close to the gasoline.

"Now then," Green said, twisting the cigar in his mouth, making the end glow red. "Tell me about the family business."

Carlo rattled off information about prostitution, which was his portion of the business, and what he knew about the drugs and numbers.

"You mentioned hotels. What's that all about?"

"We own about 10 hotels—major chain hotels that are losing money. Al funnels our money through the hotels, then reports the income to the IRS so the income is legitimate."

"In other words, you launder your drug, numbers and prostitution money through empty hotels?"

"Yeah. He buys them for a song, because they're losing money hand over fist, then fills the hotels up, on paper. It's a legit business."

"Whose brainstorm was that? Brother Al's?"

"He's the brains of the outfit. He thinks up all the schemes," Carlo said with pride.

"Well, it's a shame he didn't think of this one," Green said contemptuously, tossing his cigar into the gas-soaked pile of twigs. "It's time to go, men."

The flames started to lick through the twigs as they walked away, leaving Carlo hanging between the trees, screaming.

As the black sedan pulled away, Green looked into his rear-view mirror. Carlo was writhing as the flames had begun to lick at his clothes.

* * * *

Green had parked across the street from an abandoned warehouse and stayed in his car as he watched his men set the explosives inside the building.

"This is more fun than pushing over outhouses with the old lady inside," one of the men laughed as he closed the car door.

"I take it we're all set?" Green asked as he

picked up his cellular phone.

"Ready for Freddy."

Green dialed. The pay phone outside the Liedo rang a couple times before an irritated voice answered. "Carleone!"

"I like a man who's on time."

"Where's my brother?" Carleone snapped angrily.

"You'll meet him in a few moments. Do you know the industrial area where the old steel factory used to be?"

"Yeah. I can find it."

"Just across from the old steel foundry is a metal building with a round roof. You'll find what you want just inside the door."

"This better not be some kind of trick," Carleone warned.

"You have me shaking in my boots, brother," Green drawled. "Better hurry now, before I change my mind."

The phone line went dead.

"Phase two is about to be concluded," Green said. "So much for the Carleone dynasty. Isn't this better than wearing sheets and hanging niggers?" He laughed, slapping the man next to him on his knee. "Pass the bottle."

"It's fun, all right, but what's this all got to do with the cause?"

"It's all part of the big picture, my man. Seek, destroy and conquer. If we eliminate crooks with guns, then there will be no need for gun control."

"I knew we elected the right man for President," the guy replied, taking a swig of whiskey.

Just then a black limo pulled up in front of the metal building with a circular roof. A lone occupant exited the back seat, looked around, then cautiously walked towards the metal building.

"Looks like our package has arrived," Green said, picking up a metal box. He slowly pulled up the antenna and flipped up the protective shield covering the red button.

Alfredo Carleone walked into the building calling his brother's name. The building exploded into flames, blowing pieces of tin into the air, collapsing what was left of the building.

"I guess that eliminates the Carleone clan," Green said. "Hope that makes Murray happy."

Chapter Twenty-two

Dominic DiGivanni was correlating pieces on what he had come to refer to as the NRA-President's list. The $2 million he had lost in his drug deal correlated with the $12 million that Alfredo Carleone said he had lost at Easter. He had ably verified another loss with some local black thugs that he had learned were dealing in the cocaine trade. In each instance, not only were the drugs and money lost, but everyone involved had been killed—each in a different manner but killed, nonetheless. The date of the killings and the amount of money lost coincidentally appeared on the NRA-President's bank list, each up to 50 percent.

He had promised Don Alfredo Carleone that he would get back to him if he found any correlation. Now he was sure he was onto something. He dialed the number that Carleone had given him, one that rang through to his direct line.

There was no answer.

He re-dialed the second number, which he had said would ring through to the main house. A strong male voice answered the phone, stating that Mr. Carleone had gone out on personal business the previous night and had not returned. He sounded concerned, but gave no indication that he knew when he would return.

* * * *

"There's some serious money changing hands here," Dominic said to Joe Mann the next day as he compared the list that Joe had given him alongside the drug losses that he had confirmed. "And this has all taken place within the past few months," he said, pointing to hit dates and bank deposits.

"I want to know who these people are. Can you find that out for me?"

"I can pull up the federal directory of all government employees on the computer and run down their names," Joe told him. "It'll take time, considering all the agencies I've got to cover. This reference to NRA should pose a problem, though."

"How's that?"

"NRA? The National Rifle Association."

"That doesn't make sense. What would the National Rifle Association be doing in government banking business?" DiGivanni shook his head.

"The bank account says 'NRA: Presidential election contributions'. Maybe they're matching funds or something."

"Or maybe they are the ones hitting us and taking our drugs and money. That would make more sense. They hit us, keep the drugs for themselves and take the dough, putting half in their pocket and donating the other half as presidential contributions for personal favors."

"Why give all that dough to an election campaign? Only a fool would do a thing like that."

"Or an organization that doesn't want a gun control initiative to pass."

Mann and DiGivanni looked at one another seriously. "We could be onto something that goes all the way to the top. The question is, what do we do with it? Who's going to believe us when we tell them that our President is using drug money to get re-elected? They'll probably applaud him for squashing drug deals, and he'll get elected by a landslide for creativity."

"If I were a bettin' man," Joe nodded thoughtfully, "I'd say you're right."

"So now the question is, what do we do with what we think we know?"

"Maybe the answer lies with Green and Macaffe. Let's find out who they are. There's a significant piece to this puzzle that we don't have—from the looks of these figures, a $40-million piece. At least now we know who some of the players are."

"Except for Green and Macaffe. Let me know the minute you've got something. Call, day or night."

* * * *

Murray was seated at his desk with Grover planning his next move against the Mafia and the Cartel when his fax machine squealed, indicating that there was an incoming message. The message was short but succinct:

Molina Marquez will attend World Cup in
Palo Alto. To arrive on Pan Am 647—Tu.
TJ

"Good news?" Grover asked when he saw the look on Murray's face.

"An old friend. Actually a young old friend." He smiled. "Things are looking up, Grover. Things are definitely taking a turn for the better."

Just then the phone rang. It was Macaffe.

"That deal regarding Don Carleone?'"

Murray just listened without responding as the

name Carleone made his mind think Mafia, then visualized three caskets next to mounds of fresh dirt.

"You can cross him off your list. The matter has been taken care of."

"What do you mean, "The matter has been taken care of?'" Murray asked, irritated.

"Watch the news tonight, you'll see," Macaffe said sarcastically, using Christian's own words against him.

"Fuck the news, Mac. If you got something to say, spit it out."

"One of our operatives coerced the Carleone boys to talk. He admitted to killing Jana and the kids," Macaffe said with a tone of remorse. "They also admitted to trying to get you while you were in the hospital. Thought you would be happy to know."

Murray was silent for a moment. "Tell me the rest." His voice had a tone of reserved irritation.

"They were taken out," Macaffe said simply. "The Carleone family no longer exists. That is to say, the Carleone Mafia family no longer exists," he was quick to add, so Murray wouldn't think that their families had been eliminated, too.

"How exactly did it happen?"

"As I said, watch the late news," was all Macaffe said. It was obvious that he wasn't talking, for whatever the reason.

"And who, did you say, was the operative?" Murray pressed.

"I didn't."

"Well?"

"Well what?"

"Damn it, Macaffe. Stop playing games." Murray ground out, his hand tightening on the receiver of the phone. "I asked you a straightforward question. Who was the operative?"

"I'm sorry, I can't tell you that."

"You go behind my back and interrogate the thugs that admitted to killing Jana and the kids, and now you tell me that you've had them eliminated and you can't tell me who did it? Who the hell do you think you're talking to?" He was furious.

"You were too close to the case," Macaffe rationalized. "We needed someone less...involved."

"That's old news. You already told me the why, now I want to know the who." By this time his knuckles were white.

"I'm sorry, Chris. It's a delicate situation. It goes far deeper than I can discuss on the phone and is considerably more delicate than you could ever imagine."

"Bullshit!" was all he could say. Murray knew the drill, but he didn't like it. He slammed the phone down without further comment, conveying his displeasure to Macaffe.

That night, on the national news, there were pictures of a blown-up metal building where it was reported that a Mafia boss had been killed. The follow-up story was about the mobster's brother, Carlo Carleone, telling of him dangling from the trunk of a tree, his body burned beyond recognition. They were able to identify the corpse only by dental records, the reporter had said.

Authorities attributed the death of the two brothers to a gang-related drug war, the commentator said.

That same evening, Dominic DiGivanni sat, stoic-faced, watching the same newscast. The circle of a select few was getting smaller, and it made him uncomfortable.

* * * *

Molina and TJ arrived at San Francisco International Airport on Pan Am's flight 647. They didn't notice a lone figure dressed in acid-washed blue jeans, tennis shoes, a white Stanford sweatshirt and a flight jacket standing next to the wall by the luggage carousel. They were accompanied by a tall man dressed in a white suit, his long black hair combed straight back tied in a ponytail. His eyes shifted from side to side as he led the pair to the luggage carousel.

They gathered their luggage, then headed to the outer concourse, where a white limo was waiting for them. As they pulled away, the figure in jeans waved to a parked black van to pick him up.

* * * *

Molina's first stop was Fisherman's Wharf. TJ was dying to have lunch at Scoma's. The food was everything she had said. Molina was fascinated with America's fixation with football. Every wall of the restaurant was adorned with pictures of Joe Montana and the '49ers football team. "In Colombia, there would be pictures of soccer players." He smiled. "I don't know how you Americans can get excited about a sport that plays only a few seconds at a time, then rests before the next play. In soccer, the action is constant, non-stop."

"Kinda like some men I know," TJ smiled. She enjoyed boosting his ego, although he certainly didn't need it. It was like a mind game she played with him, to see how much she could manipulate his mind without him being aware that she was doing it.

"After we eat, how would you like to walk down to Pier 39 and look around? There are loads of interesting shops and unusual things to see. They have these street performers—"

"I have a little unfinished business to attend to with my cousin who lives nearby," he interrupted. "Why don't you do your shopping and I'll meet you back at the hotel at, say, 5:00?"

"Oh. That means you won't get to see everything," she whined, tugging at his coat sleeve. "I do so want you to see the wharf."

"We'll have plenty of time to see everything. We don't have to be at Monterey for two days, so we'll have ample opportunity to visit your Fisherman's Wharf," he said, patting her on her back like a small child.

"You promise?"

"I promise. Now, can I take you someplace before I leave?"

"No. I think I'll just walk around, if you don't mind—sort of re-Americanize myself, if you know what I mean."

"See you at 5:00, then," he said, bending down to kiss her lightly before leaving. "I'll take Rene with me if you don't need him."

Neither Molina nor Rene paid any attention to the man in jeans and a white Stanford sweatshirt throwing what was left of a cold sandwich into the garbage as they left Scoma's.

Molina instructed the driver of the limo to take them to Francisco's condo, which, as it turned out, was a mere four blocks away, overlooking Fisherman's Wharf and the bay. The limo parked under the porte-cochere of the condo and waited while Molina and his bodyguard entered the building.

The black van parked in the visitor's parking area and waited. After Molina went up the elevator Murray entered the lobby and watched as the elevator dial indicated that the car had stopped at the eleventh floor. He looked at the directory. One of the tenants on that floor was Francisco and Gloria Regalado.

Murray rushed out of the building and sped back to the wharf, just in time to see TJ round the corner from where the street vendors had set up shop on the sidewalk near Scoma's. She was walking towards Pier 39. He drove to the Franciscan restaurant parking lot and waited.

He fell into step behind her until she paused by the wooden fence fronting on the marina to watch the sea gulls and sea lions barking as they fought for position to sun themselves on the ramp.

"Have you enjoyed your vacation in Colombia so far?" Murray asked with a hint of sarcasm in his voice. He leaned on the railing with his foot resting on the first rung as he looked out at the seals.

TJ shot the man next to her a sharp glance, then quickly looked around as her face became flushed. "Murray! What are you doing here?" she asked through clenched teeth, still looking straight ahead. A sly smile crept across her lips.

"I thought you invited me," he said, nudging her with his hip. "Don't you remember?"

"Not exactly."

"What about that fax? Any prudent man would have taken that as an invitation."

"I didn't expect to see you at the airport," she said jokingly.

"I thought I was doing a good job at being conspicuous."

"You stood out like a sore thumb."

"Your husband and his bodyguard didn't see me."

"With me around, they have eyes only for beauty," she said, laughing.

"Speaking of eyes, I noticed he went to the towers where Francisco Regalado lives. What can you tell me about that?"

"Nothing."

"Nothing? I thought you were his wife."

"Listen, he hasn't even told me that he's a member of the Cartel and raising cocaine. He thinks I think he's raising coca leaves for medicinal purposes."

"Are you that dumb?"

"He thinks so."

"I was surprised when I got your fax saying he was coming to the games. Doesn't he know that he's walking on thin ice here?"

"Soccer games cloud all Colombians' reasoning. Do you know that they've actually been known to kill an official for making a call that goes against one of the Cartel's teams, especially if the call results in their losing the game?"

"They take their fun and games seriously."

"You'd think serious if you saw his villa. It would take a small army to even get on the grounds, let alone get to Molina. In the short time I've been there, I've learned that he's got the police wired, the judges so scared that they never convict anyone from his army irrespective of the crime, and the rest of the Cartel thinks he's Napoleon without a horse."

Murray looked around before standing. "I've got to get going. I need to talk to this Gloria Regalado to see what Molina is up to, as long as you don't know," he said, looking at her. "We've had her husband in jail for the past month. He claims your husband wants him dead and asked for protection. So we arrested his ass," he laughed.

She looked into his eyes. "Like I said. He won't tell me shit. I might as well be barefoot and pregnant."

"See you at the games," he said, starting to walk away.

"What's the plan?" she asked. There was a hint of regret in her voice.

Murray studied her pretty face. *She's matured since she went to Colombia,* he thought to himself. "After I find out more about your love's connection with Regalado, I'll be able to answer that question. You'll know when I know, if you're not barefoot and pregnant, that is." The last comment had a bite to its tone.

"I hate a smartass."

"Peace," he said, holding up two fingers in a "V" sign, then walked back to the van.

* * * *

Murray drove back to the towers just as the limo was pulling away. He debated following him before snapping open his cellular phone. "Grover. You there?"

"Right, Chief."

"Follow the limo. I'm going to see what our Colombian friends are up to. It would appear that I may have overlooked an important piece of the puzzle by ignoring this Regalado fellow when he turned himself in for protection. Check with me when they reach their destination. And, Grover—"

"Yes, Chief?"

"Be careful. This man is one of the most feared people in Colombia."

"We're not in Colombia."

"Just the same."

* * * *

Gloria Regalado only partially opened the door, keeping the door chain in place as she peered through the opening. "Yes. Can I help you?" she asked tentatively, peering past Murray to see if he was alone.

Murray identified himself as Tom Miller, DEA agent from Washington as he opened his wallet, displaying his gold DEA badge and new photo ID. "Your husband came to see me a while back, asking for protection from his cousin, a Molina Marquez. I just saw Marquez leave the premises and thought maybe we should talk."

She hesitated for a moment before opening the door. She was a short woman, dressed in shorts and a faded blue sweatshirt. Her jet-black hair was swept off her face, held back by a blue scarf. *She's very attractive,* Murray thought. Bright, too, he guessed by looking into her eyes, which seemed to dance with brilliance.

He decided that being forthright and upfront was the best approach, given the circumstances. "I should tell you that since your husband came to see us—you know that he came to see us for protection, don't you?"

She nodded, but said nothing. *A smart woman,* Murray thought. *She knows when to talk and when to listen.*

"Well, as I started to say, since Mr. Regalado came to us asking for protection from his cousin, we've been keeping tabs on this fellow Molina Marquez. We know that he's in the country, and now that he's been here to see you, I thought you might need our help." *May as well lay all our cards on the table,* he thought. *There's no time to pussyfoot around.*

She nodded. "He was here just a few minutes ago," she said, looking tired and apprehensive.

"Do you know what he wanted?" He needed to know if Francisco had been honest with his wife.

"He wanted Francisco."

"Did he say why?"

"Apparently Francisco owes him money—a lot of money, and Francisco is..." She didn't finish her sentence. "His cousin just said he should get in touch with him as soon as possible."

"But he didn't say what he wanted?"

"No," she lied. "From the tone of his voice, I got the impression that it was serious. He scared me, the way he looked at me when he was talking. He left a note saying where he could be contacted while he was in San Francisco," she said, showing Murray the handwritten note.

"The Mark Hopkins. Figures," he said somewhat to himself. "He's a very dangerous man, Mrs. Regalado. You would do well to avoid having further contact with him if you can. You may consider staying with a friend until he leaves town. Here's my card. If he does get in touch with you, please call me immediately."

As soon as Murray had left, Gloria Regalado called the holding pen where Francisco was being detained.

"Francisco! Your cousin was just here looking for you. Then a man from the government with a badge came afterwards. I'm scared, Francisco. These men scare me. Isn't there anything you can do? Can't you get your cousin to leave you alone?" She was in tears, trying to maintain her composure.

The phone line was silent for a few moments. When Francisco spoke, it was with carefully chosen words deliberately spoken.

"Listen to me, Gloria. The court has set my bail at $25 thousand. There is $5 thousand hidden behind the large red dictionary. Take the money and find a bail bondsman and get him to put up my bail immediately. He will charge you $2,500 and ask you to sign a paper securing our condo. Do it! When you've done this, meet me at the detention hall as soon as possible. Now go!"

* * * *

Three hours later, Gloria Regalado was at the entrance of the jail waiting to pick up Francisco. He drove her straight back to the condo, stopping under the porte-cochere to let her off. It was late in the day and the sun was fading behind the hills, coloring the sky in hues of orange and purple.

"Go upstairs and pack whatever you can get into two suitcases," he said nervously, his words spoken so fast that they ran over one another. "Be ready to leave the minute I return. Have the suitcases waiting for me in the lobby. Don't bother with things like dishes and stuff. Hurry," he said, waving her out of the car with his hands.

"You're scaring me, Francisco. What are you going to do?"

"Save our lives," was all he said as he drove away.

Gloria was left standing alone, feeling scared. She was crying silently.

* * * *

"The bird of paradise just settled into the nest," Grover said to Murray over his portable phone. "Shall I stay here or return home?"

"I see no reason to hang around the Mark. I suspect they're in for the evening. It's been a long day since they left Colombia. I suspect they'll want to retire soon. May as well go home and get yourself some grub. Check back in the morning."

* * * *

Francisco pulled into the parking garage of the Mark Hopkins Hotel and found the entrance to the elevator. He backed his car into the yellow passenger loading zone and dialed information on his car phone. The operator gave him the number of the Mark Hopkins Hotel.

"Mark Hopkins Hotel. How may I direct your call?"

"Molina Marquez, please."

"One moment, please."

"Mr. Marquez's suite," a male voice answered.

"Give me Molina."

"Who is calling?"

"His cousin. Francisco."

There was a long pause.

"Cousin! I'm so glad that you have called." Molina's voice was guarded. "I believe we have some unfinished business to attend to. $500 thousand?"

"Yes. I am ready. I apologize for the delay. Can you meet me at my place?"

"But of course. When would it be convenient for you?"

"I have the money now. I dislike having so much cash on hand. Would you mind coming now, if it's not too late?"

"Not at all. I'll be right there."

Francisco rolled the window of his car down and swung the sun visor over to the driver's side so no one could see his face if they were to look in his direction.

A few moments later a bell rang, announcing that the elevator had reached the parking garage.

Francisco rested his automatic weapon on the frame of the door with just the barrel sticking out.

He closed one eye as he looked down the sights.

He squeezed the trigger lightly.

He knew he would have only a moment before they would see him. Molina's bodyguard would certainly have a weapon to protect his boss. A moment. That's all he needed, he thought as he squinted down the sight.

The elevator doors opened.

Francisco held his breath and squeezed the trigger tighter.

At that moment, four young women emerged from the elevator, talking and giggling amongst themselves.

Francisco released his breath. He had almost killed four innocent women. Beads of perspiration broke out on his forehead as he wiped it with the back of his hand.

A few more moments passed and the bell rang again. This time the doors opened to the figures of his cousin Molina and his bodyguard. They emerged from the elevator without a thought of danger.

Francisco gritted his teeth as he emptied the magazine on the pair, then sped out of the garage without stopping to see if he had killed his cousin or not. It was but a matter of minutes before he screeched to a halt in front of the towers, where his wife was waiting with four suitcases and several garment bags.

"I thought I told you two suitcases," he barked, as he threw them into the trunk and over the back seat. A moment later they were screaming down Van Ness towards Highway 101.

Molina Marquez and his bodyguard lay at the base of the elevator with its doors banging against their bodies, trying to close.

Chapter Twenty-three

Dominic DiGivanni was watching the 6:00 news when he saw the image of the two bodies lying in a pool of blood in the parking garage of the Mark Hopkins Hotel. The news commentator said the men had been identified as Molina Marquez, a drug czar from Colombia and a member of the Cartel, and his bodyguard. His wife, who had accompanied him, was not available for comment. "It would appear that this slaying was drug related," the commentator concluded.

The camera then cut to a handful of women marching in front of the hotel carrying signs that read, "WAG (Women against Guns)" and "Down with Guns and Drugs."

The news commentator closed by saying that this was the second drug-related slaying in the past month, again graphically showing pictures of Alfredo and Carlo Carleone where they had been slain.

The two incidents seemed too coincidental for DiGivanni. "The tie is too close to home," he said aloud as he switched off the television. He retrieved the list from his desk again. He had to have more answers. Time was running out.

* * * *

Murray was just toweling off after taking a hot shower when he heard the news on his bathroom radio that a member of the Medellin Cartel and his bodyguard had been executed at the Mark Hopkins Hotel. The newscaster said there were no witnesses and no immediate suspects.

His first thought was that Francisco Regalado had killed them, but he was in custody. Then he thought of TJ. Could she have been caught in the fire fight and been killed, too? The news hadn't said anything about her.

He was about to dial Grover when the phone rang. "Did you hear the news?" Mark asked.

"Just now. Any idea how it was done?"

"My money goes on Francisco Regalado."

"Can't be. He's in jail."

"Not anymore. His wife made bail this afternoon. I took the liberty of going by their condo before calling. They're gone, boss—lock, stock and underwear. They apparently left in a big hurry, because all their furniture, dishes and personal items are still in the condo."

"The woman too?"

"Both. There's not a stitch of clothing left. I don't think they're comin' back, boss."

"Shit!' Murray hit the ceramic tile with his fist. "I should have listened. I had him in the palm of my hand and let him go. We would have had Marquez in custody today."

"We had no grounds. Look at it on the positive side. At least this way, a member of the Cartel has been eliminated and the drug dealer is runnin' for his life. And the best part is, the job was done and it didn't cost the system a cent."

Murray thought for a moment. "I suppose

you're right. What about TJ—I mean Mrs. Marquez? What of her?"

"Vanished. I would imagine that she's fearful for her life, too, especially now that Marquez is gone. You know, battles over territorial rights, the Cartel and all that."

"Got to run," Murray quickly said. "Put the word out that I need to find her. She's not to be hurt under any circumstances. Understand?" His voice was firm, but had a panicky edge to it, too.

There was silence on the other end of the phone, as if Grover was trying to read between the lines.

"She's family," Murray explained, feeling Grover's hesitation.

When Grover still didn't respond, he added, "She's one of us. Her father worked for Alcohol, Tobacco and Firearms. The mob had a mole inside, and they were tipped off about one of his busts. They laid a trap and killed the whole team." He paused for a moment while the image of what must have happened danced through his mind. "She wanted revenge and was forceful enough to work her way into a position in the system. They found her an inside spot."

"Next to the most powerful man in the Cartel? What a spot."

"It's a long story. When we're old and gray, fishing on the Snake River, I'll fill you in. Meanwhile, go find her!"

* * * *

The next morning the phone rang just as Murray was about to walk out of the door. "TJ?" he anticipated as he ran to pick it up.

"Chris? Macaffe here. We've got a serious development down at the plant in San Francisco. I want you to handle it. Can you be at headquarters in half an hour?"

"I was just walking out the door. What's up?"

"You remember the hit on Manuel La Torre's men earlier this year?"

"TJ's father?"

"Yeah. Well, they think they've got the mole who's been leaking information to the Mafia. His name is Joe Mann."

"Never heard of him."

"He's just a clerk, but apparently he's been taping into our security lines and has been feeding data to the Mafia, for a handsome fee, I would wager. Apparently all those recent Mafia killings have gotten him spooked."

"If he's a weak link to the Mafia and there's fear of a breakdown, he may have good reason."

"Especially if he can be a witness against the Mob," Macaffe added.

"Why pick on me? You've got dozens of agents here who can handle the case."

"You're dead, remember? Only they don't know that in San Francisco. If it calls for a decisive action, a non-existent Tom Miller from Washington could come in handy, if you get my drift."

"Who's in charge?"

"You're to see an agent Larson. He's completely trustworthy and a loyal employee with aspirations for advancement. He'd like your job." He smiled.

"A boot licker."

"Be nice."

"All right. I'll put this guy Mann's balls in the nutcracker and see what develops."

* * * *

Joe Mann appeared to be much younger than Murray had expected. He took him into one of the interview rooms without windows or ears.

Murray was more interested in finding TJ than interviewing a mole who was already in custody, but something told him to take the time to interrogate him. He introduced himself as Tom Miller, showed him his ID, then said, "All right, Mann. I'm short on time here. Tell me what you've got and what you want. And make it snappy," he demanded impatiently.

Mann studied his hands for a few moments without saying anything. He did not meet Murray's eyes.

"Come on, man, I don't have all day!" Murray shouted impatiently. "I didn't come down here to babysit. They can do that in jail."

It was obvious that the boy was scared. *If he's got any knowledge of the Mob, he's got reason,* Murray thought as he studied the young man's face. "All right. I'll get you jump-started," he said sympathetically. "They tell me you've been feeding federal information to someone on the outside. Tell me how you get your information, what you feed and to whom, and maybe I can help save your ass from the firing squad."

"Firing squad!"

"Yeah. In your case, you got two choices. Take your pick. You got the people of the United States for selling secrets to the enemy. They call that treason, I believe—Benedict Arnold and all that, you know? You're up on your US history, I trust? Or we could save the country a ton of money on trials, appeals and prison housing by simply turning you over to your employer. I'm sure they would love to put a bullet through the center of your head," Murray said, twisting his forefinger in the center of Mann's forehead, "just to keep you quiet." He paused, letting the visual image sink in. "Your choice," he said simply, sitting back with his hands folded.

Joe Mann squirmed in his chair, his eyes looking scared. He glanced up at Murray momentarily before putting both elbows on his knees with his head hanging down in desperation.

"You want a lawyer?" Murray asked. "A lawyer will tell you not to say anything. Then, of course, the press will find out that we're holding a man connected with the Mafia. They eat that shit up. Once they learn that you aren't talking they'll just make up some stuff. Publicity sells, you know. I suppose you don't mind your friends and family reading about you in the paper or seeing your picture on TV." He looked at Mann, who was squirming uncomfortably in his chair. "And, of course, they'll want to interview everyone you know, to find out what they know about you. You understand," he said, patting him lightly on the shoulder as if consoling him.

"Since you're not talking, the judge will have no choice but to put you in jail, not that that matters much, because you're going to jail anyway. The only question is, for how long?"

He took out a piece of gum and took his time unwrapping it, giving the boy time to think. "By this time, the Mob will get one of their men to bust someone in the chops and have them thrown in jail. Someone will bribe a jailer to have him share your cell. The next thing you know, you're lying on your bunk with your eyes open, but they won't see nothin'. And they never will. Is that what you want, Joe Mann, employee of the United States Federal Government that's been stealing secrets and selling them to the Mob?"

Joe Mann looked up at Murray with pleading eyes. "Please help me, Mr. Miller. I'm so nervous I don't know what to do!" he said, rubbing his eyes erratically.

"You should have thought of that when you first got in bed with those scumbags," Murray said, gently putting a hand on Mann's shoulder in a fatherly fashion. "Now, if you please, let's start with a name. Who have you been dealing with?" he asked gently.

Mann closed his eyes for a moment, then quietly said, "Dominic DiGivanni."

Murray stared at him. "The Dominic DiGivanni? Of the DiGivanni Mafia family?"

"I guess so. I just know his name. All I know is that he's got a daughter named Virginia."

"How long have you known this Dominic DiGivanni?"

"Since I was in college. His daughter had the hot pants for me, but her father didn't think I was good enough for her, so he offered to pay for my college if I agreed to move out of town."

"You're certainly blasé about it, letting him talk you out of his daughter. Of course, she may not have been worth it," Murray taunted, shaking his head.

"I was a realist. I knew I couldn't make it on my own. When he offered to put me through college plus give me spending money, I took it."

"And when you graduated?"

"He helped me in getting a job with the government working on computers. He said if I would tell him things that would help him in business he would give me a car and a place of my own."

"That's DiGivanni, all right. He gets his hands on your vital organs, and when he wants something all he has to do is squeeze."

Murray paced the room for a few moments, looking at Mann periodically. "Let me guess. He started out asking for little tidbits and eventually got you to feeding him whatever he wanted?"

Mann looked at Murray, but didn't say anything.

"How did you gain access to security files?"

Mann smiled for the first time, obviously satisfied with himself. "I always considered myself a good hacker. I enjoy the challenge. It was a game to me, nothing more."

"A hacker?"

"One who gains access into other people's computers by cracking their entry codes."

"Did it ever occur to you that you may have been giving away security documents, even endangering lives as a result of this 'hacking'?"

"No," Mann admitted softly.

"So, you preferred to hide your head in the sand so long as you got your perks," Murray said angrily. "What sort of things has he been asking you to get for him recently?"

Mann shrugged his shoulders and looked at his hands. "I was just hacking around one night like I usually do when I accidentally gained access to a file that made no sense to me, but I gave it to him anyway."

"And that was?"

"I don't know. It was something that excited Mr. DiGivanni, though. It was a list of moneys deposited into some bank with account numbers and names that he said were the same amounts and dates that he and his friends had stolen from them, as he put it."

A cold chill went down Murray's back.

"He said that he and some of the other families have been hit and they've lost a lot of money, too. He wanted me to see if I could find out who was doing this to him and his friends."

Murray studied Mann's face for a moment. He had no idea what he had stumbled onto, but Mann was obviously a scared young man, fearing for his life. Whatever it was, it had to be important enough to turn himself in and face jail.

"Which brings me around to why you called us—for protection, I believe you said?" Murray looked at Mann square in the face. "That's why you turned yourself in?"

"DiGivanni said some of the people on those lists have been killed," he said. "I was scared that maybe I had gone too far. Mr. DiGivanni said that there's something about that list that's causing people connected to it to die. I figured if that was the case, it would only be a matter of time until something happened to me, too."

"This Dominic DiGivanni—do you know how to get a hold of him?"

"Sure. I just call him when I have something."

"All right. Here's what I want you to do. I want you to call him and tell him that you need to meet with him. Tell him that you've discovered something very important about that list that you feel he would want to know. If he wants to know what it is, say that you can't talk about on it on the phone but it's important enough that you meet with him as soon as possible. Understand?"

He handed Joe Mann the cellular telephone. Mann dialed a number and relayed the message to DiGivanni. A time was set to meet him at Mark's hot dog stand at one o'clock that same day.

* * * *

Murray was standing by the stand eating a hot

dog when DiGivanni walked up, looking around for Mann. Not seeing him, he took a seat on the park bench.

"Buy you a dog?" Murray asked, nonchalantly, holding out his hot dog as he sat down next to him.

DiGivanni looked through him as if he didn't exist.

"I hear that they're excellent. Price is right, too."

"Look! Buzz off, if you don't mind," DiGivanni said curtly, looking harshly at Murray.

"Did we get up on the wrong side of the bed this morning?"

"Look, fella, if it's conversation you're looking for, go feed the pigeons."

"Speaking of pigeons, I spoke to your boy Mann this morning," Murray said as he cracked the top off a can of Pepsi. "Boy. Mann. Sounds like a contradiction of terms, doesn't it?" he said, taking a sip from his drink. "Sure you don't want a dog?" he asked, extending the half-eaten dog under DiGivanni's nose.

DiGivanni continued looking ahead. "Who are you?" he demanded.

"For the time being, let's just say that I'm a go-between. An interested party."

"If it's a cut you're looking for, you've tapped the wrong man," DiGivanni said, opening his overcoat and showing the butt of a revolver.

"You got a permit for that?" Murray asked, nodding towards the weapon. Then he noisily took another sip from the can.

"Why? You a cop?" DiGivanni sneered.

"Close." Murray removed the leather carrier from his vest pocket, where he carried his shield. "Miller, from the DEA." He looked at DiGivanni's startled face as he replaced the case into his breast pocket. "As I said, I was talking to Joe Mann earlier today."

"So, what's that got to do with me?" DiGivanni asked, his voice becoming cold and distant, yet guarded.

"So, that's how it's going to be? Playing fat, dumb and stupid?" Murray finished his can and smashed it before tossing it into a trash receptacle 10 feet away. "Two points," he said, holding up two fingers. "Let me refresh your memory. Joe Mann is the fellow who was dating your daughter, Virginia, and you paid his way through college to get rid of him. Okay so far?"

No response from DiGivanni as he shifted his weight on the bench nervously, looking at the pigeons.

Murray finished his hot dog before continuing. "Then you got him a job working for the Feds. In the computer department. Very clever. Then, the piece d' resistance. You bought him a house and fancy car if he would simply get you a few insignificant pieces of information. Nice touch. Now you've got him hooked."

He paused as he looked at DiGivanni. "How am I doing so far, Ollie?" He wiped his hands on a paper napkin and threw it at the can. "Missed! Now comes the interesting part. Quite by accident, he breaks into a federal security system and uncovers something that's far more delicate than he knows, but he gives it to you anyway. Or did you send him on a fishing expedition?"

"You're the one who's fishing," DiGivanni said coldly, crossing his arms and legs. Murray noted the change in his position. *He's really feeling insecure*, he mused to himself.

"Well, maybe yes and maybe no. Let's see what I've got so far. I have one Joe Mann locked up in a holding cell, pending the outcome of 'Let's Make A Deal', and I've got a Mafia boss whose dick is sunk so deep in the government's business, ranging from extortion, stealing security documents, bribery of a government employee, to tampering and who knows what else. All that's worth at least a hundred years in Club Fed. Now, you tell me who's fishing and who's cutting bait."

"What do you want from me?" DiGivanni asked again, very slowly.

"For openers, I want to know what you're looking for and what you found."

"And if I tell you that, what are you going to do for me?"

"Let you walk the streets for another day."

"And if I refuse?"

"Let's understand one another here, DiGivanni. I don't give a rat's ass about guys like you that suck the life's blood out of innocent victims. If I had my way, I'd drop you where you stand and save the taxpayers a bundle of money trying, convicting and then caring for you at Club Fed for the rest of your life."

"You arrest me, and I'll be out on the street before you can start your car."

Murray smiled. "Maybe I won't arrest you. Maybe I'll just turn you over to the boys that took care of the Carleones. You did hear about them, didn't you? Fellow members of the Scum Club."

DiGivanni's face showed visible signs of stress for the first time. "You wouldn't dare."

"I wouldn't?" Murray raised his eyebrows in surprise. "I could care less about you. My job is to clean the streets, sweeping away the likes of you. The sooner the better. Why should I arrest you only to have you out on the street, how did you put it, 'before I could get my car started?'"

"Let me see that badge again," DiGivanni demanded. "You're no DEA agent. Who the hell are you?"

Murray smiled. He took DiGivanni by the arm. "Let's go for a ride. You drive," he said, as he reached into his coat, relieving DiGivanni of his weapon.

DiGivanni jerked his arm away. "No! You can't do this! You have no right!"

"Watch me."

"All right! All right! I'll tell you what you want know." DiGivanni reluctantly pulled a folded sheet of paper from his pocket and handed it to Murray. "This is what Joe Mann gave me."

"And what's so important about this single piece of paper?" he asked before looking at it.

"That slip of paper contains names, bank accounts and dates of bank deposits." DiGivanni hesitated while Murray studied it.

"And?"

"And some of the amounts of money and the dates on that paper correlate with certain sums of money that I have privileged information about."

"In other words, you're saying that you lost money to the government, say on a drug bust or some similar civic undertaking, and you think those amounts appear on this list?"

"I don't think, I know. I've confirmed the dates and amounts with other parties who have..." He didn't finish the sentence, realizing that he might have said too much already.

Murray looked at him, then looked at the list more carefully. Apparently the startled look on his face betrayed his thoughts, as DiGivanni asked, "See anyone you know, aside from the President, that is?"

He faltered for a moment, ignoring DiGivanni's

comment. He recognized one entry as being the first banking day after Easter. The sum total of the two deposits equaled the amount taken from the Italians and Colombians that fateful day that his family had been murdered. The handwritten note at the end of the entry read "Carleone". Murray's fist tightened as he thought of Jana and the family.

There was a line with arrows drawn under the date which was of apparent special interest to DiGivanni. *Another one of our hits,* Murray thought as he studied each date and the deposit amount with familiarity

He frowned when he read the account headings: "Presidential Election Contributions" and "Green-Macaffe". The account numbers made no sense to him, but then again, there was no reason for them to.

"What else, aside from this list, that's of special interest?"

"That's about it."

"Like the crocodile taking a rabbit for a ride across the lake."

"What do you mean?"

"Think about it, DiGivanni. I'm going to let you go, for the time being. Under normal circumstances I would arrest you and throw away the key, but I have neither the time nor the inclination to expose you to the obvious danger that you would be in if you were in jail right now."

"I'm afraid I don't understand," DiGivanni said, looking at Murray with a frightened, confused expression.

"Play dumb on someone else's time, DiGivanni. I don't have time for your feigned stupidity. There's bigger game afoot. For the time being, get your ass home and consider yourself under house arrest.

As of this moment, I want you to shut down your entire operation, lock, stock and whore. I get wind that you're dealin', pushin', bookin' or pimpin', I'll throw your ass to the wolves in the blink of an eye."

"Who do you think you are, talking to me like that? I have friends in high—"

Murray grabbed him by the tie and brought his face within an inch of his own. "Now listen, and listen good. Remember the Carleones and that guy from the Colombian Cartel at the Mark Hopkins? If you want to join that elite group, I can assure you, I can arrange it."

He released him with a force that propelled him back on the bench. "Now get out of sight before I lose my lunch all over that nice London Fog you're wearing."

Chapter Twenty-four

"Mr. Macaffe, Mr. Murray to see you."

"Tell him I'll be out in—"

Murray walked through the door with Marcie trailing closely behind, protesting.

"I tried—"

"That's okay, Marcie," Macaffe said, holding up his hand. "Close the door, please.

"So what's so damned important that brings you to Washington without notice, Christian? I could have been out on business, you know," he said, obviously irritated, "and you would have made the trip all the way from California for nothing."

"There's a matter that's best discussed just between the two of us," Murray said, studying Macaffe's face closely, as if trying to read his thoughts.

"I'm listening."

"Joe Mann. You recall that name?"

"The California mole that turned. Of course. Why? What's happened? Did the Mafia get to him?"

"No. I've got him in custody. Turns out he was working for the DiGivanni family."

"Dominic DiGivanni? The Mafia?"

"The same. A real nice guy."

"You've met him?"

"We had a nice long chat yesterday. Turns out he groomed this Joe Mann kid, and that's what he is, just a kid. Anyway, he apparently had enough pull to get him into the system, and after buying his soul with a house and car, got him to feed him company information."

"Are you suggesting that's how La Torre got hit?"

"No. I don't think he made that connection, although I'm not sure what all he's fed DiGivanni. I haven't had time to dig that far into the matter yet."

"If you haven't had time to do your research, why are you here?"

"Does the name Green mean anything to you?"

Macaffe almost broke the wooden pencil he had been twirling in his hands. "Green? Is that a name or a color?"

Murray studied his boss' face intently. He had obviously hit a nerve. "You tell me. It seems that his name is connected with you and the President and certain overseas bank accounts."

Macaffe examined his fingernails, then sat back with his eyes closed. After a moment, he looked Murray in the eyes and said in a quiet voice, "I can't discuss the matter with you. It's too sensitive. Sorry."

Murray nodded. "Then maybe you could tell me this. All the money that we've been collecting from our hits, over $40 million now, what happens to that dough?"

"Why, we stash it in the bank, just like I said."

"Whose bank? What account?"

Macaffe said nothing.

"Isn't it customary to put government money into government-controlled banks? Under government accounts?"

"It's customary."

"This money went into overseas accounts."

"How do you know that?" Macaffe said, now sitting up with his hands folded on his desk. Murray could see that he had gotten his attention.

"I've got names and account numbers."

"You've got what?"

Murray slid the paper that DiGivanni had given him across the desk to Macaffe. He studied the paper, scanning the items quickly at first, then slowly again. "Where did this come from?" he asked dryly.

"Joe Mann pulled them out of someone's computer."

"That's impossible."

"If it's impossible, then you're holding the impossible in your hands."

It was obvious that Murray had caught Macaffe with his guard down. He was uncertain where this conversation would lead, but was bound to follow it to the end, no matter what the cost.

Macaffe took a deep breath and closed his eyes. Murray watched him closely and was surprised to see a tear escape his eye.

Macaffe took out a handkerchief and wiped his eyes, then blew his nose. "Sorry," he said as he stuffed the handkerchief back into his pocket. "You have no idea how terrified I've been that something like this would turn up. When Green killed the Carleone brothers—"

"Who the fuck is Green?" Murray asked, irritated. "This is the second time I've asked you about him. The first time you didn't know his name, and now..."

Macaffe took a deep breath again. "I don't know his real name. Green is his operative name. He's tied in with the NRA," he said with a sigh.

"The National Rifle Association?"

Macaffe nodded.

"What the hell is the attorney general of the United States doing in bed with the likes of that lot?"

"It's a long story."

"I've got the rest of my second life," he sat back in his chair, obviously waiting for Macaffe to speak. His eyes were fixed on his boss.

"It started a long time ago, before I became attorney general. The details are immaterial, but needless to say, my inadvertent blunder allowed the NRA to get their claws into me.

"For a long time things were quiet and I thought that they had forgotten about me, but—"

"Green never forgot..." Murray offered.

"Well, when the President began making noises about the crime bill, which obviously meant gun control to some degree, a collective shiver ran down their spine. They could foresee the time when the citizens of the country would demand that all guns be limited and registered."

"And no one would be allowed to have automatic weapons," Murray added.

Macaffe blinked an acknowledgment.

"So, they wanted you to exert your magnificent influence on the President with donations from the NRA," Murray guessed, studying the deposit list headed NRA Presidential Election Contributions."

"That's only a part of it—the most insignificant part, as far as I'm concerned."

He studied Murray's face again. "I've lost a family serving this God-forsaken administration, Macaffe. If anyone deserves to know the truth, you're looking at him. Now out with it!" It wasn't a request.

"Green thought that if we could cut down the crime in this country by attacking the source—"

"The people would lighten up on the gun control bill and the NRA would have won on all fronts?"

"That's about it."

"How could you get sucked into..." Murray was so mad he was at a loss for words. "And to think, all this time I thought I was working for God and country, when in reality it was the NRA who was pulling my chain."

"It was Green's idea to form the team concept. You've got to admit it worked."

"Oh, shit, Macaffe. Shut up, will you? You make me sick!" Murray closed his eyes for a moment to collect his thoughts. "How much of this does the President know?"

"He doesn't know anything."

"Man, can you imagine what the press would do if they got wind of this? This would make Nixon look like a choirboy. And the senate—they'd fry his ass so fast they'd have the barbecue right there on the senate floor."

He looked at Macaffe. "And you and I would be serving time in Club Fed. You can depend on that. If heads are going to roll..." He didn't finish the sentence.

Macaffe just sat behind his desk in silence.

"And you know the NRA's story. They were innocent bystanders who thought they were assisting the President's election and were duped by corrupt politicians," he said, pointing at Macaffe.

He could see the frustration on Macaffe's face. He was trapped in a corner with nowhere to go. "What are we going to do, Chris?" he pleaded.

Murray thought for a moment. "There are only three people who can sink our boat: Green, DiGivanni and Joe Mann. You let me handle Joe

Mann. Green will inadvertently handle DiGivanni, and then all we have to do is figure out how to deal with Green. When the time comes, that shouldn't be too difficult." His face was stoic, with a hard, determined look in his eyes.

"You're talking murder," Macaffe said, his voice cracking.

"What the hell do you think Green did to Carleone? What do you think we've been doing these past few months? Kicking ass and taking names? Our reputations are at stake here, Macaffe. Hell, our very lives. This is no time to go soft." He was talking to Macaffe like a drill sergeant.

"How do we get Green to get rid of DiGivanni?"

"Simple. You tell Green that DiGivanni had a mole in the company, and we found him. That much is true up to the present. I'll fake a hit on Mann and make sure the media picks up on it and that it makes the papers so DiGivanni will be sure to see it. Then you tell Green that DiGivanni is scared for his life, which he is, and in order to save his bacon is willing to turn state's evidence in exchange for immunity and a stint in the federal witness protection plan.

"Then you tell Green that unless DiGivanni is silenced he'll expose the whole plan, again which is probably true, and everyone will go down in flames, including the NRA."

Macaffe looked at Murray in admiration. "Did you ever consider running for President? With a devious mind like yours, the opposition wouldn't have a chance."

"I've got too much larceny running through my veins."

* * * *

Murray flew back to San Francisco and arranged to have Joe Mann in the holding room when he arrived. Joe was nervously pacing the floor of the small interrogation room when Murray arrived. He had a look of apprehension as he studied Murray's face.

"Well, I had a meeting with your Dominic DiGivanni. A real quality fellow. The sort of upstanding criminal that keeps every justice system busy."

Joe Mann was in no mood for Murray's dry sense of humor. "What did he say? Was he mad at me? Do you think he's after me?"

"Well, let's examine the facts. The Carleone family in Virginia, one of the names on the list, a Mafia family just in case you didn't know, was exterminated like so many cockroaches. Then one of the Cartel from Colombian, the supplier of cocaine for the Mafia, I might add, comes to this country to watch the World Soccer Cup games, and he gets blown away. All of the deceased are present and accounted for and, in one way or another, are represented on that list you pulled out of the computer. In short, you're the only link that can tie DiGivanni to any or all of the above. I'd say it's in his best interest that you disappear permanently—and the sooner the better."

"Well, what's going to happen to me now?" Joe looked up at Murray like a child who knows he's been caught stealing. "You have to help me."

"As I see it, you have three choices. We could simply turn you loose and save the taxpayers and the government a lot of embarrassment and expense."

"Turn me loose? But what happens if he finds me?"

"That's the whole idea, if you get my drift."

Mann studied Murray's face with frightened eyes. "Are you telling me that you would turn me out on the streets and let DiGivanni hunt me down and kill me in cold blood?"

"Look at it from my point of view. He kills you, then we arrest him for murder and put him away for the rest of his life. Sort of simple when you think about it."

"I don't think I care for that option," Mann said, forcing a weak smile.

"I didn't think you would."

"Give me another choice," Joe pleaded, leaning closer to Murray, hanging on his every word.

"We could try you for treason, selling security documents and a bushel of other federal crimes. Not a great choice, either. You'd get a few lifetimes of hard time in Club Fed and the government would be stuck feeding and housing you until you die— or get killed, whichever came first. Knowing the Mafia, you'd probably last a month or two at the most. They have tentacles that even reach into federal prisons."

"I'll pass on that one, too. What's my third choice?"

Murray looked at him for a moment, then took out a piece of gum and slowly unwrapped it before folding it and putting it into his mouth. "Your last choice is to let us kill you in order to get the Mob off your back," he said flatly.

Joe Mann suddenly jumped up from his chair and backed into a corner. His eyes were as large as they could possibly get. The blood visibly drained from his face. Murray could see that he was in the beginning stages of shock.

"There is one glitch to the third choice, however," Murray added, motioning for Mann to sit down again.

"I get to kill myself?" Joe asked facetiously.

"No," Murray grinned, despite the seriousness of the situation. "We'll do that for you. And I can guarantee it will be painless."

"You're such a sport."

Murray thought he had toyed with him long enough. "Ever hear of the federal witness protection plan?"

"Only in the movies."

"It's like your own home movie. We give you a different identification and a secret place to live and you get to pretend that that's who you are for the rest of your life. You can make up any story you want and no one will know the difference."

"So what are you telling me? That you're going to fake my death and ship me out?"

"That's the gist of it," Murray nodded curtly. "Are you up for it?"

"In a minute."

"There is just one small hitch."

"Why am I not surprised?"

"It's not what you think," Murray assured him. "If you're dead for us and the Mafia, you're dead for everyone. I mean everyone, including your friends and family."

"I can't tell my folks?"

"You can't tell anyone. As soon as someone knows you're alive, the Mob will track down a phone call, a postcard or letter and 'bang', you're really dead."

Joe's eyes went glassy as he thought about how his mother and dad would take his death. It would be a terrible ordeal for them to go through. "No, I couldn't do that to them," he said, his eyes looking blank.

"Then you're free to go," Murray said, opening the door.

"You've been stripped of your federal security pass, so you can't go back to your desk. The only way out is through the front door. You won't mind if I don't accompany you, do you?"

"You wouldn't, would you?" Joe wanted to know.

"Do what?" Murray asked innocently. "I'm dropping all charges and releasing you. You're a free man, Joe Mann. Good luck," he said, extending his hand. He then purposely looked at Mann's feet.

"What?" Joe said looking at Murray, then at his own feet.

"Oh, nothing. I was just looking to see if you had on running shoes. When you leave, I doubt if you would want to start your car. It's probably rigged with a bomb. That's how they got my family."

As soon as he had said the words Murray knew that he had made a mistake. A shiver went down his spine temporarily as he thought of the consequences if the underworld found out he was alive and operating. *What the hell*, he thought. *This kid's too preoccupied with his own problems to ever check up on me and my fake ID.*

"The Mob killed your family?" Mann asked, shocked.

"My wife, son and daughter."

Joe sat down again. "I guess I better think this through," he said, closing his eyes and rubbing his forehead vigorously. He looked up at Murray. "All right. We'll do it your way. What do I have to do?"

* * * *

Joe Mann was lying face-up in a pool of blood

when the photographer entered the room. He took several snaps from all angles, making sure the face was visible in all shots. When he was finished, Murray accompanied him out of the room. "I want you to get copies of these pictures to all the local television stations and newspapers, along with this copy explaining how he was killed. You're not to answer any questions. Just deliver the copy and disappear."

"Got it," the man said, removing the film from his camera.

* * * *

"All right, Joe. You can get up now," Murray said, handing him a towel to wipe himself clean. "Here's a pair of coveralls you can wear. Put this wig on and wear these dark glasses. Agent Lehman will accompany you through the plant and out the service entrance. You will be transported in a van to your new destination."

He watched as the six-foot-six-inch, long-haired worker dressed in coveralls with the Sal's Air Conditioning Service embossed on his back ambled down the corridor. "Good luck," Murray said, more to himself that to Joe Mann.

* * * *

The next morning Murray sent a Federal Express package to Macaffe, the contents of which were copies of the *San Francisco Chronicle* and the *Examiner*, as well as the *San Jose Mercury News*.

Within each edition, in various places, was the picture of Joe Mann lying in a pool of blood. The *Mercury News* had it on the front page. There were bloodstains on his shirt, indicating that he had

been shot several times with an automatic weapon.
The news caption was "Mafia Mole Murdered".

* * * *

When Murray got back to his office there was
a fax transmission waiting for him. It read simply:
Returned home, the safest place
for the time being.
The firm hand of a man is going
to be needed shortly.
TJ

Chapter Twenty-five

"Mr. Green to see you, Mr. Macaffe."

"Send him in."

"Did we have a meeting?" Macaffe asked, seemingly irritated as Green strolled in with his usual air of arrogance.

"Did you read this morning's *Post*?"

"Sorry. I've been too preoccupied to enjoy the luxury of reading the news."

Green tossed the paper on his desk. "It seems the President is making headway on the crime bill faster than we anticipated. That group of hysterical women who formed the WAG has been putting a lot of pressure on their constituents. They in turn have been applying an equal amount of pressure on the President to be stricter on gun control."

"That surprises you?"

"It doesn't surprise me. I think it's time that we have a meeting with the man."

"You want a meeting with the President of the United States?" Macaffe couldn't quite believe Green's nerve.

"As soon as possible."

"Under what guise should this meeting be called?" Macaffe inquired sarcastically.

"Under the guise that the NRA is going to contribute $20 million to his re-election campaign and the votes of all the members of the club. Lest you're of a mind to falter, let me not be remiss in reminding you that you have a rather heavy interest in his re-election, too." Green's voice went cold.

"I've got a lot on my mind aside from his re-election which, by the way, is more than a year away," Macaffe put him off.

"Well, the crime bill isn't," Green pointed out. "I suggest that you reprioritize your schedule." His voice carried a tone of demand.

Macaffe slid the pile of papers that Murray had sent him over for Green to see, each with the item of Joe Mann's death circled in red.

"So? Who's this Joe Mann and what's he got to do with anything?"

"Joe Mann was the mole that was feeding Dominic DiGivanni government data. DiGivanni, as in Mafia Don?" he emphasized sarcastically.

"I'm listening."

"Since you took it upon yourself to eliminate the Carleone clan, then coincidentally this Colombian Cartel guy is killed in San Francisco, which I'm sure you had nothing to do with, and now there's this Joe Mann, DiGivanni's boy. He figures maybe he's next in line."

"I still don't get it. How do all these interesting facts relate to anything?"

Macaffe slid the list that Murray had given him across the desk. Green studied it carefully.

"Where did this come from?" he asked, irritated.

"That's what I've been trying to tell you. Mann, the guy you see lying in a pool of blood here, pulled it out of our computer system."

"How the hell did he do that?" Green barked,

staring hard at Macaffe.

"He was DiGivanni's hacker and just got lucky," Macaffe said patiently. "That's the reason he had Mann working inside the system—to uncover tidy tidbits such as this."

"And you had it lying around so it could be found by this clown?" Green spat furiously.

"It wasn't 'lying around', as you put it." Macaffe said defensively. "It was locked in with a password that only I knew. Not even my secretary knows how to access the file. Mann just got lucky. That's what hackers do."

"I'll bet when he found this he was so excited that he wet his pants."

"I don't think he had a clue what he had when he gave it to DiGivanni, but unfortunately DiGivanni is no fool. It probably took him all of 30 seconds to match his lost funds with the deposits. After a few well-placed phone calls to some of his Mafia buddies, it was just a baby-step to figure out that someone connected with the Feds has been taking their drug money and was putting it into these accounts."

"How could you have been so stupid?"

"Hold it!" Macaffe was getting hot under the collar now. "I told you the data was filed under a code name. While we're throwing stones at glass houses, let us not forget that it was your idea to put the money in separate funds, identifying a portion for the President's re-election fund. Without that information, the data is just another bank account with unidentifiable names!"

Green made no comment, but continued staring at Macaffe with burning eyes.

"The fact that Mann found the file was just dumb luck. And the fact that he gave it to DiGivanni is even dumber luck. What's done is done. You can't unring a bell."

Green closed his eyes for a moment. "So, what's the bottom line?" His tone was more tempered now than it had previously been.

Macaffe made a face, indicating frustration and indignation.

"The bottom line is that DiGivanni has contacted the Feds for protection.""

"Protection! That mouse is asking the Feds for protection?"

"I don't think he knows what he's got, but he's smart enough to figure out he's got a bargaining chip. He's threatening to expose us if we don't protect him."

"By putting him in the federal protection plan?"

"You got it."

"So what's the problem?"

"How do you explain to the Feds that we're putting the number one West Coast Mafia kingpin, whom everyone would like to see in Club Fed, in the witness protection plan? We can't just tell them that he's got something on the NRA, the attorney general and a deceased member of the DEA—who, coincidentally, is alive and well, thank you—and has been fleecing the Mob and pocketing the money. All of which we want to cover up."

"Let's get our facts straight here, Macaffe," Green snarled. "No one's got anything on the NRA. The money's been delivered to you, and as far as I'm concerned, you've got control of the accounts with the allocated presidential funds, which, I might add, for all intents and purposes, are all NRA membership contributions. If heads roll, the NRA walks clean. We just want our money back." He smiled.

Macaffe looked at Green coldly, his knuckles turning white from the pressure of his clenched fists. "You're a bastard, you know that?"

"Hey, what can I say? Nice guys finish last." Green studied his fingernails for a moment, then added, "And don't forget, I know about that little charade with Murray and all. How do you think the President or the senate investigating committee would react if they learned that their attorney general was involved with all this governmental subterfuge?" He laughed menacingly.

He had a smirk that Macaffe was dying to wipe off his face, but he held his temper in check. "What about DiGivanni?" Macaffe asked, exasperated.

"What about him? He's a thug. Who's going to believe him?"

"Let him give this piece of paper to the papers and see how fast the senate investigating committee acts, Mafia or not. Can the NRA, a special interest group that's planning on donating $20 million to the President's re-election campaign, be held above scrutiny?" He looked at Green with challenging eyes.

"Do you think for a single second that any reporter in the US of A worth his salt won't put your donation and the verbiage of the crime bill together? Mr. I'm-innocent-of-all-charges, I don't think so. The crime bill would pass with so many teeth you'd think you ran into Jaws himself when it got to the President's desk for signature."

"So you have a point," Green conceded.

"So you better take care of Mr. DiGivanni before he gets any more nervous than he already is. I can only sit on this until he talks to a hungry reporter, then it's public information and a whole new ball game."

"All right, I'll fly to 'Frisco and take care of DiGivanni's bacon—after my meeting with the Pres," Green insisted.

* * * *

Robert Macaffe and Mr. Green were waiting outside of the Oval Office when an aide to the President told them he would see them. Macaffe was dressed in a dark blue pinstriped suit with a red tie. Green was wearing a black suit with a black tie, the first time Macaffe had ever seen him in anything other than his black leather jacket.

"Bob! Come in. It's such a pleasure seeing you again. How's the Missus? And the kids, I'll bet they're growing like weeds," the President said as he greeted Robert Macaffe in the middle of the room. "Come, sit over here. Care for some coffee or tea?" he asked, still not acknowledging Green.

"A cup of hot tea would do wonders," Macaffe said. "Mr. President, this is Mr. Green." He didn't elaborate on the purpose of the meeting, nor why Green was in attendance.

For all intents and purposes, Macaffe was calm and his usual charming self, but his stomach was in knots. He knew that this could well be the last day he served on the administration, if things didn't go well.

"A pleasure to meet you, Mr. Green. We've never met, have we?" the President asked, studying the man's rugged face.

"Oliver. Oliver Green. No, sir. We've never met, but I can assure you, it's a pleasure. I hope when this meeting is through you will feel the same."

"Coffee or tea?" the President asked Green.

"Tea would be fine, thank you."

A man dressed in a suit brought in the refreshments, poured each a cup of tea, then departed.

"So tell me, Bob, what brings you up on the Hill?" The President was smiling, but the attorney general knew that he was all business. He had precious little time to sit around exchanging pleasantries, what with the world starvation situation, Cuban refugees flooding into the country, North Korea threatening to arm itself with nuclear weapons, not to mention the constant pressure of daily meetings on the crime bill, and his wife's pet project—National Health Care, ad nauseam up to and including the Boy Scouts complaining that girls wanted to be admitted into their exclusive club.

He had been in office almost three years now, and the stress of running the country had already begun to take its toll on his usual boyish physical features. He had bags under his eyes and gray hair that hadn't been there before the election had begun to crop up around his temples. He still dressed impeccably and his hair was coifed to perfection. His greatest fear was to be a one-term President. That was Green's trump card.

"You see, Mr. President," Green said, taking control of the conversation, "the people I represent feel it's of great importance that you get re-elected. We've—"

"I appreciate your interest in my re-election, Mr. Green, but—"

"Oliver. Call me Oliver."

"Oliver, I appreciate your interest in my future, but that's a long way off. There are many fish to fry before I even think about facing that issue."

"If you will permit me, Mr. President, I think that everything you do is with the thought in mind of being a second-term President," Green said confidently, with a knowing smile.

The President was obviously irritated by the brashness of this man, but held his tongue. He looked at Macaffe and asked, "As to the purpose of your visit?"

Macaffe started to speak, not having a clue as to what he would say, but was again interrupted by Green.

"The membership of our group is extremely interested in assisting you in formulating the anti-crime bill, Mr. President. They've entrusted me with a substantial amount of money to be donated towards your re-election, along with their 100-per-cent support to ensure your continued presidency."

"And what group might that be, Mr. Green?"

"Oliver. I represent the National Rifle Association, Mr. President. We have virtually millions of members in every walk of life in every state of the—"

"I appreciate your support, Mr. Green—"

"Oliver."

"Can I assume that there's a message here? A message relative to gun control?" the President asked, masking his irritation.

Green leaned forward in his chair, emulating an air of importance. "As you know, the constitution of the United States clearly states the right of citizens to bear arms, Mr. President. It's our firm stand that the anti-crime bill should incorporate that right as a firm deterrent against those who would violate any citizen's right to protect himself and his family."

"I appreciate your concern, Mr. Green," the President said in a condescending tone. He shifted his eyes to Macaffe, who was sitting with his legs crossed and his arms crossed as well, looking somewhat like an insecure human pretzel. There was a fixed glaze in his eyes and a tight-lipped formation that betrayed his inner conflict. "Bob, how does the attorney general's office fit into all this?"

His voice carried a tone of a disappointment. It was obvious that the tone of the President's conversation just took on a serious overtone.

"Mr. Green here," he nodded towards Green, "first contacted me with the request to make a substantial donation towards your re-election campaign, and I thought it best that you hear it from his own lips."

"We're talking $20 million, Mr. President," Green said with definition. "Clearly the largest donation in the history of the presidency."

The President sat back in his chair with his hands clasped on his lap. He was going to choose his words carefully.

"Mr. Green—Oliver," he added quickly before Oliver Green could repeat his first name again. "I represent the totality of the population of these United States. We have a crimewave sweeping across the land that can be attributed to two facets of our society, the first being television.

"There hasn't been a man, woman or child between our two great shores who owns a television set who hasn't seen at least 100 killings in the past year, who doesn't know what an automatic weapon is, and what kind of havoc it can cause. Because of that knowledge, people have not only been taught violence, how to be violent, and how to react to violence, but they've become numbed by it to the point that they see it happening on the streets and ignore it as if it were on television.

"The second facet attributed to the present crimewave is the accessibility and ownership of weapons. If I had it in my power, right now, regardless of the political consequences, I would outlaw the use and ownership of every handgun and automatic weapon in existence. To even own a hunting rifle or shotgun a person would not only have to have a license to own that weapon, but would have to pass a rigorous firearms test in order to even use one, as we do when we put an automobile in the hands of an adult."

The President's voice was quiet but firm, with a definite tone of finality. He left no margin for argument. "And there you have it, Mr. Green—my stand on gun control as it relates to the crime bill. You and your group can take solace in the fact that the crime bill, once it has been passed—after hours of heated arguments and attention paid to special interest groups such as the NRA—will not parrot my will, but it will be as strict as I can make it."

"Am I to take it then, Mr. President, that you refuse our offer?"

"You can take it as gospel, Mr. Green, that I will not be influenced by anyone for any reason, much less a donation, irrespective of the amount, to detour my goal."

He switched his eyes to Macaffe, looking sternly at him before saying, "Now then, gentlemen, if there is no further business, I must get back to my duties."

"May I say, Mr. President, that my people are going to be very disappointed," Green said. The tone of his voice carried an unmistakable, thinly veiled threat.

"Bob, will you remain for a moment?" the President said, ignoring Green's comment, concluding the meeting.

Macaffe looked at Green, dismissing him with his eyes, then looked back to the President. He knew what was coming and didn't have a clue as to how to defend himself.

After Green made his hasty but obviously angry retreat, the President said, "Bob, I'm very disappointed that you don't screen your constituents more carefully. This Green fellow is a dangerous man. I can tell that just from the tone of his conversation. If he and his group had their way, every man, woman and child would have an automatic weapon and we could revert back to the good old western days, where if you called a man a SOB you would have to back it up with a hail of lead. That's great for population control, but that's about it!"

"I'm sorry, Mr. President. I—"

"I want a full report on that man and his activities with the NRA on my desk first thing Monday morning. I'm going to instruct the CIA to look into his dealings as well. Come in here like a little Napoleon and try to shake my tree! I'll teach him a lesson he won't soon forget."

"Yes, sir."

* * * *

Green was waiting for Macaffe outside the Oval Office when he came out. "That sorry son-of-a-bitch will rue the day he crossed me," Green spat, looking back at the door to the Oval Office.

"You have to admit that you were more than a little brash with the man."

"Brash, shit! I was trying to get the ungrateful wimp re-elected and solidify our country at the same time." There was a glazed look in his eyes that scared Macaffe when he looked at him. "What did the pompous bastard have to say behind my back?"

"He thinks you're a loose cannon, and I have a tendency to agree with him. He wants a full report on you. He wants it on his desk first thing Monday morning. Shit! Now what are we going to do?"

"Don't concern yourself," Green said, with a wave of his hand, dismissing the importance of the issue. "I'll take care of everything. Fortunately, the VP has a different mindset than that..."

Macaffe stopped short in the hallway. He grabbed Green by the arm, spinning him around. He looked around to see if anyone was within hearing distance. "What do you mean, fortunately the Vice-President has a different mindset?"

"You'll see." Green had an evil smile on his lips. "Go back to your little office of tin solders and leave the work to the real men of this country!"

Chapter Twenty-six

Christian Murray was in Washington in a meeting with Robert Macaffe when the attorney general said, "Chris! I'm scared stiff. Green demanded a meeting with the President and he—"

"He what?" Murray asked, incredulous.

"I showed him the newspapers you sent from the San Francisco Bay Area with the pictures of Mann's demise. After I explained the role that Mann played, I drew him a picture of DiGivanni's position. As expected, he said he would take care of the matter, but first he insisted on seeing the Pres."

"Why?"

"I think he wanted to assure himself that his pitch of trading votes and money for a position on the crime bill was going to be effective."

"And?"

"And the President shot him down in flames."

Murray smiled. "Didn't know he had it in him."

"Well, he does. But that's not the worst of it. Before we left it was obvious that Green was pissed. He all but said that he was going to try to get rid of the President, Chris."

"The President? Are you sure?"

"As sure as I can be without having a signed colored picture. His exact words were, 'Don't worry,

I'll handle it. Fortunately the Vice-President has a different mindset..."

"Meaning that if the President is killed or inca-pacitated, the Vice-President would succeed him and he would be receptive to a deal with the NRA."

"For $20 million. You got it. I'm scared, Chris. This thing has gotten so convoluted and far out of hand my brain is about to explode."

"Let me think on this, Bob," Murray said, pat-ting him on the back.

"There's one more thing." He looked at his friend.

Christian waited for a moment, then when Macaffe seemed to hesitate, he asked, "Do I get a clue or should I just start guessing?"

"Green threatened to expose us, too."

"What do you mean?"

"He wasn't clear, but probably would leak to the press the fact that you're not dead and are operating under a pseudonym."

"Try not to let it get to you. I'll come up with something."

"Great. I got Napoleon on one side and Custer on the other. I'm surrounded by military idiots."

"Don't forget who started this mess, Bob," he said firmly. "I don't have my name on any govern-ment bank accounts."

"Don't rub it in."

* * * *

That evening Robert Macaffe was sitting at his desk. The staff had gone home and the office was dark, save for the light from a single desk lamp. An empty bottle of Jack Daniels sat in the middle of his desk next to a half-filled crystal water glass. A .38 Walther lay next to the bourbon bottle. A single bullet stood next to the bottle like a small missile.

Robert Macaffe had just sealed a legal-sized envelope addressed to his wife and family. He set it against the base of the lamp, next to the one addressed to the President of the United States. His glassy eyes stared at the envelopes for a moment as he wondered what everyone would say when they heard. He wondered what the papers would say. He was ashamed—too ashamed to face the inevitable dire consequences of his actions.

He emptied the remaining bourbon in the glass with one big gulp, then gently set both his glass and the empty bottle in the garbage can. He picked up the Walther as if it were fragile. He turned it over in his hand as if examining it for the first time. With the flick of his thumb, the magazine ejected.

Macaffe picked up the lone shell, then studied it for a moment before inserting the deadly missile into the magazine. He inserted the magazine, then hesitated for a moment before slamming it home. A flick of his wrist, and the bullet entered the chamber. Macaffe studied the envelope with his wife's name on it for a moment. A tear rolled down his cheek as he placed the gun against his right temple. He closed his eyes, then squeezed the trigger. The last image in his mind was his picture in the newspaper with the caption, "United States Attorney General, Robert Macaffe, kills self to escape prosecution."

* * * *

The following morning, Christian Murray awoke with a plan of how to stop Green from to killing the President. The threat of DiGivanni no longer bothered him. He knew that DiGivanni would either fade into obscurity or he would retire to a fortified retreat. After all, it wasn't like the man was destitute. The last thing he would want, Murray thought, was publicity.

No, he no longer posed a threat. In the event he was threatened with incarceration in the future, Murray knew DiGivanni would use the information he had gained from Mann as a bargaining chip. If matters deteriorated even worse, well, he would cross that bridge when the time came.

"Marcie, Christian Murray here. Put me through to Bob, will you?"

There was a stunned silence, then Murray listened to Macaffe's secretary as she tearfully relayed the gruesome scene that the cleaning crew had found late last night. Without comment, he quietly hung up the phone as if not wanting to disturb anyone.

* * * *

"This is the man we're looking for," Murray said, passing photos of Green to his men. "I don't have to tell you how important it is that we bag this guy. He's vowed to take out the President, and it's our job—our last job—to take him out first. I don't care how it gets done, so long as we succeed.

"The one thing I do want to avoid is publicity. We cannot afford to let the situation get out of hand. If you see him, wait until he's alone before you take him out. If you're about to lose him, use your silencers, exterminate him and disappear. I want no witnesses."

He looked over the serious faces of his men. "Any questions?"

Each man had a somber look the likes of which

Murray had never seen before. This was not only their last job as a team, but the most important job they'd ever been assigned. Once it was completed, there would be no credit, no parades, no promotions, just the satisfaction that they'd done their job and saved the President's life.

* * * *

Murray divided the Team into sub-units who were assigned sectors around DiGivanni's residence to watch for Green. In the meantime, Grover and three members of the Team were to fly to Washington, DC, to try to locate and tail him. If he made a move on the President, they were to drop him where he stood. The problem was, they didn't know where to find him. All they had was the name Oliver Green and a photo of the man. The rest would have to be dumb luck.

Murray flew with Grover and his men to Washington to meet with the President. He had never been in the Oval Office, so he knew just gaining admission would be a feat, let alone facing the man he had to tell that his life was in danger. A meeting was arranged by Marcie through Macaffe's office.

Murray entered the hallway which led to the President's office, where he was met by two Secret Service men. They searched him to be sure that he had no weapon, then allowed him to proceed to the Oval Office.

He knocked on the solid wooden door and was met by a stocky man dressed in a dark nondescript suit with a stoic look on his face. Murray introduced himself and was admitted.

The President rose to meet him as he entered the office. The man dressed in a dark suit took a seat on the far wall without comment. Murray's eyes took in the richness of the dark blue carpet with stars surrounding the Presidential Seal located in the center of the room. The room was larger than he had expected and was indeed oval.

"Mr. Murray?" the President asked, extending his hand.

"It's a pleasure meeting you, sir. I'm just sorry it has to be under these circumstances."

"The message is that you're from the DEA and were working with Bob Macaffe."

"A terrible thing, his death. The country will miss him. He was a great man."

The President opened a rather large blue file that was lying on his desk. Inside the file was a picture of Murray and a photo of the limousine in which he had staged his death. He slid the photos over to Murray.

"According to this file," he said, thumbing through the top section, "Christian Murray was killed earlier this year by a bomb in front of Bob Macaffe and the media. I recall seeing it on the news myself."

Murray glanced at the pictures of himself and the exploded limo without touching them. "Yes, sir." He paused for a deep breath. He had expected this. "I can explain."

"I wish you would. I've never talked to a dead man before," the President said as he closed the file. There was no humor in his voice or in his face.

Murray relayed how his family had been killed on Easter Sunday, and that the Mob had intended to kill him but had gotten his family instead. After that, he explained, he had lost his will to live. He just sat in his chair for days, until he had apparently slipped into a coma.

The next thing he knew was when he found

himself in the hospital. It was there that he had decided that if he was going to be effective in his fight against crime and drugs, he needed to attack crime on another level—to go underground. That was when he had decided to stage his death and change his personal appearance. That was when it was agreed that he assume the name of Tom Miller, just in case he needed to be operational, like in the Mann case.

"You can check my fingerprints if you have any doubts as to my identity," he offered.

"No, I believe you. Only someone from the inside would have the information you have about Macaffe and the workings of the DEA that you possess. So what brings you here?"

Murray knew that the President wouldn't have met with him unless he had checked him out first. "I understood you've met one Oliver Green?"

The President frowned. "A disagreeable chap, that one. He and his NRA friends think they can buy control of the crime bill with muscle and money."

"Don't fault the whole NRA for one bad apple. That would be like condemning the whole German population for Hitler's insanity, or the Japanese for Pearl Harbor." Murray smiled. "I have to admit, I used to be a card-carrying member of the NRA myself. But I had nothing to do with Green," he added quickly.

"You should have been a politician," the President smiled.

"Funny, those are the same words Macaffe used when I last saw him."

"And Oliver Green?"

"Before Macaffe killed himself, he called me and said that he thought Green was going to make an attempt on your life."

"And you want me to lay low." The President shook his head. "If I went into hiding every time some nut case disagreed with me..."

"It's not the same. Trust me. Green had something on Macaffe that was so terrible that it made him take his own life. Now, he thinks if he can eliminate you, the Vice-President, who would then obviously be President, would be receptive to his money as well as his way of thinking."

The President thought to himself for a few moments. "He could have an argument there," he agreed.

"That's why you've got to be particularly careful, at least until we hogtie this Green character. I know you don't need me to tell you to be cautious, but in this case extra security wouldn't hurt. Remember, this man is a weapons expert, and like Hitler, he's not only cunning but commands a large following."

"Yes, I know," the President said solemnly.

"We have confirmed information that he was responsible for the death of the Carleone brothers, one of your local Mafia families."

"Yes, I read about that. They had a strong toehold right here in DC. If Green did away with them, he can't be all bad." He smiled.

"We think he's going to try to hit another Mafia family on the West Coast. It's his sick way of eliminating organized crime so the politicians will let everyone own guns, if you follow that logic. I've got men tracking him both here and on the West Coast, but so far we haven't been able to locate him."

The President rose and extended his hand. "Well, thank you for coming. I'm sure the country is grateful for men such as yourself, Mr. Murray. I'll have security notified immediately," he said, nodding towards the man still sitting in the corner. Murray had all but forgotten about him. "And thank you for coming so soon. Perhaps, when this is all over, we can meet on a more favorable basis."

Murray just smiled and shook the President's hand.

"Oh, Christian? Do you mind if I ask a personal question? Just for my own edification."

"Shoot."

"A bad choice of words," the President smiled. "I couldn't help but notice as I was reading through your file that your grandparents came from Colombia. You don't have to answer this if you don't want to, but does it bother you to be warring with what could well be your own countrymen? I mean, given your lineage and all?" He was obviously a little nervous about asking Murray the question.

"You've got some English blood in your family, don't you, sir?"

"Yes…"

"How do you feel on Independence Day?"

The President smiled. "I see your point. Good of you to come, Christian." He watched with a look of admiration as Murray departed his office. "We need more people like that man," he said aloud to himself as he went back to his desk.

* * * *

It was late in the evening when Murray checked in his office. He had no sooner walked in the door when Macmillan, one of his team members assigned to watch DiGivanni's house, called. Green and some men were parked in a van outside the DiGivanni residence. "Any instructions?" he asked.

"Did you ID Green for sure?"

"It's him, all right. All of us ID'd him just to be

sure. From what I hear about this animal, he wouldn't miss out on the fun."

"Keep your eye on him. If he makes a go at DiGivanni, let him be. Maybe we'll get lucky and solve two problems at once. I'll be there as soon as possible."

* * * *

The door of the van quietly slid open and Murray emerged.

They had parked across and down the street from DiGivanni's mansion. There was an eight-foot stone wall that surrounded the well-manicured grounds. An unguarded iron gate secured the grounds. Two men in the front seat scanned the grounds with night vision binoculars.

"Anything going on?"

"Yeah, plenty. There were four men in their van," Macmillan said, pointing in the direction of the van. "Each was carrying a rocket launcher."

"A rocket launcher!"

"Yeah. They dispersed, one on each side of the villa. My guess is they're going to bombard it from all four sides, blowing up everything inside and collapsing the structure in the process."

"Do we know for sure if DiGivanni is in there?"

"Oh, he's in there, all right. Saw him arrive in the limo about an hour ago. That's when the activity heated up." Macmillan nodded towards the van.

"Anyone in the van now?"

"Nope. They're all out hunting."

"How long do you suppose we have before they return?"

"If they were to hit him at this moment, I'd guess two minutes."

"All right, here's what we do..."

* * * *

They had just enough time to leave Green's van and get back before there was an ear-splitting explosion. Although the rock wall obscured the first floor of the house, a ball of fire could be seen for miles as the explosion lit up the sky and everything around the grounds. Immediately after the explosion, which was actually several simultaneous explosions sounding as one, the house was engulfed in flames.

"I'll be surprised if anyone survives that," Murray said. "Look!"

Four figures could be seen racing towards the van, each carrying a long tube affair which were the rocket launchers.

They piled into the van, and a moment later it screamed down the road with its lights turned off.

The van was about 100 feet from what used to be DiGivanni's place when Murray said, "Now!"

The man in the front seat aimed a small black box towards the van and pushed a red button.

Green's van exploded into a ball of fire, catapulting it end over end until it landed right-side up, blazing like an inferno.

"I think we can safely say that ties up any loose ends concerning Mr. Green. I'll notify the President first thing tomorrow that he can rest easy."

* * * *

All of Murray's men were present when he walked in wearing a black leather jacket and faded blue jeans. There was an air of anticipation as his eyes slowly scanned his team.

"If I never told you before, let me say it now: I'm proud of you guys and proud to have been associated with you."

They looked at óne another with uneasiness. This was beginning to sound like a farewell speech. He smiled as he looked at the loyal-yet-somber faces of his men.

He put his foot on the chair and leaned on his knee, looking intently at his men. "In eliminating Green, our job has been concluded. You've unselfishly devoted a greater portion of your youth to serving your country, and for all intents and purposes, all that you've received has been a sign of relief from the public."

He paced around the table behind his men, touching one on the arm, another on the shoulder, and mussing the hair of a third. "The funds we collected from our busts were drug money, of course. We've taken in $40 million and change during Operation Team. The money is sitting somewhere in foreign banks, where Macaffe and our buddy Green stashed it. Half of the funds have been earmarked as 'President's Election Contributions', compliments of the NRA. The balance of the $20 million and change is earmarked 'Green-Macaffe'. Neither will be needing it, so I want you guys to divide amongst yourselves. Call it hazard pay."

He handed each of them a copy of the computer bank statement Mann had retrieved. "Your only task will be to find in which country the banks are located. I don't have a clue where it is, but I would start with either Switzerland or the Cayman Islands."

There was stunned silence, followed by a loud whoop amongst the group. In an instant, they were dividing $20 million by 11 to see how much each man would get.

"You're doing it all wrong," Murray said, holding up his hand. "You don't divide by 11. You divide by 10. This is your take. I'm out of here."

There were unanimous words of protest, but again Murray held up his hand to silence the men. "Don't concern yourself with me. I've got one final fish left to fry, which I'll take care of myself. The money is yours. No argument.

"I would suggest, however, that you designate a leader to coordinate your efforts. You've got the account numbers, so finding the bank should be a simple matter of a few well-placed phone calls. After that, a cooperative, intelligent, coordinated strategy, along with a few forged documents, and you should all have, shall I say, about $2 million each, tax free."

In a moment they had elected Grover to be their leader. Murray nodded in agreement, winking at his pal. While the men talked excitedly about how each would spend their fortune or where they would go, Murray quietly slipped out of the room.

He loved those men as if they were his own children. He would miss them and hoped that they would not soon forget their leader. Their Coach. The Colombian.

Chapter Twenty-seven

The commercial airliner wove through the high mountains, seemingly just missing the hills. There was no landing area in sight until the plane rounded the final hill. There in front of them lay the city of Medellin and the airport.

The passengers disembarked, some rushing to meet loved ones, others meeting business associates. A young, deeply tanned, tall woman with sea-green eyes wearing a white cotton dress with a blue sash around her small waist stood by a white Rolls Royce convertible with the top down.

She looked in anticipation as the passengers deplaned one by one, until finally the last passenger stood at the door, searching the area below. He wore white pants and a blue Hawaiian shirt and a white Panama hat with a red headband. His skin was conspicuously white.

He spotted the tanned young woman and ran to her, embracing her at the edge of the tarmac. "What, no luggage, Mr. Miller?" TJ asked, emphasizing his name. She was all smiles as she took Christian Murray by the arm, leading him towards the Rolls.

"I figured what I have on my back was all I needed," he said, hugging TJ. "Thought I would get some local duds... Kinda try to blend in. Know what I mean?"

They laughed, then kissed and hugged. She drove them towards the villa, which was securely nestled against the backdrop of the rugged blue mountains on the outskirts of town. There, they would have their own swimming pool and tennis court. Money would never become an issue.

"Did you dispose of the land?" he asked as she drove up to the gate of the villa.

"I deeded it to the workers and their families, just as you suggested," she said, activating the newly installed electronic gate opener. "They are going to start planting vegetable crops on it as soon as the land has been plowed, no more coca plants or marijuana." She laughed.

"I trust you disposed of the underground factories as efficiently as you've taken care of everything else?"

"Nothing but large craters. The way the jungle grows, it'll be grown over before the next rain."

"And the servants?"

"Retired," she replied wistfully. "It's just you and me, pal." She smiled at Murray, squeezing his hand.

"You're so efficient. And with all that wit and charm, I'll bet you even play tennis." He laughed.

* * * *

The President was re-elected by a landslide on his get-tough crime platform. He had passed the toughest anti-crime, gun control bill this country had ever seen.

Several Mafia families had been put out of business by virtue of inter-family wars, such as the Carleones in Vermont and the DiGivannis in California.

The DEA was credited with the extermination of an important Colombian Cartel member, sending a strong message to any country supplying drugs to the US.

The relationship between Colombia and the US took a major step forward as the two countries came to a mutual agreement to fight drugs. Colombia demonstrated their first good faith gesture towards their mutual effort to eradicate drugs by sending to the United States videotapes of the destruction of the largest cocaine lab ever found in Medellin.

Crime was down in the United States and drug usage had declined dramatically. The people of America were beginning to feel more at ease on the streets again.

About The Author

Howard Losness, a father of three boys, was born in Fargo, N.D., of second generation Norwegian parents. He has been the president of his own real estate company, selling and syndicating commercial real estate for the past thirty years. His formal education includes seven years of college in pre-med and psychology. He has earned outstanding achievement awards playing the tuba for twelve years, and has played with the U.S. Army Band. An active athlete, he has volunteered ten years of his time to coach youth basketball, football, softball and baseball.

To date he has written seven novels and is an accomplished artist in African wildlife and northwestern art.

The father of Molina Marquez was executed by a Colombian drug lord for stealing a marijuana plant to buy his son a pair of shoes. Molina would avenge his father's death and eventually become the most powerful force in the drug cartel.

The Mafia has executed the family of Christian Murray, head of the Drug Enforcement Administration, the DEA, in attempt to assassinate him.

A rogue member of the National Rifle Association who has an unbreakable hold on the U.S. Attorney General takes it upon himself to involve his office in an assassination plot against the President of the United States when he refuses to yield on his position of his anti-crime bill.

TJ Escobar, whose father was killed by drug dealers, will play both sides of the field in the deadly game of love and deceit. All will collide on the battlefield of drugs, money and power. Only one can survive.

The Columbian

by

Howard A. Losness
